THE
DISAPPEARANCES

Another spirited novel by the bestselling Amish author!

LINDA BYLER

THE DISAPPEARANCES

SADIE'S MONTANA
Book 3

Good Books
New York, New York

Cover design by Koechel Peterson & Associates, Inc.,
Minneapolis, Minnesota

Design by Cliff Snyder

THE DISAPPEARANCES
Copyright © 2012 by Linda Byler
International Standard Book Number: 978-1-56148-775-2
Library of Congress Control Number: 2012941170

Good Books books may be purchased in bulk at special discounts for sales
promotion, corporate gifts, fund-raising, or educational purposes. Special
editions can also be created to specifications. For details, contact the Special
Sales Department, Good Books, 307 West 36th Street, 11th Floor, New
York, NY 10018 or info@skyhorsepublishing.com.

Good Books is an imprint of Skyhorse Publishing, Inc.®,
a Delaware corporation.

Visit our website at www.goodbooks.com.

10 9 8 7 6 5 4 3

Publisher's Cataloging-in-Publication Data

Byler, Linda.
    The Disappearances / Linda Byler.
    p. cm.
    Series: Sadie's Montana, Book 3.
    ISBN 978-1-56148-775-2
1. Amish --Fiction. 2. Love --Fiction. 3. Montana -- Fiction. 4. Horses --Fiction.
I. Title. II. Series.

PS3602.Y53 D57 2012
813.6--dc23   2012941170

Printed in the United States of America

Table of Contents

The Story   1

Chapter 1

Now that the snows had come, Sadie missed Reuben the most. Oh, it wasn't that she was lonely or discontented. After all, she could go home whenever she wanted, as long as the snow was not too heavy.

It was just Reuben, his guileless blue eyes, the way he tossed his blond-streaked hair away from his face, that often brought a lump to her throat.

She was a married woman now. Somehow, she felt no different than she ever had, except for the love that had come to fulfillment with Mark Peight, her husband of exactly two months and five days.

Sadie Peight. Or Sadie Anne Peight. Sadie Miller no more.

In the Amish world in which she lived, that close-knit community of plain people in Montana, she was "Mark Sadie" now—not "Mark's wife, Sadie," in the proper way. Just plain "Mark Sadie." No last names were needed. Everyone knew who "Mark Sadie" was.

Her family, the Jacob Millers, had moved to Montana when she was 15 years old. She had had to give up her beloved palomino riding horse, Paris, as well as her best friend and cousin, Eva, moving thousands of miles away from her home community in Ohio.

In time, she came to love Montana, working at Aspen East, the huge ranch that employed dozens of men, cattle drivers, farmers, horsemen, the list went on and on. She cooked large meals in the kitchen with Dorothy Sevarr, whose husband, Jim, transported her to and from the ranch. The Sevarrs came to be beloved friends, as well as Richard and Barbara Caldwell, the wealthy owners of Aspen East Ranch.

Sadie had met Mark when a horse appeared from seemingly nowhere in a snowstorm, falling sick and disabled in front of Jim Sevarr's pickup truck. Sadie opted to stay with the horse, a beautiful but dying paint, while Jim went for help. Mark Peight and his driver found Sadie in the snow with the dying horse. There was an instant mutual attraction between Mark and Sadie. A long, imperfect courtship followed, imperfect due largely to Mark's troubled, unusual past.

Wild horses had been a danger, running uncontrolled through the isolated areas, terrifying the Amish community. The large, black leader of the herd threatened unassuming horses and buggies traveling the countryside.

Sadie and her brother, Reuben, had spent many weeks on a grassy hill taming the few remaining horses. Among them was the outstanding palomino mare Sadie now owned, which she named Paris, in memory of her beloved horse from Ohio. The palomino had been given to Sadie as a gift of appreciation from the owner of the wild horses, which turned out to have been stolen by clever horse thieves in Laredo County. After the thefts, someone started going around the county randomly shooting horses, Reuben's among them. Paris and Sadie managed more than one harrowing narrow escape. But the sniper—or snipers—remained at large and the motive for the shootings a mystery.

She felt safe now, snug and cozy in the house Mark was renovating. There had been no sniper activity for almost four months. The Amish community breathed a sigh of relief. People went on with their lives, shaking their heads at the seeming incompetence of the local police, but, in the Amish way, taking it all in stride.

The home Mark had bought before the wedding had been a forsaken homestead nestled at the foot of Atkin's Ridge. The buildings were covered in old, wooden, German siding, the framework amazingly sturdy, but almost everything else was crumbling with age.

When you came in the driveway, the unique shape of the barn, with its series of gable ends and various roof slopes, was so completely charming that you forget to look for a house, which was farther up the slope in a grove of pine trees. Despite its lamentable state of disrepair, the property was as cozy and attractive as a nursery-rhyme house.

There was an L-shaped porch along the front, dormers on the roof, and a low addition on the right side. Besides the broken windows, sagging porch posts, and torn floor boards, sparrow nests were built into every available crack of the decaying lumber, the floors littered with their feces. Bats flew in and out of the upstairs dormer windows at will, and mice scurried in terror at their approach.

Mark had put in long hours repairing the barn first. His hard labor resulted in a remarkable building with a beautiful forebay, horse stalls on either side, wide enough to drive a team of horses attached to a manure spreader through it, for easy mucking out. There was a workshop in another section and room for the carriage, spring wagon, and various lawn tools in another, all on top of a solid, new, concrete floor.

The barn was their pride and joy, especially when Paris adapted so well, becoming quite sleek and flirtatious with Mark's horses.

Sadie would stand at the wooden fence, her arms propped on the top board, one foot on the bottom, watching Paris nip at Truman, the new horse, then squeal and bound nimbly away.

She still loved Paris and rode her as much as ever. But whenever she went to visit her parents, she drove Mark's steady, brown standardbred driving horse hitched to the shining, black carriage. Since the sniper incidents had quieted down, she felt safer and often returned home with the back seat of the buggy full of items that had been left behind after the wedding.

The house was not finished; only the lower floor was livable. Mark's original plans changed after his mother passed away from bone cancer, leaving them a substantial amount of money to be shared with his five siblings when they had been located.

Mark hired a cabinetmaker and a crew of carpenters to finish the main floor, resulting in a well-crafted home.

The kitchen was all done in oak cabinets, with wide plank floors also made of oak. The countertops were a speckled black and gray, so Sadie had chosen to paint the walls a gray so light it was almost white. Three windows side by side provided a full view of the driveway, the sighing pine trees, and the barn.

Sadie placed her furniture where she wanted it in the house, then told Mark she was unworthy to be the housekeeper of such a beautiful home. Mark ran a hand through his black hair. He said nothing, just grabbed her and swung her around. His glad brown eyes and perfect smiling mouth told her everything he thought she should know. Their love was an all-consuming flame, their marriage a union of God—a blessing that, after all they had been through together, they would never take for granted.

Oh, they had their times, like Mark's sliding into his silences, becoming absorbed in a sort of blackness when she least expected it. She would always revert to self-blame, her shoulders tightening, a headache developing, watching his morose face with a sort of hopeless intensity. What have I done? What have I said to bring this on?

She would be completely miserable, afraid to approach him, until she remembered his past and the awful times after his mother left with a real estate agent, leaving eight-year-old Mark to care for his five younger siblings.

The slightest put-down, often going unnoticed by Sadie herself, could bring on those quiet times. A dark fog, as impenetrable as the proverbial pea soup and about as messy to clean up, surrounded him.

Sadie had been raised in a secure, loving home, imperfect perhaps, as most homes tend to be, but completely normal. Her three sisters, Leah, Rebekah, Anna, and one brother, Reuben, all younger than herself, had been loved, disciplined, and nurtured.

Their mother, Annie, endured mental illness that resulted in hospitalization. In the end, it only bound them closer, enveloping the family in a shroud of thanksgiving for Mam's well-being.

Sadie was often quick to speak her mind, the words tumbling out happily before she thought of their consequences. Mark would be hurt, returning to that place where only he knew, leaving her floundering, reeling from the rejection in his eyes.

The latest bout had been brought on by her happy evaluation of the oak kitchen cabinets. Sitting back in her chair, wrapping her soft, white robe securely around her waist, she crossed her legs, kicking her slipper-clad foot, shaking back her long, dark ponytail, saying simply how no one could build cabinets the way a cabinetmaker could.

"They just know exactly what they're doing, don't they? Such perfect raised panels on their doors!" Forgetting, like a dummy, that he had built the ones in the office and had been terribly proud of his accomplishment and the money he had saved by doing it himself.

He had nodded his head, agreed, using words to that extent, finished his coffee, and abruptly left the table, returning to the recliner. He stayed there without offering his usual Sunday-morning dish-drying assistance.

Amish people hold church services in a home every other Sunday. This is an old tradition, allowing the ministers and deacon to visit other communities if they feel so inclined. Church members have an in-between Sunday, allowing long sleep-ins, leisurely breakfasts, a day for resting, visiting, Bible-reading, studying German, or, as is often the case, simply relaxing and doing nothing.

Which is exactly how that Sunday turned out. Doing nothing. Not one thing. Finally her insides were in knots. The book she was reading gave her the creeps. Her legs became so restless she thought they might run away by themselves. She wished she had never married Mark Peight. She wanted to slam doors and spill a whole container of water over his head or pound her fists into his chest.

What she did do, finally, was kneel by his recliner and beg him to tell her what was wrong. But he feigned sleep, grunted, stuck up an elbow as if to shake her off, rolled on his side, smacked his lips in the most disgusting way, and resumed breathing deeply.

Sadie got up and walked blindly to the kitchen, then stood in the middle of it. She wanted to go home. She wanted to lay her head on Mam's shoulder and, smelling the talcum powder that always wafted from her, cry great big alligator tears and ask Mam why she hadn't warned and better prepared her little girl?

She felt like a buoy anchored to the sea floor, tossed about by the waves. But she stayed right there in the middle of her kitchen, anchored to the beautiful floorboards by her marriage to him. Oh, he made her so mad!

It wasn't right, this anger. All her life, she had been groomed to be a submissive Amish housewife. The husband is the head of the house, and his wishes are to be respected. Your life is now no longer your own.

No doubt.

Your life is doled out in portions by his moods. If he falls into a black one, your life could be measured by the tiniest measuring spoon. Approximately one-eighth of a teaspoon. Barely enough to keep a person going. No cup runneth over here.

Ah, well. She knew their life together would not be perfect, the way he had always been so hard to understand. But this? This standing in the middle of the kitchen, completely afloat, by that tall dark stranger sunk into a vile mood for which you were unprepared.

Then he would get over it, usually by going off to work the following morning, his lunchbox swinging in one hand, the red and white Coleman jug of ice water in the other, his faithful driver and coworker, Lester Brenner, waiting at the end of the yard, idling the diesel engine of his pickup truck.

Mark was a farrier and a good one. He shod all of Richard Caldwell's horses, as well as those of the Amish who owned more than one horse, and still the telephone messages kept coming.

After he spent a day doing hard physical labor, getting out among people, talking, forgetting himself, he would return home a changed person. Smiling, his arms enfolding her, her head fitting so perfectly into that hollow of his shoulder, she would smell the rich odor of horses and his own musky, salty essence. She would close her eyes and thank God for her husband, forgiving him another time of blackness.

That was when the eighth of a teaspoon turned into immeasurable quantities, and Sadie's life made great, big, happy sense, like a tree filled with great rosy-cheeked apples, its roots by a blue lake, watered constantly by the love of God.

So when it was Tuesday morning, and the snow was coming down thick and fast, too fast to attempt a drive to her mother's house, she decided to unpack some of her extra things and wash the dishes, fold the towels, and store them in the bottom drawer of the bureau in the living room. It was a job she had meant to do at least a month ago and still had not accomplished.

She was unwrapping a set of salt and pepper shakers, the newspaper around them aged and crumbling from being stored in her parent's attic for many years. Mommy Hershberger had given them to her on her tenth birthday. Purple grapes with green leaves swinging from a sort of tree, all made in shining ceramic. Oh, my. And she had thought they were so cool back then.

Smiling, she put them on the countertop to be washed in soapy water, then she retrieved a small white basket filled with yellow plastic roses, the greenish faces having changed color from the heat of the attic, waxy, smelling like old plastic. Grimacing, she pulled out the artificial flowers and threw them into the trash can with the old newspapers, then set the white basket by the purple salt and pepper shakers.

She had just found a small cedar chest with a glossy top, a gray and white kitten smiling from the lid, surrounded by pink flowers and a red handkerchief. Ugh. A gift from a names exchange in seventh grade. Oh, dear. She should keep it.

Barking from Wolf, Mark's large gray and silver dog, brought her head up, her gaze automatically going to the driveway. His bark was deep, full-throated, but not threatening. She watched as a black Jeep, (four-wheel drive, she hoped) made its way slowly up to the end of the yard before stopping. The driver shut off the engine.

Sadie stood up, smoothed her white apron over her stomach, adjusted the sleeves of her lime green dress, then checked her appearance in the mirror above the sink in the laundry.

Covering straight.

Wonder who would come visiting in the snow?

Three men slowly opened the doors of the vehicle as if hesitant to subject themselves to the cold wetness of the snow. They all wore some semblance of the usual Stetson hats so common in Montana—brown, black, slouched, but seemingly clean. Their clothes were presentable, clean blue jeans, tan Carhart coats. Adjusting their jacket zippers, they looked to the boards leading up to the porch.

No sidewalks or strips had been built yet, so the boards leading from the porch floor to the ground would have to do. Covered with snow, though.

Why were all three of them coming in? Usually, only one person could state their business.

Well, no use getting all flustered, she'd be okay. Once fear invaded your life, it could easily take control and make you subject to it. She'd be okay.

The leader was evidently heavyset, his large form rocking from side to side with each purposeful stride. His gray mustache hid all of his mouth, his hair tied in the back, a long gray ponytail hanging down the back of his coat.

He stopped, evaluating the slope of the boards, the accumulation of snow, before turning to his friends, saying something.

Sadie started to go to the door to advise them, then decided against it. They'd find their way.

The other two men were smaller in stature, with clean-shaven faces, not unpleasant. One wore glasses low on his nose, which he pushed up every time he squinted toward the house.

Wolf kept barking but followed them, his tail wagging. Sadie knew he was friendly, but one command from Mark could change the situation entirely, and he would attack a person or animal if Mark wanted him to.

None of the men seemed to be bothered by Wolf, completely unafraid, barely acknowledging his existence. That was odd.

They were all up on the porch now, huddled, talking in hushed tones. Should she simply disappear, glide noiselessly away, up the stairs or into the bedroom, and hide? No, that was cowardly. She was here by herself except the days she still worked at the ranch with Dorothy and Erma Keim, the garrulous spinster who had been hired to make the work load easier.

A resounding knock. Nothing timid about them, that was sure.

She wasn't afraid when she opened the door, and when they greeted her with friendly smiles, she invited them inside, the man with the glasses still pushing them up, squinting at her as he did so.

The heavyset man introduced himself as Dave Sims, the other two shaking hands with her politely, saying their names, which she promptly forgot.

Sadie gestured toward the kitchen table.

"Would you like to sit down?"

"Actually, we will."

Silently, they all pulled out chairs, Dave grunting a bit as he folded his large form into the chair that had appeared quite sturdy before but looked very small and feeble now.

"What we're here for…" he began. Then, "How much do you know about the two children who came to the Caldwell place?"

Whoa. How did they know she worked there? Why come here? Why not talk to Richard Caldwell? Or Jim and Dorothy?

Taking a deep breath, Sadie said carefully, "Not very much."

"You work there?"

"Yes."

"Were you working when they arrived?"

"Yes,"

"What did they look like?"

"Just…well, two very dirty, poor children. Their clothes were in tatters. Too big. They just hung on their thin shoulders."

No answer, just a nodding of three heads in unison.

"Where are they now?"

"Why don't you talk to Richard Caldwell, the owner of the ranch?" Sadie asked, a bit hesitantly, yet braving the adversity she felt would come.

"We did."

Instantly, Sadie felt more at ease. She visibly relaxed, let go of the hem of her white apron, which she had been twisting between her thumb and index finger. If they talked to Richard Caldwell first, and he sent them here….

Yet, there was a lingering doubt.

"They are adopted, the way we heard."

"Yes, I think legally."

They nodded.

Then, they all showed their identification. They worked for the government, some kind of detectives who handled special kinds of cases. (Sadie didn't completely understand it.) Apparently, the children had disappeared with their mother. The father was a fugitive, a person of interest who was running from the law. The mother was also under suspicion, although her complete disappearance was the only reason. They needed information. Everything would be recorded. How much did she know?

Sadie told them everything from the moment the children appeared at the kitchen door, about the bag of costly jewelry, the safe where it was held, their impeccable manners, their names.

When she mentioned their names, two of them shook their heads.

"No, no. Not their real names."

Sadie's eyes opened wide.

"Really?"

"No. Their mother, or whoever took them away, did a good job of masquerading the real kids. Their names are Sebastian and Angelica Hartford, of the Dallas Hartfords?"

Sadie shrugged her shoulders.

"Ever watched the TV show, *Dallas*?"

"No."

"Well, there's more money than you can ever imagine involved."

"These kids are victims of a serious ring of horse thieves. The only thing they ever did wrong was to have eyes and ears. They know too much, and, we're surmising, so does their mother. There is an old, old bloodline running in the veins of some of these horses, an Arabian strain, that makes them worth thousands and thousands of dollars. There was one stable here in Montana that unknowingly housed a stallion carrying the bloodline. The horse thieves knew this. Stole a lot of horses. I think what happened, it was a mistake gone completely haywire."

Sadie swallowed hard. The room spun, then righted itself, her breathing came raggedly now, as she acknowledged the fact that she knew a whole lot that could help these men tremendously.

But...should she?

With all her heart, she longed for Mark. He would know what to do. She had seen the identification. But why the ponytail? The mustache? Their clothes did not fit her mind's description of a detective. Was that only the Amish way instilled in her?

You expected people to dress a certain way, to look the way you think they should. Men wore hats and suspenders buttoned to broadfall trousers. Older women combed their hair flat, wore larger coverings, wore darker, plainer fabric and colors. Young girls arranged their hair in nicer waves, wore smaller coverings, brightly colored dresses. Little boys wore straw hats, denim trousers. Everything was in order and expected to appear a certain way.

People who worked for the government wore uniforms and cut their hair close to their heads, didn't they? She would have to know. So she asked them. Hesitantly at first, but gaining strength as she talked.

"What do you think 'undercover agent' means?" the heavyset man asked, a broad smile on his face, widening to a likeable grin.

The man with the glasses, (what was his name?) pushed them up again, squinted more than ever, but smiled genuinely.

So she told them everything. The black stallion's return, Cody, Paris, the shootings, the close calls, the Amish people's frustration with the local police.

At the mention of Paris, Dave Sims' eyes bore into hers. He shook his head from side to side as she mentioned the narrow escapes.

"Do you have any idea of the danger you are living with?" he finally ground out, his face turning a dark shade of red.

"Are you here alone, every day?" the thinner man asked, keeping himself professionally in check.

"No. I work at the Caldwell...Aspen East. Aspendale," she stammered.

"Your husband?"

"A farrier. Works for Richard Caldwell."

"Where is this horse named Paris?"

"In the barn."

They all looked at one another, compressed their lips.

"Do you have the registration papers?"

"Yes. In fact, I do. They were one of the last things I brought from my parents' house. I'm ... it's been a bit over two months since we've been married."

"That's wonderful. Congratulations."

"Thank you."

"Can we see the papers?"

"Yes, of course."

She found them in the pocket of the notebook, where she had filed more important documents until she could arrange them properly in Mark's bottom file drawer. When she produced the papers they needed, Dave Sims extracted an envelope from an inside pocket of his coat. They all bent their heads, clucked their tongues, read portions out loud, then sat back. Dave Sims told Sadie she was the owner of an extremely valuable horse who was in grave danger and would have to be taken away if she wanted the horse to stay alive, or wanted both herself and Mark to remain safe.

"But you can't take Paris!" she burst out, unashamed now, her only thought how much Paris would miss her, how unhappy she'd be away from Truman and Sadie and Mark and Wolf. In the end, she gave in. There was no other way.

Chapter 2

WHEN MARK ARRIVED HOME SHE THREW HERSELF into his arms and cried and sniffed and mumbled and blew her nose, her eyes red, her nose swollen, her hair disheveled, until he led her to the new beige-colored sofa with the gray cushions. He told her to stop crying, calm down, and start all over.

He held her hands and stroked her back reassuringly as she repeated her story much slower this time, hugging him and begging him to try and do something about Paris. They simply could not take her away.

"And the thing that worries me just as much—what in the world will happen to Dorothy if she finds this out? She'll be beside herself without those children."

Mark said she wouldn't have to know, and Sadie said that wasn't one bit fair, that it was better to tell her, which is what she did when she went to work the next day.

She went straight to Richard Caldwell's office, glad to hear his voice welcoming her in, glad to hear every word he had to say about her and Paris.

Yes, he believed it was as serious as the men had said. Paris would have to go to an undisclosed location, despite

Sadie's vehement protests that Paris would be perfectly all right in the barn.

"Who knows I got married and live with Mark now?" she finished, a note of rebellion hanging on the question.

"You want my personal opinion, Sadie? You better do what you're told. Until this whole thing is cleared up, anyway."

Sadie said nothing, still hoping for a chance to keep Paris in the barn where she would be perfectly all right, thank you very much.

However, they agreed to tell Dorothy about the children together. When she was called into the office, she waited a good 10 minutes before making her appearance, then blew through the door, prickly with irritation, sat solidly on a leather wing chair, then almost slid off, her short legs putting a halt to it by digging into the carpet, definitely not helping her dignity.

"Now what do you want, Mr. Caldwell?" she said, putting all the impatience she could into the "Now."

"This is very important, Dorothy," Richard Caldwell said soberly.

"Hardly more important than my roast of beef. That Erma don't know how to trim it, so she don't."

Sadie squelched a giggle. Erma Keim had only one name here at the ranch, and it was "That Erma."

Continued combat, she thought.

Richard Caldwell assured her it was much more important than roast beef and proceeded to tell her in a level, quiet voice everything that had occurred, which left poor Dorothy rocking from side to side in agitation.

"Oh, come on now, they can't take my babies. They're in school! You can't take kids out of school. They're mine. I don't care if those men say they're the government, you can't take kids out of school."

With that, she pulled a bobby pin out of her gray hair and dug so viciously in one ear that Sadie was afraid she'd never find it again. Dorothy remembered what she was doing and put it back in her hair, clearing her throat self-consciously.

A wave of pity rolled over Sadie's heart. Dorothy was so small and plump, her polyester slacks too short around the ankles, her beige shoes from the Dollar General splattered with bacon grease, her multicolored shirt exposing too much of her wrinkled neck, a cloud of bluster and sense of self riding solidly on her gray head.

Richard Caldwell went on explaining patiently. If they found the mother of their children and she was proved innocent, Dorothy would have to give them up.

Shaking a plump finger in Richard Caldwell's direction, Dorothy told him the Lord had sent Marcelona and Louise; they were her beloved angels sent straight from heaven, and he'd not allow them to be taken away. And don't you kid yourself, she was going to go back to her roast beef, and if he wasn't going to do anything about Erma Keim trimming off too much fat, then she'd have to do it herself, or he'd be eating a roast beef that had the taste and texture of good shoe leather, and she meant it.

She slid off the leather chair after that display of territorial words and bustled straight back to the kitchen, leaving a vapor of martyrdom behind her. Richard Caldwell shook his head, then exploded in a volcanic bellow of laughter that brought one just like it from Sadie.

They wiped their eyes, smiled, then agreed to let it go. They had told her the truth, and now it was up to Dorothy to accept it.

Sadie vacuumed and dusted, scoured bathrooms, and

as always, thoroughly enjoyed cleaning this grand house. There was just something about being in a home as beautiful as this that fulfilled a sense of longing for the finer things in life.

In her circles, Sadie knew this lust of the world, this lust of the eyes, was accompanied by a firm denouncing of it. She was admonished to take up the cross, deny herself, and follow the narrow path of Jesus, which she felt was good and right. Sadie wanted no life other than the one she led, the goal of which was to live in a way that would lead to heaven.

That was how she was born. Amish. To parents who wanted this way of life, this security for their children. The heritage passed on from generation to generation.

It was hard to explain when English people asked questions, implying the senselessness of driving a horse and buggy or having no electricity. And if it was so wrong, why ride in a car at all?

It wasn't wrong for Richard and Barbara Caldwell to have their beautiful home. They were living their lives the way their parents lived theirs, doing what, to them, was right. That was fine.

Sadie loved her employer and his wife, defending their lifestyle if anyone dared say anything negative. They were kind, caring people, who did what was right for their employees, even if they lived lavishly, according to Amish standards. She would never judge them.

She stopped in the upstairs bathroom to lift the slatted wooden blind and gaze out across the snowy ranch land. It spread as far as the eye could see, the scenery so beautiful it could take your breath away, especially in winter.

She would have to ride Paris this evening. One more time before they took her away. Paris loved the snow, taking great plunging strides, spraying clouds of it when she ran, the cold air slamming into Sadie's face, Reuben at her side, yelling and laughing.

She'd have to leave a message for him on her parents' phone. Maybe he could ride over tomorrow after work.

As it turned out, Reuben had to work late. Dat started a new log cabin that needed the concrete poured for the footer before the next snow arrived.

A week later, the government men came and took Paris away. Sadie refused to watch, throwing herself on their bed, shutting out any sound with the pillow clamped over her head as tightly as possible. She lifted it cautiously to listen for any sounds before emerging from the bedroom, her ears red, her eyes swollen from crying.

Catching sight of herself in the mirror, she was shocked to see how old and careworn she appeared. So she took a shower, changed to a dress the color of cranberries, brushed her teeth, and decided to grow up and stop being so immature about Paris. She was just a horse.

Then Sadie thought of Paris stepping down from that trailer after a long cold journey, her large brown eyes with the thick, bristly lashes looking at everyone and everything with so much trust in them. Sadie's lips trembled, her nose burned, and she started sobbing all over again.

Mark told her to go home and spend the day with her mother and sisters. She needed it.

And that's exactly what she did, being greeted with cheers and hugs and coffee and French toast, maple syrup and chipped beef gravy, fried cornmeal mush, and Mam's perfect dippy eggs.

Leah was working at her cleaning job, but Rebekah and Anna were at home. They caught up on the latest news, the life of dating, being with the youth, their work,

Reuben turning 16 before too long, and Mam's concern about Reuben's time of *rumspringa*, literally translated as "running around," which is exactly what the youth did after they turned 16.

Mam was in high spirits, making them all laugh with stories about the last quilting she had attended. She had to get started piecing Leah's Mariner's Star quilt, with the feeling goading her that Kevin had marriage on his mind.

"But, can you imagine, a Mariner's Star in black and beige? It's enough to give me the blues. All that black!"

"Get Fred Ketty to piece it," Rebekah suggested.

"Fred Ketty?"

"They said she did one with black and ... I forget what else, but she got over 900 dollars for it."

"Where?"

Mam was so incredulous her mouth formed a perfect O, then closed tightly after she pronounced the "where."

"She sold it at the fire hall, remember? That auction in August."

"See, that shouldn't be allowed. That's too much display ... of ... Well, it's just too worldly, parading a quilt like that at a fire hall. Likely it was raffled off or whatever, and that's too much like gambling, and that's strictly *verboten*, you know that."

Mam became so agitated she started scraping leftover crusts of French toast into the garbage, her face with heightened color, her nostrils flaring.

Rebekah winked broadly at Sadie, with the sort of look that said, "Mam's just jealous," but in a loving way. You could never hate your mother. You could get irritated, even angry for a short time, but if she had a whole list of failures, you sort of loved even the shortcomings. Mam so obviously prided herself in her own ability to piece outstanding quilts that this sort of news was a bit much.

After the conversation lagged, Anna got up, saying she had a dress to sew, so Rebekah and Sadie could do the dishes.

"What color are you making?" Sadie asked.

Anna brought out a three-yard piece of fabric, the color a hue of brilliant magenta with a decided stripe in it.

"Mam!" Sadie gasped. She was clearly shocked.

Why would Mam allow a color that bold, a stripe that pronounced? She obviously hadn't. Calmly, Mam laid down her plate, then came over to peer at the offending color and texture.

"Where did you get this, Anna?"

"Walmart."

Anna's eyes were very large in her too-thin face, the angle of her beautiful cheekbone so pronounced, her chin so tiny, the cleft in it showing so plainly. Her dress, as usual, hung on her thin frame, gathered about her tiny waist by the broad belt of her apron.

Anna was the youngest and battled eating disorders. With little sense of self-worth, always appearing overweight and ugly in her own eyes, she had taken to purging. Sadly loathing herself and her pitiful ability to be a friend, she felt she had nothing to contribute to a conversation or any circumstance in which she found herself. Anna was one of the reasons it had been difficult for Sadie, often acting as a mentor to her troubled sister, to leave home.

Mam pursed her lips now and said evenly, "I hope you know I can't let you make a dress with that fabric, Anna."

It was all Anna needed to release the spring of tension, the bottled up volcano of rebellion against Mam, or

Sadie, or anyone who tried to take this dress away from her. It was completely essential that she wear this dress, the object that would surely grab and keep Neil Hershberger's faithful devotion.

"Oh, no! You're not taking this dress away from me!" she shouted, her beautiful eyes already forming tears. "I paid for it with my own money! No. You're not. I'm going to wear it!"

She turned, sobbing, running up the steps, the priceless magenta-colored fabric clutched tightly to her thin chest.

Mam started to follow, a hand out, calling her name, but Sadie stopped her. "I'll go after awhile."

"I don't know what to do. She is so different from all you other girls. I plum don't know how to handle it."

With that, Mam sat down wearily, suddenly overcome with her daughter's rebellion coupled with Fred Ketty's 900 dollar quilt.

"Mam, you know her whole problem is that she has to be on top of the pile," Rebekah said harshly.

"Ach, Rebekah," Mam said sadly.

"I'm serious. She can't give up. If that would have been me, you would not have been overwhelmed very long. Bingo! In the trash! Subject closed!"

Mam laughed, her plump stomach shaking with mirth. "Now stop it," she said, still laughing.

When Sadie got to Anna's room, she found it hard to see her sister that way, lying on her stomach, as close to the wall as she could get, her fingers in her ears the minute Sadie opened the door. Human nature made Sadie feel like smacking her, calling her a big baby, and telling her to get off that bed this minute, go eat something, and stop obsessing about yourself and Neil Hershberger. Maybe that's what Sadie should have done.

There were too many big girls in the family while Anna was growing up. Somehow, she had been shorted, whether it came from Mam's mental illness, or whether she was born with this decayed sense of her own worth. Whatever the cause, she needed help.

"All right, Anna. Stop it. Get your fingers out of your ears. Look at me."

"Go away."

"All right, I will."

She walked away, closed the door firmly behind her, then heard it open and Anna calling, "Come back, Sadie."

"Not unless you're *chide*." (nice, normal)

"I'll try."

Sadie picked up the fabric, took it over to the window, parted the curtains and looked at it, peering closely, as if it were a foreign object.

"You weren't really going to make this, were you?" she asked, kindly and unaccusing.

"'Course I was."

Her words were hard stones pinging against Sadie's flinching face. Somehow that answer was a solidified thing, an assurance that Anna was no longer the harmless little girl who ate great dishes of Lucky Charms cereal. She was actually a concern, a problem to be addressed, like a broken porch step or a refrigerator that stopped working. You had to acknowledge that it needed fixing and then apply yourself, even if it put you in a state of despair. This thought swam into her consciousness, like a shark in a peaceful barrier reef.

Softly, but firmly, Sadie addressed her sister. "Wouldn't you be afraid? Ashamed to wear it to the hymn singing?"

"Huh-uh!"

"I bet you would."

"Hah-ah." So pronounced, her words were almost guttural.

"Come on, Anna. It's way too bright. The parents would have a fit."

"Hah-ah."

"Tell you what. I'll buy you another one if you'll go shopping with me."

Anna rolled over on her back, then sat up, pulling her knees to her chin, wrapping her arms around them. Her dark hair was disheveled, a lock hanging into her large, dark eyes and the dark shadows of ... what? Tiredness? Lack of good nutrition? Her eyes made her appear older, much older in fact, than her years.

Anna said nothing and just looked at her steadily, unflinching, with a cold look Sadie could not fully perceive.

"I want the dress I chose." The voice was flat, the words hard as nails.

Sadie said nothing, sighed, turned toward the dresser, picked up a small bottle of cologne, winced, gasped in shock at the words written diagonally across it. Still saying nothing, she plucked off the cap, spritzed a small amount on her wrist, rubbed it with the palm of her hand, and sniffed. "Mmm."

Anna's face brightened.

"You like it?"

"Yes, it smells ... different. Where did you buy it?"

"Neil gave it to me."

The defiant note in her voice is what gave away the lie. There was an angry retort on Sadie's tongue, but she caught herself just in time, knowing that a thick, suffocating confrontation would follow, driving a wedge of cast iron into the fragile relationship between them.

"He did? No birthday, no nothing?" Sadie turned, her eyebrows raised, surprise in her voice. "And you're not dating?"

Anna came up off the bed in one movement, her face darkening as anger propelled her. Standing boldly, one thin hand on her hip, her pelvis jutted out in defiance, she clipped her words short.

"No, we're not dating. Which I hope you know is none of your business. If I remember correctly, you weren't dating Mark for a very long time. Just sort of creeping around."

It was the sarcasm that did it. Turning, she felt the heat rise in her face, did nothing to stop it. She stepped within a foot of her sister, thrust her face close to hers, and let her words fall where they would.

"Anna, you know Neil did not give you that cologne. You also know that you are on a dangerous road, completely obsessed with a person of ... of questionable intent. You can't do this, Anna. He doesn't seem like someone you should be spending time with."

"You don't know him."

"Yes, I think I do. When I saw you two at my wedding, I could tell. You have no idea how you two appeared. The..."

She was cut short. "Shut up!"

Sadie's mouth fell open in disbelief. "Anna!"

"Get out! Get out of my room and stop talking. Go!"

Sadie opened her mouth, closed it, turned, and walked

through the door, closing it firmly behind her.

The remainder of the day passed in a blur. Mam prattled away happily about Kevin and Leah, how absolutely wonderfully he treated her, how much money he made, being the same as foreman on that logging operation, but then his father always was a good manager. Everything he touched turned into money.

Mam said this innocently, but Sadie caught the underlying pride. She wanted to tell Mam to be careful, but she was suddenly too tired, too beaten down by Anna's outburst to try and remedy anything at all. She just wanted to go home. Home to Mark, to her clean, uncluttered life, where the unpleasantness came only from Paris's absence, which would turn out all right in the end, she felt sure.

She hitched up Truman with Rebekah's help. She waved good-bye as he pulled the carriage down the drive, and a deep sense of anticipation settled over her.

There was no need to question whether it had been God's will for her to become Mark Peight's wife. With a deep, abiding knowledge, she knew the rightness of it, of returning to him with this joy after spending a day with her family.

She would worry about Anna, the magenta-colored dress, Neil, the questionable cologne, but she would be able to put all of it out of her thoughts, for a time, anyway. Perhaps it was just a phase.

The cream-colored SUV passed her from behind, traveling so slowly she almost had to hold Truman back to keep from catching up to it. Annoying driver... Why didn't he accelerate? Just get going? She did pull back on the black leather reins then, or she would have driven too close. Probably an elderly couple afraid of the snow-covered back roads. Truman wanted to run, so Sadie held back firmly now, glad to see the car ahead of her pick up speed.

Driving horses were all the same, she thought. When you got them out of the barn and hitched them to the buggy, they trotted along willingly, took you where you wanted to go, settling down to a level trot, even if they felt a bit spunky at first, dancing around, balking a bit, or crow-hopping sometimes. But if you let them stand at a barn, or along a fence, or tied to a hitching rack for any length of time, then hitched them up to return home, they pricked their ears forward and clipped along at a much better pace, knowing a good cold drink out of their own trough, a nice pile of oats, and a block of good hay awaited them at home.

Home was where all horses wanted to be. Me, too, Truman, Sadie thought, smiling to herself. She had some cold chicken breast in the refrigerator. She would make the chicken and rice casserole for Mark this evening. No broccoli, so she'd substitute peas. She had a whole pumpkin pie in a round Tupperware container under the seat, a gift from Mam, bless her heart. Pumpkin pies were complicated to make. She smiled to herself, thinking of Mam's distaste for any uncovered, or loosely covered, food items put under the seat of a buggy. No matter how hard you tried to avoid it, there was always a certain amount of horse hair floating inside a buggy, always finding its way to the top of a container. But not one hair would be on the pumpkin pie. Mam double-checked the famously secure Tupperware seal.

The beige-colored SUV approached her again from the opposite direction, driving as slow as before. The windows were tinted, so there was no use checking for the occupants. That was some expensive vehicle, Sadie guessed.

She wondered vaguely what she would drive if she was English. She smiled at the thought of turning the ignition key, stepping on a pedal, and moving off. Wouldn't that be different?

She wished she had sunglasses to wear. The late afternoon sun was blinding. That would be different, too. A pair of black sunglasses on a face framed by an Amish bonnet. Likely she'd get her picture on the front page of the local newspaper.

Truman was gathering speed for his dash up the side of Atkin's Ridge, so Sadie relaxed the reins, letting him have his head, knowing he had to make it up the hill on his own terms, rounding the curve on top like a racer, leaning to the right.

She pulled back in alarm when the same SUV roared past from behind, disappearing up the side of the ridge in a whirl of snow and grit. Boy, for all the time they wasted going back and forth, probably looking for a certain road sign, they must have suddenly decided they knew where they were going.

And when she came upon this vehicle parked across the road, she hauled back on the leather reins as hard as she could, thinking they should have been more careful, having suddenly hit an icy spot. She hoped no one was hurt, and she was glad to see the vehicle had not turned over. There was no way around it, with the high bank on one side and the steep incline on the other, so she opened the window, calling "Whoa."

Chapter 3

TRUMAN OBEYED, ALTHOUGH HE RAISED AND lowered his head, pulling at his bit, impatient at the obstacle in his path.

Sadie was surprised when the doors flung open and two men wearing black ski masks quickly ran to the buggy. Her first thought was about their lack of common sense, wearing ski masks this time of the day when the temperatures weren't that low. Later, during the night, the temperature would hover below zero. It was only when she saw the small black pistol in the fat man's gloved hand that she felt the first stab of fear.

"Don't give us any trouble and you won't get hurt."

The words were muffled, as if the opening in his mask was at the wrong place. His breath was coming fast and hard, like he had been running. The barrel of the pistol was so tiny. It looked like a toy, actually. Maybe it was. That thought was fleeting, instantly replaced by the knowledge of danger and the alarming position in which she now found herself.

Truman's ears flicked back, he lowered his head and tested the reins.

"You're coming with us."

She knew she couldn't do that. Who would care for Truman and the buggy? What about Mark? His chicken-and-rice casserole? Her eyes sought an opening, a way through. Not enough room. Could she jump out, make it on foot? Not in this snow. Panic spread its oily fingers across her chest, squeezing her lungs till her breathing was only coming in shallow puffs.

"Get down." The words were garbled, surprisingly mild, and, in a way, mannerly.

"I can't." Her voice was hoarse, her dry throat now aching with a sort of despair, an acceptance that this time she could not go dashing away on Paris. She didn't even know where Paris was.

"You will get down." The words were forceful now, spoken much louder. The gun was positioned again, shoved up against the frame of the buggy where the door had been slid back.

Wildly now, her eyes darted, searching for an escape route, realizing there was none. Slowly, methodically, she lifted the lap robe that kept her legs warm.

"I can't just let... Truman... the horse, loose."

"Get down now."

There was nothing to do but obey. Not with that pistol stuck in her face and the two men waiting for her. It was when she laid the reins across the glove compartment, slid the lap robe away from her legs, and grasped the frame of the buggy to lower herself that a total loss of hope clenched her heart. Here, on Atkin's Ridge, again. This time, would it be her last? She was too afraid to pray.

Like a robot, she moved. Her foot hit the step, then the ground. She was immediately seized on either side, her elbows encased in gloved hands like vices clamping down and propelling her forward. Stumbling, sliding, looking back at Truman, she begged them to let her take care of the horse and buggy. Yanking on her, they stuffed her into the back seat. She saw a roll of duct tape appear.

"No!" She screamed, then kicked, flung her arms, and hit the fat man with every ounce of her strength.

"Get in and drive!" The fat man's accomplice instantly slid behind the wheel and locked the doors. Still she fought until the fat man shoved the sinister little pistol to her face.

Sadie became more terrified. She was being taken to an unknown destination, to an unknown end. And for what reason? She shuddered and slid back against the leather seat as the fat man encircled her wrists and ankles, the sticky tape digging into her flesh. The car was moving now, going down the side of the ridge.

Oh, Mark. It was then that she cried. If this was the way her life would end, then she was deeply aware of having had these short months with Mark and so very grateful of his love. That he had chosen her to be his wife still seemed like a miracle. The days they spent together were idyllic, except for the bad times, which, so far, had proved to be temporary.

What would he do? If there is such a thing as telepathy, a sort of mental communication, just let him know I'm safe, so far.

Then she remembered God. Of course, God was here. He knew where she was. Her fate was in his hands, not the hands of these men. He had the power to rescue her, keep her safe, or end her life. It was all in God's hands.

How often had she heard that phrase? *In Gottes Hent.* Over and over, the Amish people used that phrase. It was the way they lived. The way they believed. Everything happened for a reason. To God on his throne, it all made perfect sense, so they lived simply, peacefully, not having to under-stand everything, their faith a substance of things not seen.

Like one of Mam's homemade, pieced comforters, his presence wrapped itself around her shoulders, loosening the clutches of fear. As if God wanted to comfort her, she clearly remembered the story of a girl who had been kidnapped and knew to remain friendly, talkative, com-plying with her abductor until they became friends of a sort. They finally agreed on a compromise. The man who abducted her acknowledged that he needed help and became a much better person in the end.

Well, there were two kidnappers, and as far as she could tell, they were still hurtling along on an interstate. The joyous thought entered her mind of the driver going far over the speed limit, a police car overtaking them, being rescued, and these men being caught. Hopefully, the driver was pushing about a hundred.

She couldn't swallow without straining, the duct tape biting into her cheeks and jaw every time she did. She des-perately needed a drink and wondered how long a person could go without using a restroom. She thought of a tall glass of sparkling lemonade with chunks of ice, which made her swallow, bringing much more discomfort.

"Better watch it. Cops'll be after you." The driver slowed down.

Sadie was lulled to a stupor, a sort of gray area, nei-ther asleep nor awake, but always aware of the moving vehicle and the men beside her. The emotions of fear and panic were blanketed with a fuzzy warmth, a dissociation from reality.

She didn't know how long she stayed in this posi-tion; she only knew they were slowing, then came to a stop. The men exchanged a few whispered comments.

The driver got out. She smelled gasoline, so she knew they were filling up at a service station. Was it dark outside? What time was it?

Please, please, let me have a drink of water. Her throat was beyond dry; it was ravaged with thirst. Any saliva she could summon was instantly absorbed by the rags, sponge, cotton, or whatever it was that they stuffed in her mouth.

The driver returned; they moved on. She heard tractor trailers moving slowly through the parking lot. Cars moved, honked their horns. The men were drinking something. She heard the crack and hiss as the fat man opened a bottle of soda pop, the liquid gurgling from the bottle down his throat.

She was so thirsty that she cried. Tears squeezed from between her lashes, wetting the blindfold. She was glad of the blindfold, absorbing the tears, her sign of weakness. She would have to be stronger. She would be. She would will away her thirst.

Her feet were going numb. The duct tape dug into her ankles and cut into her black stockings. Her hands throbbed. She imagined them growing twice as big and turning purple, then falling off. That's what happened if you banded a little piggy's tail. After the circulation was shut off for a length of time, it simply shriveled away to nothing and dropped off. She hoped it took hands a long, long time.

Her ears were pressed so hard against the side of her bonnet, she could barely feel them. If she moved her cheekbones, or imagined moving her ears, it helped. So she knew she could actually change the position of her ears, even if it was only for a short time before the numbness and tingling returned.

All night, they drove. Sadie alternated between sleep and a half-awake stupor. Her thirst raged in her throat now, a constant thing she could not escape. As a child, she had often imagined being kidnapped, the pain of fetters, but never could anyone imagine the cruelty of her thirst. No wonder people died of thirst way before they succumbed to hunger.

The vehicle stopped. The back door opened. She lurched awake, strained against her blindfold, screamed a silent scream of alarm when rough hands seized her.

"Get out."

Sadie tried to wiggle the duct tape loose, leaned forward, swung her legs over the side of the seat. The air was cold and wet, sharp as a knife against her senses.

"Loosen her feet."

Sadie brought her teeth together, clenched her jaw, willing herself not to cry out. If she moved as much as a tongue muscle, the pain was excruciating. The tape made a tearing, sticky sound. She felt it being unwound, the blood rushing into her feet, a thousand needles pricking like a swarm of yellow jackets from the swamp in Ohio.

"Get out. Walk."

She slid down, her feet hit the ground, and she crumbled into a heap, crying in her throat, raw from the thirst and pain and hopelessness.

"Get up." The fat man was angry.

"She can't with the tape," the driver said.

"Get her."

Two hands went under her arms, lifted her, but she crumbled into a heap the same as before. The fat man snorted with impatience. Grabbing her, he threw her across his shoulder, the same way any man would pack a hundred-pound sack of feed or bag of potatoes. The blood rushed into her head as she bobbed along, being carried up one flight of stairs, then another. Doors opened and closed. It was warm. Something smelled good, very good, in fact. Like pine woods or the first of the wild flowers.

The fat man dumped her on a soft sofa or bed. She lay completely still. Somehow playing dead like a possum seemed safe.

"Unwind her hands. The duct tape."

Again she heard the grinding sticky sound. Her hands fell into the bed, containing no strength of their own.

"We need to talk. We're going to unwind the tape around your mouth. We will loosen the blindfold if you promise to stay. Any attempt at leaving will mean death. We are serious. You are of no consequence to us."

Her head turned from side to side by the force of the tape being removed. It was all irrelevant. No matter. The pain was bearable. She'd be able to see, to swallow. Would they allow her a drink? She gagged when they removed the object in her mouth. But she recovered quickly, summoning her courage and resolving to remain strong.

When they removed the blindfold, she untied her heavy black bonnet with groping, numb fingers that felt as big as bananas and about as clumsy. She kept her eyes closed, afraid to open them. Where was she? Slowly, through shaking eyelids, her eyes focused, bringing the room into view.

At first she saw only beige walls, then the ornate molding in a darker shade. Slowly, as her eyes cleared, she saw that she was in a bedroom, sort of a guest bedroom. The carpeting was beige, as well as the bedspread, the curtains, and pillows. There was a red sofa, a glass coffee table, and red objects of art. Black lamps cast a yellowish light into the corners, and huge, navy blue, plaid pillows were strewn across the sofa in the glow of the lamps. Very pretty, she thought wryly.

"May I please be allowed a visit to the restroom?"

She tried to say this, but her voice was only a whisper, her vocal chords refusing to accommodate her. The fat man pointed to a door behind the bed. Slowly, carefully, Sadie set one foot on the carpeting, then the other. Clutching the side of the bed, she moved around it, bent over, wincing with the pain of the returning circulation.

She never knew a person could drink so much water. She cupped her hands beneath the gold faucet and drank and drank and drank. Water seeped between her fingers. She sucked at it greedily, hating to wait until her cupped hands were filled again so she could slurp at it like an animal dying of thirst.

It was only after her thirst was sated that she knew how hungry she was. She looked at the pink guest soaps in the white seashell dish and considered eating them. She had to have something to eat. They'd have to feed her. Allow her some kind of food. Did kidnappers starve their victims to death? Who knew?

Tentatively, she opened the door of the bathroom, hobbled out, still clinging to the side of the bed.

Immediately the fat man began. "You cooperate, you're fine. If you act stubborn, you're not. Got it?"

Sadie nodded, her eyes on the carpet.

"Where's the palomino mare?"

"I don't know."

With the speed of lightning, his hammy fist smacked her mouth, snapping her head back. Sadie didn't cry out. Tears came to her eyes, and blood spurted from a torn lip. She lifted the hem of her blue apron to sop up the flow.

"I told you. You work with us, you're fine."

The driver shifted uncomfortably, his gaze wavering, clearing his throat as if he wanted to say something, then thought better of it. From behind the apron, Sadie shook her head.

"They took her away."

"Who?"

The fat man's eyes bored into hers, a sick light of greediness shining.

"Four men came to my house. Was it a week ago? Something like that. They said I was in danger. So was Paris."

"Who's Paris?"

"The horse."

"The palomino?"

Sadie nodded. "They said they were taking her to an undisclosed location."

The two men looked at each other and nodded. "Are you telling the truth?"

"Yes. Why would I lie? I just want to go home. You can have the horse if you spare my life. I don't want to die."

"We ain't killin' anybody," the driver burst out before the fat man held up a hand, giving him a scathing look.

"Looks as if you're gonna be here awhile, young lady. We want the horse. At any cost. We figure we'll get her if we use you to acquire her."

At this, the fat man's eyes glittered again. "There's more ways than one to acquire our needs," he chortled.

"All right," Sadie said, not unpleasantly. "If you have to keep me here, am I allowed to know where I am? How long I have to stay? Will I be able to have some food? You're not going to tie me again with that duct tape?"

The driver shook his head wildly behind the fat man's back.

"You're a long way from home. You'll be staying until we can persuade them, whoever it is, to give us the palomino. We'll feed you, and if you stay cooperative, we'll keep you locked up in here, but no duct tape.

Sadie nodded. "Thank you. I am appreciative of this freedom. I won't attempt an escape as long as I'm treated decently."

"If the people hand over the palomino, you're good to go."

Sadie nodded again. She lifted her head then, "Am I alone in this house?"

"This is a big place. No, you're not alone. This place is full of housekeepers, gardeners, cooks. It's a big place," he repeated.

So her imprisonment began. The digital clock read 11:09. The big red numbers against the black face were her only companion. There was no telephone, radio, or television. She went to the window, parted the heavy curtains, pulled on the cord that raised and lowered the blinds. Yes, as she thought, she was housed in a palatial home. Looking down from her third-story room, she saw there was no doubt about the immensity of the gardens, pastures, and the vast corrals and barns. It made Aspendale East seem quite ordinary.

The snow was thinner here, with brown tufts of grass showing like eyebrows on an old man's face. As far as the eye could see, there was only flat earth, a level landscape with rows of fences and trees creating a crisscross pattern that looked like one of Mam's homemade comforters.

Sadie had no communication with the outside world, only the fat man or the driver appearing with trays of food at whatever hour they chose. Her first meal had consisted of cold cereal, milk, and an apple, blistering in its sourness on her raw tongue and throat. The cereal tasted heavenly, savoring each sweet, milky bite the way she did. Sometimes she fared well, eating good, hot, Mexican dishes. Other time she went to bed hungry, dreaming of Mam's breakfasts.

She tried to keep her thoughts away from Mark. She always ended up sobbing into the pillow if she let her mind wander to him. She missed her family. She hoped Mam and Dat would be okay. She figured Reuben would waver between anger and indignation, between bluster and little-boy tears.

She paced the room, did sit-ups, stood at the window for hours on end. She was always thankful for good, hot baths, the ability to wash her clothes in the bathtub, to have clean towels, soap, and a good bed to sleep on. Her situation could have been so much worse.

She prayed for her rescue. She prayed the government agents would deliver Paris. She cried about Paris, too. But if it meant her life…

Had she been too *gros-feelich* (proud)? Didn't the Bible say we reap what we sow? Had she sown pride and arrogance with her beautiful Paris? Why had God allowed this to happen? How long until this ordeal ended?

Then one day, when she felt as if she would surely lose her mind if she had nothing to do, she decided to houseclean the room. It would give her exercise, keep her occupied, simply save her wandering sanity. She shaved some of the pink soap into the vanity bowl, grabbed a heavy, white washcloth, dunked and swirled it in the soapy water, then wrung it out well.

She started with the bathroom cupboards. She carefully took out towels, soap, a hair dryer, and what she guessed was a hair-curling apparatus, an assortment of combs and brushes, a box of guest soap. She washed each shelf thoroughly, replacing the objects, before tackling the bathroom closet. She stood on the vanity stool to clean the top shelf, pushing aside a stack of perfectly folded blankets.

Ouch! Her fast moving hand struck the corner of a hard object. Pulling out the stack of blankets, she let them fall to the floor before procuring the cause of her pain. She held it in her hands, incredulous. A radio! It must be. She didn't know much about electronic devices, living all her life without them, but she did know what a radio looked like. Eagerly, the blood pounding in her ears, she unwrapped the long, brown cord, plugged it in, then turned the dial with shaking fingers.

Nothing. Her disappointment was palpable—big and heavy, black, as dark as a night without moon or stars. The depth of her disappointment fueled her anger, her desperation. She jiggled wires, shook the radio, twisted and turned dials with a sort of viciousness, yet there was nothing.

Then she thought of Jim Sevarr's old rusted pickup truck and the wire coat-hanger stuck on the end of his broken antennae. Oh, dear God, let it be. Dashing to the closet, she flipped frantically through a long line of plastic or wooden hangers. Just one. I just need one wire hanger. Over and over, she went through them, finally acknowledging that there were none.

When a knock sounded, she had time to close the bathroom door. The fat man called her name; she told him she was in the bathroom and would he please wait until she came out. Her evening meal consisted of a great, steaming pile of roast pork and corn tortillas with tomato sauce, which absorbed her tears as she ate.

Chapter 4

Richard Caldwell and his wife, Barbara, were at their wit's end. They had already run the gauntlet of emotions in the weeks that Sadie had been missing. They had badgered every police department in the state of Montana. The computer was never idle, searching relentlessly for new avenues of discovery.

Dorothy's way of dealing with Sadie's disappearance was blaming the country, the president, Wall Street, the love of money, the devil, and most of all, the local police for not being able to track down the horse thieves, the snipers, the whole crazy lot of them in the first place. Erma Keim nodded her head, pursed her lips, and worked like a maniac, saying her nerves couldn't take this if she didn't use her muscles. She agreed with Dorothy on most subjects but stopped at Wall Street and the president.

The news media had posted regular news about the disappearance that first week, leaving the Amish community reeling. They had to be very careful, as being on TV was strictly *verboten*. So was speaking on radio or other forms of "worldly" news.

They were most comfortable "doing" for Jacob Miller's family and Mark. People came in great, caring buggy loads. They cleaned the stables, washed Mam's walls and windows, cooked so many casseroles and baked so many pies, half of them were thrown out.

Dat's face aged week by week. They all feared for Mam the most. Hadn't she been emotionally weak? Hadn't she been mentally ill? Yes, she had. But her strength now was amazing. She was a matriarch, a fortress of long-suffering and patience. She assured her family it was that palomino; the money or the horse would eventually show up. She prayed for Sadie's well-being. The only thing that set her face to crumbling now was the thought of Sadie having to suffer.

Anna became steadily more fragile. She blamed herself. She was afraid of God. He was up there on his throne, raining fire and brimstone down on her family because of her magenta dress and the secrets about her and Neil Hershberger. She roamed the house, a sad ghost of her former self, disappearing when company arrived. Leah and Rebekah hung posters on the local store windows. They prayed together, cried together, tried to include Anna, and were always supportive of Dat and Mam.

Mark moved in. He couldn't live in their house without Sadie. He lost weight, and deep lines appeared beneath his eyes. He had come home that evening, found Truman hitched to the buggy by the fence, shivering with cold. He became irritated. Why hadn't she unhitched him? He took care of Truman, noticed his leg bleeding, found the pumpkin pie, and Sadie's purse. Alarmed, Mark ran to the house, called for Sadie, and tried to stay calm.

Wolf had whined, and Mark even asked Wolf where she had gone. Men and dogs searched for days that turned into weeks. Helicopters throbbed in the sky. It was all a bad dream. He would surely wake up soon. But things like her nightgown hanging on a hook in the bathroom are what made him move in with her family. He simply couldn't take it—the sight of the boots she wore to help him do chores, the smell of the soap on their vanity, the essence of his darling Sadie.

They talked a lot, Mark and the Millers. They said things they probably never would have said if this had not occurred, leaving an impenetrable bond that would always hold.

Reuben got mad. He said Sadie was foolish, driving her horse and buggy around the way she did when she knew her life was at risk. The whole thing was—she had no fear. She never did. She should have taken a warning way back when she had that near-accident with Paris and the spring wagon and that guy from Lancaster County. It probably had something to do with that fat guy in the dentist's office. He reasoned with a lot of common sense for a youth of 15 years old.

He almost had it down pat; the only thing missing was more information. Which, with the hand of God moving in mysterious ways as it always does, was partially supplied when Richard Caldwell asked Reuben to come help Louis and Marcellus get the tack ready for the horse fair in February. There were piles of silver buckles and rings to be taken off the saddles and bridles, polished with silver polish, and reattached. It was a perfect job for Reuben, and one for which he'd be paid the astonishing amount of $12 an hour. In his eyes, he was amassing a fortune.

Dorothy fussed about that, too. She said the tack room was too cold. The children were too little to work, but Erma Keim told her they were not either. Little Amish children did lots of chores at that age, and Dorothy got her dander up and told her they were no better than English kids, and who did she think she was? Erma went home in a huff, slid down the washhouse stairs, and scraped her backside on the concrete steps, which Dorothy never learned of.

As it was, Dorothy supplied the young workers with cranberry juice and ginger ale, warm chocolate chip cookies, and ham salad to eat on warm rolls, all packed in a tin basket, telling them to come into the kitchen to warm up if their feet got cold.

Louis warmed right up to Reuben. They talked nonstop. Reuben asked Louis where they really came from, and Louis dropped his voice and told him the whole story in his little-boy wisdom.

"We're from far away. The town of Santa Fe, New Mexico. It's a big town. My parents owned a ranch. We had too many horses to count. My dad got greedy, and I think he stole other rancher's horses. My mother became very sad. After that she became angry. They were always fighting. Bad men came to eat at our table."

Louis paused, wiping absentmindedly on a buckle.

"There is a big fat man with a mustache and very long ponytail. His name is Oliver Martinez. He steals the horses. Him and a whole bunch of other men. They appeared at our door and continued to do that for many months. Mother would cry.

"My dad would not listen. Then she had to go away and said she would be back for us, but she never came. That's why Jim and Dorothy—they're our parents now. We love them okay, only they don't look as nice as our real parents. Our house isn't as nice. Our dad's name is Lee Hartford!"

Marcellus chimed in, laughing. "Grace Hartford!"

Reuben laughed, then shook his head. "Whoever they are, you probably have a wise mother."

When Richard Caldwell paid Reuben, he asked if there was any news of Sadie. Reuben shook his head, but related Louis's story, giving him the name of the man named Oliver Martinez. When Richard Caldwell's eyes became quite big and round, and he swiveled his chair immediately to his computer, Reuben figured he was onto something.

He rode home, fast and hard, the bitter cold searing the skin visible between his coat sleeve and his glove, Moon throwing the snow in chunks. He found Mark slumped over the kitchen table, his head in his hands, waiting for supper to be ready.

"Hey, guys! I think we're onto something!"

Mam turned sharply. Mark lifted his head, his two big eyes piercing into Reuben's, his face devoid of color.

Reuben related the story, finishing with, "I bet you anything that Oliver guy is connected here somehow. Richard Caldwell is already on it. He wants to search all the old police files. I mean, that little Louis and Marcellus are likely victims of this whole horse thieving thing, don't you think?"

Far into the night, Richard Caldwell sat hunched over his computer. Mark lay sleepless. Reuben knelt by his bed in his T-shirt and flannel pajama pants, put his head on his hands, and prayed like never before. He had to see Sadie again.

✿ ✾ ✿

Erma Keim walked out to the tack room to take some hot chocolate to Reuben, (still her favorite buddy, she told him) and met up with Lothario Bean, who promptly began bowing and scraping his feet in his total delight at seeing her again. Reuben watched them both in bewilderment, Erma giving off those loud guffaws of pure delight at Lothario's antics.

Wasn't he married? Reuben shrugged his shoulders, went back to polishing saddles, but held very still when he thought he heard the name Oliver.

"Very big. Very big!"Lothario Bean stretched his arm up high above his head to show Erma how big Oliver was, then extended his arms out in front of his stomach to show the size of his girth.

"He a good friend of ours. My wife cook up wonderful Mexican food for him. He won lottery. Lucky fellow. Bought brand new SUV. Cream color. Look like Dallas people on TV. Bought it at Gregory Cadillac in town. Nice man. Like to eat. Oh, yeah, love hot chocolate just like this. He marry a person like you. Make him hot chocolate this way."

Reuben froze, then began slowly polishing buckles, his mind whirring like Mam's egg beater when she made lemon meringue pie. He got up, stretched, and casually walked to the house, straight to Richard Caldwell's office.

"Gregory's Cadillac. In town! Oliver Martinez bought a new car there. He's a friend of Lothario Bean!"

Reuben leaned over his desk, his hands reeking of silver polish, his eyes very big and blue, desperate with longing.

"I'll call the police immediately, Reuben."

✿ ✡ ✿

The police came to interview the family and found Lothario Bean, who gave them all the information they needed. Then they went to Jim and Dorothy's house, where they found Louis and Marcellus in their pajamas, having their evening bedtime ritual of graham crackers and milk.

Still as mannerly and well-spoken as ever, they answered questions forthrightly with childish sincerity. They proudly produced their address label on the inside of their drawstring duffel bag, having discovered it only the week before and told Dorothy, who refused to look at it, saying no one knew whose address that was.

The police were onto something, and they knew it immediately. They went back to the Miller home, found Mark still awake, pacing the kitchen floor, and delivered the good news. Mark bent his head, nodding, his mouth working as he fought to control his emotions. At last, a thread of genuine hope. With promises of keeping him posted, they left, but there was very little sleep for him the entire night.

Sadie was finished cleaning. She felt as if her mind was slipping, slowly leaving her without the good foundation of genuine reality. Had this all happened? Was it a bad dream? This couldn't have happened in real life. Amish girls driving around in horses and buggies were not accosted on rural roads. Another car or truck would have passed them, been aware of a suspicious-looking situation, stopped, and helped her out.

She checked her appearance in the mirror. She still looked the same, only thinner, circles casting shadows beneath her dark eyes, and definitely like someone who was, yes, slowly losing her mind.

If she only had something to write on or something to read. She had asked but was refused. Why? Why couldn't they let her have something to read? She wrote poems in her mind. She thought of words, put them together in a sequence, sort of, until she memorized verse after verse.

She considered kicking her way out of the door. Not the door. The drywall would break easier. Just kick and pound, bludgeon the wall with whatever she could find, and sneak out. Or, like a rat, chew slowly away at an opening, slip out during the night, and run. Run wildly, crazily, screaming for help.

Another scenario that held more logic was knotting the bed sheets, the bedspread, the towels, and whatever else she could use, hanging them down the side of the great house, and slipping away during the night. But who could measure how many sheets it would take to reach the ground? What if she stayed dangling halfway, unable to climb back up, and the distance too great to drop down? The alarm system in a home this grand was another thing to be reckoned with. Probably not even a cat could roam these grounds without someone being aware of it.

She stood at the window, watched the wind blow the brown tufts of grass, prayed to be allowed to feel the wonderful breezes caress her face. Sometime she felt as if she was riding Paris, Reuben beside her, laughing, the wind tearing at her *dichly*. She would smile, remember, and then tears would rain down her cheeks, missing Reuben.

The fat man was becoming increasingly forgetful, leaving her without breakfast, and sometimes without anything to eat until evening. Once, she received only a stack of stale saltines and a warm bottle of Dr. Pepper without apology. He seemed to become more agitated as time went on, peering over his shoulder before he entered, his fingers drumming on the window pane as he stood, parted the wooden slats of the blinds, then turned sharply.

"They're not responding yet."

Sadie looked up sharply. "Who?"

"The people we think have the palomino."

"Maybe they don't even have her."

"Do you know more than you're telling us?"

"Absolutely not. I told you the truth."

"I don't believe you."

"Please. I don't know where they took her or who the men were."

"Why wouldn't they respond?"

Suddenly Sadie became physically ill, her stomach churning with fear, the knowledge hitting her, slamming into her with the force of a hurricane: the kidnappers must not have alerted the police or government agents, or they would have responded a long time ago. It was becoming clear to Sadie that these men weren't really interested in the horse. Paris had little, if anything, to do with her abduction.

Sadie felt a cold sweat break out on her back and shoulders. Her hands shook of their own accord as she clenched them in her lap, desperately trying to still them before the fat man saw her fear. Play dumb. She would need to be an opossum, playing dead. It was the only way.

"Perhaps they don't have her."

"That's what I'm thinking."

The fat man was pacing now, extremely agitated. "So, if we can't get the horse, and we take you back, I'll spend time in jail for having taken you in the first place. It's not looking good."

Sadie nodded.

"And…if you were to disappear…Just weighing my options here."

Another lurch of Sadie's stomach was followed by her mouth drying up, her breath coming in shallow puffs, the color draining from her face. Play dumb. She heard the words this time. She forced herself to meet his eyes, found his sliding away, furtive, sensitive, unstable.

"You mean you'll let me go, right?" she asked, as normally as she could possibly manage.

"No."

"Why not?"

"You'd turn me in."

"What does that mean?"

He gave her a look of disbelief.

"You mean you don't know?"

"No."

Sadie squared her shoulders, sat up, took a deep breath, summoned her courage. "Don't you have a wife, children, anyone you care about?"

"Used to."

"Did you love her? Or your children?"

"Yeah, at one time I did. But I got to messing with this…uh…operation, and they left."

"Who left?"

"They did."

"You mean your wife and children?"

"Yeah."

"Do you own this house?"

"No! Who do you think I am?"

"I have no idea who you are."

"No. I don't own this place. I just work for the guy who does. Things are just so out of control right now. I mean, he always dealt in horses. Done real good for himself. Beautiful wife and kids, found out about the...I can't say...and plumb lost his mind. Started thievin' and doin' illegal stuff just to get his hands on these horses. Offered me...I can't say."

"So, if you just work for this man, why can't you let me go? Does he know I'm here? Does anyone know why?"

"Yeah. Well, in the beginning he did. But I'm not sure he didn't...I can't say."

"Well, if you don't know how I can go home, why don't you just put a stop to this whole deal and let me go?"

He looked at her, and she saw the wavering in his eyes, the doubt, a certain dipping of his eyelids.

"Because I'm getting a bunch of money if we get that horse. I mean, a lot. And...I thought if I have so much money, maybe Adele will come back to me. See, she needs money to keep her happy, and I just couldn't make enough for her. I mean, to keep her with me, happy— you know?"

He looked up. "Adele's a terrific cook. She cooks the best sausage and eggs with salsa, fried tomatoes with chil- ies, it's unreal. I loved her. Did anything I could to keep her. The kids though, that's what really broke my heart."

Sadie nodded. "Must be hard, losing your wife."

"You could live with me. Just disappear. Can you cook? We could go across the border. I don't want to go to jail."

Suddenly, he appeared to Sadie as his true self, undis- guised. A fat, lonely man, afraid, who had only been trying to make enough money to keep his spoiled wife at his side. Perhaps he was as afraid as she was, only in a different way. Was he capable of harming her? She doubted it.

Quickly, she weighed her options, measured them on the scale of pros and cons. To go with him, out of this room. To refuse, stay here, with no promise of escape. It was the confinement that was hardest. She would go. She would risk it. What did she have to lose?

"You take me, I'll go."

He looked at her, then shook his head. "Can't do it. I have to wait. Surely I'll get the money."

Sadie felt the desperation assail her, became fueled by it, burst out, "But if you don't even know if your ... your boss is trying to contact the men who have Paris ... the horse, then how is this thing ever going to come to an end?"

She was crying, then sniveling, pleading, groveling at his feet.

"Just please take me home. Get me out of here. I've done nothing wrong except own a palomino horse. Supposing I was your daughter? Your son?"

In the end, the fat man hardened his heart, became harsh, adamant, refusing to budge or listen to her cries. She knew without looking at him when she heard him heave himself from the chair, open the door, turn the key in the lock, and leave.

It was the large sum of money. Her despair felt like a heavy backpack that wore down her resolve, her hope, her courage. There was truly nothing left. They would let her die in this room.

Well, she wasn't going to die. She had too much to live for. Mark. She pictured him. Tall, dark hair tumbling over his forehead, a new line of dark hair appearing along his jawbone, growing the beard in the Amish style of the married man, so handsome, so gentle. How she loved him! And she had Mam, Dat, Reuben, her sisters, Dorothy. No, she would not give up.

Eyeing the bedspread, the towels, estimating a sheet's length, she sat on the beige sofa and planned. As her thoughts were fueled by a shot of adrenaline, she formed a plan. It was absolutely doable. Yes, it was. The hardest part was determining how to secure the end of the rope of sheets firmly enough to hold her weight. The door? The bed? The doorknob? Would it hold? Oh, dear God, help me.

As night fell, she knew it was this night or never. To pass time, she took a long hot bath, shampooed her hair, hung up the towels, rinsed the tub and bowl of the vanity. She straightened the cushions on the beige sofa, then found extra sheets, towels, whatever she could knot together to form a rope of sorts.

With her teeth, she gnawed at the sheet's end, beginning a small tear. Sometimes with fabric you could pull with all your strength and you'd be unable to tear it apart. But if you put just a tiny cut in it, you could rip it easily. Even if her teeth hurt, she kept chewing, until she had a delicate beginning.

Would he be back? He never came to check on her after her evening meal was delivered, but you never know. To stay safe, she worked on the floor on the opposite side of the bed, so if anyone did appear, she could quickly stuff it all beneath the opulent bed skirt. What a wonderful sound! That ripping, tearing sound of a sheet being torn—the sound of freedom!

She worked steadily, her ears tuned to the slightest sound from the hallway. When there was none, she continued tearing, then knotting. She knotted the sheets with the same knot she used to tie Paris or Truman to a hitching rail. The *gaul's gnipp*. The horse's knot. Over and under and around. If the knot was done properly, the harder it was pulled, the tighter it became. Sometimes, a horse could pull until it became dangerously tight, and still there was no way it would loosen.

She planned her escape route, considered the distance to the road, the crisscross of fencing, and where the fence rows and the trees were. She wondered whether she might trigger alarms and lights as she scurried across the property. There was a row of square bales and a place she hoped was a ravine.

She had never seen her coat or her bonnet after they had brought her to this room. Her only hope to keep from freezing was the white terrycloth robe that hung on the ornate hook on the oak bathroom door. It would work as a coat of sorts.

The red numbers on the clock were 10:22.

Chapter 5

SADIE LAY IN BED, HER EYES WIDE OPEN, PLANNING her getaway. How strong was she? Powerful enough to cling to a rope of sheets and lower herself to the ground? Reuben would be. So would Mark.

She tied the end of the sheet around the leg of the bed, having determined that it was made of heavy steel. She secured it to the hinge on the door as well, just to be sure, sliding a length of sheet carefully into the crack of the door when it stood ajar. Surely, secured in two places, it would hold.

Better to wait till close to the morning hours. Hadn't she heard, somewhere, that people slept most securely at four o'clock in the morning? Four o'clock, then; that was her goal.

She didn't sleep a wink. Every shadow of the room imprinted on her mind. She pictured every knot, every length of sheet. At midnight, she got up, sat on the sofa shivering. She shivered with a case of nervous energy coupled with fear. She shook out the heavy bathrobe, put it on, secured it around her waist with the belt on top of her blue dress.

She wore no covering since they had taken it with her black bonnet. She had been taught to pray with her head covered, so she laid a washcloth as a makeshift covering. She caught sight of herself in the mirror, and looking so silly, she decided surely God would hear her prayer since these men had taken her covering away and she was in such dire need of help.

What about that Magdalene, or whatever her name was, in the Bible? Hadn't she wiped Jesus' feet with her long hair? She didn't wear a covering, and Jesus said she had done him a far greater service than anyone else. Or maybe she did wear a covering, one of those long biblical cloths they wore thousands of years ago. Who could tell?

Sadie prayed reverently, tearfully, begging God to keep her safe. I'll take pain, fear, whatever, but just give me strength to do this, she prayed.

Her mind raced, her nerves jangled. She wished she had something to put in the deep pockets of her bathrobe. A package of crackers. Some pretzels. A bottle of water. It couldn't be too far to a house. A car would pass.

What about dogs? The great rangy creatures flew like agile wolves at the heels of the cattle scattered all over cattle country to protect the livestock from predators. She'd just have to deal with them. She surely did not want to die like Jezebel in the Old Testament either. That was such a tale of warning, the way Jezebel had held her own spiritual meaning far above her husband's, and he was likely closer to God than she was. Women could be such misled creatures, being the weaker vessels the way they were.

Boy, she got herself in trouble saying that to Doro- thy. Sadie had finally conceded, saying all right, Dorothy, we Amish are sort of old-fashioned in our views about women knowing their place, being submissive to their husbands. Dorothy did not go along with that. Where would her Jim be if she didn't keep him on his toes? Huh? Answer me that.

One thirty-six. Soon now. Soon she would know. The wind moaned around the corner of the house. Hmm. It hadn't been windy. She hoped there wasn't a storm coming. There was no snow, only cold.

Would a car come along before the dogs, or the fat man, or the hired hands, or whoever else was in the wealthy man's employ? She must have dozed off. Not really slept, just entered the gray zone, the way she had done while they traveled to this house.

Three forty. She jerked, her whole body froze. Twenty more minutes. Oh, dear God. What difference will these 20 minutes make? I must go. She felt a numbness, a maddening listlessness steal over her legs, her arms. You can't do this. You are weak. Tears rose from the hard lump in her throat. Yes, she was weak. No, she couldn't do this. She couldn't.

The Apostle Paul had said the same thing. He was weak, but in Christ Jesus he could do anything with his power. A warmth stole over her body, an assurance of strength. Adrenaline followed it.

She sat up, swung her legs over, secured the belt of the white bathrobe, checked the security of the knots one last time, then slowly loosened the crack of the window. In one turn, she was rewarded by a loosening scrape. She turned steadily, until the long, narrow window was propelled out, allowing enough room for the rope of sheets to be thrown over. Leaning out, she peered desperately into the semi-darkness.

Oh, no. It did not reach the ground. Well, it had to

be close. The sheets passed both windows of the second and third stories, went to the first story. She had to go.

With a deep breath, she climbed up on the windowsill, grasping the sheet. It was so thin. The actual taking hold of the sheet was much harder than she had imagined. How to do this? She finally realized she'd have to sit on the windowsill, with her legs dangling down the side while keeping her hold on the sheets. She'd have to sit forward, then take the plunge, twisting her body to keep her feet against the wall.

She looked back. Three fifty-eight. A good omen. A little before the set time. Grasping the rope of sheets in both hands, she pushed herself off the windowsill, her teeth clenched in the desperate effort to keep a firm grip.

She swung out too far. There was a tearing at her shoulders. Her hands slipped. Oh, no. She couldn't do it. She would fall. Such thoughts tumbled through her mind, but only for a moment. Then her arms rippled with strength. She propelled her body sideways, then in a turn, her feet slid against the stone wall.

Slowly, hand over hand, she lowered herself. The air was so cold. Should have thrown this bathrobe down, the way it billowed out. The first knot. On down. Ouch.

She was going too fast. The sheets burned the palm of her hand. Grasping them more firmly, she slowed her descent. Better to take her time. She didn't want bleeding palms on her hands. The last knot.

She looked down but could not determine the distance to the ground. Was that a shrub? A low tree? She had to stop or let herself fall to the ground. It couldn't be too far.

She dropped. A gasp tore from her throat as she felt nothing at all, only the air rushing past her face as she fell.

She suddenly landed on her feet, one twisting sideways with the impact of her weight.

A red hot, searing pain shot up her leg from her ankle. She lay on the ground, her hands propping her upper body, her eyes squeezed shut, her lower lip caught firmly in her teeth, as she struggled to keep from screaming out a high cry of pain and weakness.

She spun her head. A light went on. No! Oh, please, God, no. She never knew how she got up and started running, but she did. She ran with pain her constant companion. She lowered her back, pumped her arms, her knees raised and lowered, propelling her toward the ravine she projected as her destination. She didn't look back, afraid of what she might see.

Her breath was coming quickly now. She imagined herself in school, running with that effortless, little-girl gait. The time when you could run and run and run, and still you could breathe all right and keep running. She had always been good at it. She would've won every fast race if it hadn't been for that long-legged Henry Mast. They should have let the girls and boys race separately.

Still she ran. Why stop at the ravine? She ran along fences, across water-filled ditches. They would be ice at home. Headlights? A car! A blessed car. A real vehicle. She ran toward it, waving her arms. The vehicle slowed, but then accelerated.

Sadie would never know how the employee at the Quick-Mart, heading to work on the early morning shift, his face now drained of color, said he had seen a real ghost, white, flapping its arms. It didn't take him a second to step on the gas and get out of there. When his co-worker eyed him coolly and said that's how those stupid Bigfoot rumors get started, he got hopping mad and told her off, pouted the rest of the day, and wouldn't speak to her till she brought him a homemade Boston cream pie.

When the second vehicle zoomed by in all its disregarding splendor, Sadie thought of the bathrobe. She took it off and rolled it up, carrying it under her arm.

Dogs! Barking in the distance. Who knew though, if they came from the house she had just escaped from? She walked now, backward, holding out her thumb, a hitchhiker. In desperation she kept her arm out. Her breath was coming in quick succession, her fear a palpable thing. The dogs. Coming closer? Yes. They most definitely were. Were the dogs merely herding cattle? Bringing home milk cows?

What was the best thing? Revert to fleeing across the fields? No, better to stay with the safety of the highway. Another vehicle. Her teeth were chattering, the shaking spreading to her limbs as the pain in her ankle worsened. She could not keep walking backward like this.

When the truck rolled on past, not even bothering to slow down, an idea entered Sadie's mind. She would appear to be carrying an infant, a helpless baby, clothed in white. She stepped aside, rolled the white bathrobe into the form of a blanketed baby, then held it in her arms, walking backward, slowly, limping now. Would anyone have mercy? No. A tractor and trailer roared past, spraying her with an odorous sulphur, tiny bits of hard gravel, and a wave of hopelessness.

Then the dogs were on her. Clutching the bathrobe, she stepped back, which was completely insufficient. There were four. They touched her, milled about, snapping playfully at each other. They were so big. Collars. Tails wagging? Yes! Oh, yes!

"All right," Sadie squeaked from a throat gone dry. The leader, a large brown and white dog with short, heavy hair grinned up at her, his tongue lolling. The heavy black one reached up to sniff the bathrobe.

Headlights made her wince, close her eyes momentarily. She tried hard to pay attention to the dogs, any sign of aggressive behavior, so she did not really comprehend the slowly rolling vehicle coming to a stop on the shoulder of the road.

It was only when the door opened, and the form of a heavy man emerged, that she lost her courage, her resolve, everything that brought her this far.

Had the fat man caught up to her? Her legs became traitors, turning to Jell-o at the knees, her arms lost their strength until she could barely hold onto the bathrobe. Then the lumbering giant came closer, the round, ruddy face surrounded by stiff bristles of white hair, his eyes intent, assessing her predicament.

"Git! Git! Git goin' there! Ho! Git!" Waving his arms, taking control. Did God not look exactly like this?

She wasn't aware that she was crying. She talked, laughed, showed him the bathrobe, became hysterical, and wept in earnest. The dogs bounded off across the level fields, the man helped her into his car, handed her Kleenexes, offered her his cup of coffee, listened, then told her he was on his way to work, had to be there by six, but he was taking her to the police barracks and would call in late. The brilliant white lights of the police building made her shield her eyes, feeling like a castaway, a stray cat brought in until the local humane society rescued it.

Sadie related her story, saying she didn't know where she had been, only that she ran for close to an hour. The house had three stories; they had horses; she wasn't sure how long she had been held there. The officers made her feel as if she was the one who had done something wrong with their stern expressions, gun belts slung across their hips, all creased and crisp and professional. But the morning light brought a bit of understanding, like a jigsaw puzzle when you finally found the missing border section. Things began to make more sense after she was shown to a waiting area with comfortable chairs, pillows, and warmth.

Gratefully, she accepted a steaming cup of coffee but waved away the sugary croissant, her stomach rolling now. When she winced from the pain of her ankle, the policeman insisted on having it checked at the city hospital.

While the cruiser moved through the city, the sun brought everything into reality, along with a glorious knowledge that she was safe. She was here in this wonderful vehicle, protected by a man who worked for the good of humanity, in a big city filled with people who walked all sorts of different paths. The wonder of those tall buildings!

The feeling of appreciation swept through her when white-coated professionals poked and prodded at her ankle, pronounced it a torn ligament, no broken bones, wrapped it in some heavenly, soft brace, and then wheeled her out to the police cruiser. Later, she laughed softly with the officer.

To Sadie's surprise, the heavy, white-haired gentleman was waiting at the barracks till they returned, introducing himself as Harry Magill.

When she laid her head on the back of the sofa and closed her eyes, he immediately brought her a pillow and blanket, then stayed with her the remainder of the day until it was time to return home to his wife, receiving Sadie's profound thanks as a sort of benediction.

When the call came, no one answered the phone, as usual. The black telephone in the phone shanty shrilled its eight rings. But the wind was blowing the snow around in cold, painful little spurts, and Mam stayed in the house.

Dat and Reuben were at work, putting in a fireplace for a friend of Jim Sevarr's who lived in town.

Anna was down with the flu, having retreated to her room in a huff after Mam told her it was her own fault, the way she stayed out on Sunday night until who knew when.

When the second phone call came, Rebekah had just closed the door of the white minivan that took her to and from her housecleaning job, having finished early because of new carpeting going in. She thought she heard the phone, but in this wind she couldn't be sure. Better check the messages. Too cold for Mam to be out in this.

There were three. Three messages relating the same thing. The same unbelievable news that made Rebekah sit down on the cold plastic chair and cry big sobs of gratefulness, then forget to replace the receiver and close the door of the phone shanty so that it slapped back and forth in the wind, blowing snow into every crevice and chasing the calendar pages up and down all afternoon. She was hysterical by the time she reached the kitchen, frightening her mother so badly, she had to sit on the recliner, seeing spots in front of her eyes.

When the police car pulled up to the door, Mam waved

a hand in Rebekah's direction, who answered the door with tears streaming down her face and dropping on her dress front. Dat and Reuben were brought to the Miller homestead, Mark came with Richard Caldwell, clearly beside himself with joy, Richard's voice booming as if he really was holding a megaphone. The police had offered a phone to Sadie so she could call her family.

Leah, after she learned of the joyous news, told a most amazing story. Her sleep had been restless all night. But a few minutes before four o'clock, she awoke with a great and intense urge to pray for Sadie.

"All the while, I had this sensation of falling. But after I prayed, I fell asleep, deeply, better than I'd slept all night."

No one at this point knew how or when Sadie had escaped, or even if she had escaped, but they all agreed—wasn't Leah's dream something? Wasn't it awesome how God heard and answered prayer?

Next they discussed whether they should let Sadie fly home. Riding in an airplane was *verboten*. Should they confer with the ministry to see if it was allowed in a case of emergency? Dat said just fly her home. Mark said the same thing. And everyone also agreed that Mark should be the one to make a return phone call to Sadie. He was, after all, her husband.

✵ ✹ ✵

She was asleep on the sofa at the police barracks, wrapped in her cocoon of safety, when Mark's phone call came through. Gently, Cindy, the tall, thin receptionist, woke her.

"Sadie Miller? There is a phone call."

Immediately Sadie sat up, throwing back the blanket in one clear sweep, stumbling a bit, but following her eagerly to the cordless phone, taking it with her to a corner of the room where she could squeeze her eyes shut and blow her nose and sob and talk and laugh, and no one would see her.

His voice! She had forgotten that deep, gravelly baritone. She couldn't talk at all, just cry, until Mark thought there was no one there and said, "Sadie? Are you there?"

She had to answer, and all that came out was a hoarse squeak. Finally she croaked a pitiful, "Oh. Oh, Mark!"

Then he began crying, and no one said anything for quite some time, until finally Sadie took a long, shuddering breath and said she was fine and asked how soon were they coming to get her.

"No, I do not want to fly home, Mark. I had enough of being too high up in the air to suit me for the rest of my life."

✿ ✡ ✿

When they hired a driver, he figured his GPS system would get them to Brent, Colorado, in about 12, maybe 13 hours. He could leave after two o'clock. Everyone went along, the 12-passenger van holding them all quite comfortably. No one wanted to stop to eat or sleep, rolling into gas stations, grabbing sandwiches, and back on the road they went.

They encountered a snowstorm after about six or seven hours of travel, slowing them to a mind-numbing crawl across a corner of Wyoming. The driver peered through a whirl of white until he proclaimed the roads unfit for travel.

They were forced to stop and stay at a motel, the rooms reeking of stale air and cigarette smoke, the beds hard as nails, in Reuben's words, and nothing to eat except stale crackers and bitter coffee. The fact that he found the Discovery Channel on TV soon smoothed over the sadness of stale crackers and coffee, and when he discovered Animal Planet on another channel, he was quite beside himself with amazement.

Twenty-four hours later, they rolled into the Brent police barracks with the voice from the GPS as their guide. "What an absolute miracle," Dat proclaimed the small device.

Sadie had been taken to the Hilton Inn a block away. She was pacing the second-floor lobby, dressed in the much-washed blue dress, still without a covering, but showered, her hair combed neatly, running to and from the windows on the second floor.

When she saw the black van, she knew it was George Gilbert's. She went down a short flight of stairs as fast as the brace on her foot would allow, then stood rooted to the carpeting, gripping the back of the sofa, until her knuckles turned white. Mark walked up to the glass door. With a cry, she flung herself into his arms, oblivious of anyone or anything around her. They clung to each other, the amazing, unbelievable joy of being alive, safe, and having come through this together, restoring their emptiness, their hopelessness.

Dat stood back, his hands in his pockets, shy, ill at ease, as everyone held Sadie in their arms, crying, laughing, then crying again. Sadie saw him then. "Dat!"

There was no self-consciousness. It was not customary, but she needed to feel her father's arms around her to make her homecoming complete. She put her arms around him. He clutched her tightly to his denim-clad chest, his gray beard caressing her forehead, his tears anointing her head.

Her parents had aged and had both lost weight. Reuben looked terrible, but he said it was because he had been up all night watching TV and drinking that sick coffee and eating disgusting cheese crackers. He shook his hair into his eyes so no one would see the tears. He was too old and cool to be caught crying over a crazy sister.

They sat in the lobby, listening quietly as Sadie related her story from start to finish. Mark got them all rooms, and the driver, too, so he would get a solid day of sleep before the long drive home. Mam and Dat welcomed a long-awaited rest, along with the joy of having seen their beloved daughter again.

For Mark and Sadie, it was very nearly heaven on earth.

Chapter 6

It was all over the news, on every television station and in every newspaper. Richard Caldwell informed them: the horse thieves were caught. The whole ring of them would finally be brought to justice.

They had been extremely intelligent at first, but as the band of thieves grew, so did their lack of security and loopholes of leaking facts. When they abducted Sadie, it was the beginning of the end.

Reporters requested interviews with Sadie, but they were all turned down, as was the way of the Amish. No one could appear on TV, so there were no on-camera interviews, although she spoke to many other people about her experience.

The government agents returned Paris to her golden glory. Sadie laughed to Mark about how they could tell Paris was pouting, standing in her stall batting her eye-lashes, a haughty princess who believed a great wrong had been brought on her head.

Sadie bathed her and brushed her. Then Sadie bundled up in numerous layers of warm winter clothing and rode the horse across the snowy fields. The wind froze Sadie's face as tears welled in her eyes. Paris ran, kicked her heels joyfully, lifted her head and whinnied high and clear, the sound borne away on the freezing wind. Sadie leaned into her neck, reveled in the motion beneath her, that quivering mass of muscle and speed, understanding the gift of freedom as never before.

Mark rode with her sometimes on Duke, the new gray gelding he purchased from Sam Troyer. Duke was a magnificent animal, a bit raw around the edges, perhaps, but with careful training, he would improve. Sadie winced, however, when Mark began using the quirt. How she hated that evil-looking little whip! It only served to increase Duke's nervousness, being a bundle of alarm waiting to implode as it was. Mark was short on patience. He was too quick to use that hateful quirt, as Sadie explained to him, gently trying to keep from deflating his always fragile ego.

The thing was, life was so good, and, like a delicate egg, she carried their relationship with care. The specter of his dark moods served to put a hand over her mouth, an ear attuned to his derisive snorts of annoyance. It was one of his quirks, this tumble into darkness where he would stay, entombed in a silence of his own making, brought on by who knew what.

"Mark, that Duke is absolutely fearless. After the snow melts, we're going to race. Reuben could bring Moon."

They were in the forebay of the barn, watering the horses. Sadie pushed the barn broom in a short, quick motion, sweeping loose hay and straw into the open stall door.

"Duke would win."

"Not if you don't quit using that hateful quirt on him."

The words tumbled out even as she realized their harm, but it was too late to save herself. Deliberately, Mark turned Truman, slid the steel pin into place and ground out, the words serving to box Sadie's ears. "You think you know more than I do about horses, Sadie. You don't. Paris is spoiled rotten."

Uh-oh. When he spoke in that tone of voice, the harm was done, so she may as well have her say. Besides, she couldn't avoid it, her anger serving as the propeller that lent wings to her hot words.

"Paris is not spoiled. She listens to anything I want her to do. Without using a *quirt*."

She turned, flounced her skirt, steamed her way through the snowdrifts, thumped up on the porch, her cheeks blazing with the lust of her indignation.

They ate supper in silence, dipping spoons into the home-canned tomato soup, then lifting them to their mouths. They dipped grilled cheese sandwiches cut in half into the steaming tomato-y goodness, but they spoke no words. Sadie swallowed water from her glass noisily. The only sound beside Sadie's clumsy gulping was the ticking of the clock. It wasn't that she didn't try. She did.

"Do you have plenty of horses to shoe this week?"

When there was no response, she tried another tactic, wrapping her arms about his waist. But they were firmly loosened and set aside as he made his way to his recliner. With a heavy heart burdening the slightest task, she slowly washed the soup bowls, each seeming to weigh 10 pounds now.

Everything had been so perfect, their love elevated to new levels after her escape. The homecoming, and now here she was, sunk to the bottom again, her life draining away because of what she had said. It was all her fault. That realization, like light entering a darkened room through a slowly opening door, was more and more apparent. She needed to be careful. No words of correction, no unkindness, no rebuke. She would be perfect soon.

When Mark spent the night on the couch, his dirty work clothes covered with their beige throw with their wedding date, names, and "Love Is Forever" monogrammed on it, his stocking feet sticking out like two questioning gray puppets, a fear arose in her throat. Would it always be like this now?

She slept well enough, but at 5:30 her heart raced, wondering why he wasn't up, the propane lamp lit, going to do chores. Was he dead? People passed away in their sleep. Was he so angry that he would leave or just stay lying on the couch all day? Perhaps, like Mam, he was depressed, and it was all her fault.

Nervously, she cleared her throat, waiting for Mark to come into the bed, lifting the covers the way he always did, taking her into his arms, apologizing, clearing the air. This would never happen again. Never.

But he didn't. He showered and shaved, banged doors, slammed drawers, and said absolutely nothing. Sadie's heart wavered within her. She tried meeting his eyes, but they were flat, black, unseeing. Breakfast was as silent as the evening meal had been.

"But Dorothy!" Sadie wailed at work, sitting at the table, her untouched coffee turning cold in its ironstone mug.

"You need to stand up to your man. He's controlling

you with his temper. Huh-uh. You ain't allowin' it. It ain't gonna happen."

"How can I love him so much, and yet last night when he lay on our clean, new couch with his dirty work clothes ignoring me, I...I almost hated him. He makes me so mad I don't know what to do. Just because I told him about that stupid quirt."

Dorothy buttered a warm biscuit, her arms beneath the too-short sleeves of her white T-shirt flapping with each stroke.

"Sounds a lot like marriage to me," she chortled.

"But what causes it? Why can't he take any correction or...Oh, whatever."

Sadie's voice ended in a wail.

"What'd I tell you? He's a tough one. Most men don't like for their women to tell 'em what to do. The normal ones. Your man ain't normal. So keep yer mouth shut."

Sadie winced. "What if I don't like the way he uses that quirt?"

"Shut up about it, or learn to live with his moods, then, if yer not going to stand up to him and tell him to grow up."

"What do you mean, grow up? Reuben is 15 years old, and he never ever acted like Mark."

"Reuben had a normal childhood."

"But how can Mark go through life like this, always blaming his childhood?"

Sadie lifted her hands on each side of her head, bringing down two fingers of each hand, mocking the word *childhood*.

"I mean, it's a crutch. Suppose I would go lay on the couch and pout because he did something I disapproved of? There wouldn't be a whole lot going on at our house."

Dorothy's arms wobbled along with the rest of her as she shook with glee, infused in her own delight of finding out how human Amish people were, obviously. She buttered another biscuit, popped half into her mouth, then flipped the bacon on the hot griddle.

"I ain't no shrink. I don't have all the answers."

She looked at the clock.

"Five more minutes and it's Erma Time."

Dorothy shoveled bacon into the steel pan, and Sadie lifted herself off the chair, placing her mug of coffee into the microwave and punching the minute button.

She was busily flipping pancakes when Erma Keim breezed in, her red hair frozen and her covering smashed beyond help by a brilliant purple head scarf. The freckles on her nose were unforgiving, doing absolutely nothing for her very white skin.

As usual, her mood was ebullient, which was about the only word to describe Erma. Gregarious was another, Sadie thought wryly, watching her with tired, creased eyes.

"Good morning, my ladies! Top of the morning to ya! Did you hear the Chinook, Sadie? Waters going to be running shortly. Snow melting! Whoo-ee!"

Dorothy shook her head, then turned to watch Erma as she fairly danced to the coat hooks and shimmied her way out of her black wool coat.

"Ya musta slept good," she observed dryly.

"Oh, I did! Pillows from Fred Ketty's store. Did you know she has super-good quality foam pillows? She's really getting that little dry goods store up and running."

Suddenly a wave of longing wrapped itself around Sadie, bringing with it a sort of wanting, an unnamed but nonetheless real feeling of wishing. Yes, to be straightforward, she wished she was Erma Keim. No one else to worry about. No relationship as tricky as a cracked egg to juggle continuously.

She shouldn't have married. The thought squashed her whole day. The vacuum cleaner clogged, she broke the leaf off a rabbit statue, her back hurt, her head swam with a million negative thoughts. Black crows of unsettling resolve about her future and her past added to the mountain of unscalable heights growing out of this one incident.

She told Erma Keim her apple pies needed more brown sugar and hurt Dorothy's feelings when she criticized her ability to keep the refrigerator organized.

"You don't need butter in three places, Dorothy. The butter goes in the door. The one to the left."

She swiped furiously with a cloth wrung from a bucket of Mr. Clean and piping hot water. Her hands were red, chapped, and she had a nasty hangnail, that annoying little piece of skin that got so painfully in the way of every task.

"Well, ain't we Miss Hoity-toity, now? That butter to the right is old. Outdated. I'll use it for bakin'. So don't tell me where to put my butter. I know what I'm doin'."

Sadie knew she should have apologized, but she was too upset to do it. Why was one's whole life upside down and strewn about when you fought with your man?

She didn't want to go home. She wanted Mam. She wanted to be in her old room, giggling with Leah and Rebekah and Anna, not a care in the world, except who was cute, who they would like to date, while eating sour cream and onion powder on a big bowl of freshly popped corn.

Why did she ever think Mark was handsome? How disturbing was that? Those huge feet sticking out from

the much too short afghan, unwashed socks, smelling—
no, reeking—of his work as a farrier.

Bouncing home in Jim Sevarr's rusted old pickup
truck, she slunk against the door, her face pale, her mouth
an upside-down "U" of disenchantment. Jim shifted his
toothpick, watched her sideways, turned the steering
wheel with gnarled fingers, then sighed.

"Wal, Missy, ya look under the weather, now, don't
cha?"

"Oh, I don't know."

"Honeymoon over, eh?"

"I guess."

"We is all alike, honey. Black, white, suntanned, or
Amish, Chinese, or Tippecanoe. Two people git hitched,
problems follow 99 percent o' the time. Ya gotta work
through 'em. See what works. See what don't. Learn by
it. Appreciate what you got. My Dorothy's a salty one,
now ain't she? Tells me off, but no more harm than a fly."

Slowly Sadie turned her head, watching the lined features, the creases opening and closing like an accordion
as the words slowly came from his mouth, the toothpick
disappearing as he shifted it to the other side. That was
quite a speech for Jim. The equivalent of an hour, actually.

"Well, Mark is more harmful than a fly," she burst
out.

"I doubt it."

"He is!"

"What happened?"

In brief detail Sadie told him, finishing with Mark's
black silences.

"It's a tough one. I used to do that. Hang in there. It'll
get better as time goes on."

The truck ground to a halt, and Sadie hopped down. "See you in the morning," she called.

Jim touched his hat brim, ground the gears of the truck, and was off down the drive. Wolf bounded up, his nose snuffling the creases of her coat. She ruffled his ears, stroked the broad face, and walked slowly up the melting, snowy path to the door of the washhouse. Mark wasn't home yet.

Laundry hung on the great, wooden rack, waiting to be folded. In winter, clothes were dried on lines in the basement, if there was a woodstove, or on racks in the washhouse or kitchen.

There were many different kinds of clothes-drying racks. Some were round and made of PVC pipe, with wooden clothespins attached to the ring by a small chain to hang small articles like socks, washcloths, or underwear. Wooden racks mounted to the wall had arms you could spread out. These held all the laundry you could fit on them. Clothes dried quickly by the wall behind a good stove. The large adjustable wooden folding racks that sat on the floor were used for hanging larger items like T-shirts and denim trousers. Dresses on hangers were all drip-dried in the washhouse beside the gleaming new wringer washer.

Whenever possible, Sadie hung clothes outside in spite of the cold, even though she'd bring in half-dry, half-frozen laundry. It still retained that outdoor scent. The clean, sun-washed fragrance never ceased to make her heart glad.

Today, however, the laundry didn't stir any gladness at all. It just hung there, stiff, still damp in the armpits and hems, smelling vaguely of old Snuggle and residue of Tide and bleach. She noticed the gray stains on the heels of

Mark's socks, which increased her feeling of inadequacy.

The kitchen was dark. What was that smell? Going to the waste can, she flipped back the lid, bent, and sniffed. Eww! She remembered then, the plastic wrap of the tray of chicken legs and thighs, the yellow Styrofoam tray containing the heavy padding of chicken juices and blood. When did they have fried chicken? Saturday evening. Her stomach churning, she grabbed the top of the waste can, fairly hurled it onto the countertop, hauled the garbage bag out, and swung it through the door and out to the garbage can, replacing the lid with a bang.

Now what to make for supper? If Dorothy wouldn't have been quite so testy, she would have asked her for a small portion of the chicken and dumplings she made in the gigantic cauldron, as Sadie called it, for the ranch hands' evening meal. After Sadie had complained about the unorganized refrigerator, Dorothy sizzled with displeasure. Her mouth a thin line, her eyes snapping, she did not stop to have her afternoon tea and leftovers, but moved grimly, methodically, until Sadie felt like screaming at the top of her voice, especially when Erma Keim began singing, "When the Roll is Called up Yonder" in a reedy, high voice that sounded like tree frogs in the early spring.

Opening the refrigerator, Sadie found a square Tupperware container of leftover spaghetti and meatballs. She'd warm that in a saucepan with a bit of water, open a can of green beans, and use Mam's leftover homemade bread for garlic toast, all possible in 10 or 15 minutes.

She set the table, pleased with her supper, her thriftiness, the cheese and garlic wafting from the oven making her hungry at last. When Mark did come home, her heart skipped, then plodded on, giving her a headache in her right temple. Eagerly she searched his face, ready to welcome him home, put the ugliness behind them.

He put his lunch bucket on the counter, followed by his Coleman water jug, then disappeared through the laundry-room door. She heard him wash up, wanted to follow him, plead with him, but stayed where she was. Quickly, she dished up the steaming spaghetti, added a pat of butter to the green beans, and arranged the garlic toast on a pretty platter. Mark came in and sat at the table, averting his eyes. Nervously, Sadie poured the water from the blue pitcher in the refrigerator, spilling some beside Mark's glass. With a gesture of annoyance he got up, yanked a paper towel from the roll, and wiped at the spill before throwing the towel in the trash can.

They bowed their heads in silence. Mark cleared his throat. He surveyed the food, then said gruffly, "What is this?"

"What?"

"This?" He pointed to the garlic toast that minutes before had been so inviting.

"It's garlic toast. With cheese."

"It smells like feet."

"It's the Parmesan."

"You know I don't like string beans."

Sadie literally counted to 10. In her mind, she said the numbers, a first-grader in the class called "Marriage." What had Jim said? See what works. See what don't. She knew what "don't." Criticism of any kind. Ever. Was it because of the quirt? This senseless criticism of her cooking? Is this the way it works?

She watched as he helped himself to a large portion of the spaghetti and meatballs, ignoring the string beans and garlic toast. Going to the refrigerator, he bent to find the applesauce, then dumped half the container onto his plate, spooning it up as fast as he could. Like a hog.

Sadie couldn't help her thoughts. She had a notion to say it, but instantly knew she wouldn't. Well, okay. If this was how he was going to be, she'd learn from it. See what works. See what don't. Learn from it.

She spent another night alone in bed, but she did not cry. She read part of a book called *Love and Respect* she had received as a wedding gift, her feelings numb, the words jangling through her nerves that only felt dead.

In the morning, when she sprayed the couch with Febreeze and threw the beige-colored afghan into the rinse tubs to be washed, she cried great big tears of disappointment and hurt.

When she arrived at the ranch, there was an ambulance parked at the barn. She forgot all her personal struggles. A hand went to her mouth as she lifted questioning eyes to Jim Sevarr's concerned face. He hopped down quickly, disappeared behind the entry door, and reappeared after a heart-stopping few minutes.

"It's Lothario Bean. The Mexican. Got kicked by the new mustang. Better git off to the house."

Sadie did as she was told, finding Dorothy and Erma by the window, their eyes wide with concern.

"It's Lothario Bean. He was kicked."

Erma's hand went to her mouth, her eyes opened wide, popped out the way they did when she was concerned or surprised. There was an air of solemnity about the three of them all morning after the ambulance careened out the drive, lights flashing, sirens screaming, sending chills of dread up Sadie's spine. When Jim Sevarr came slowly into the kitchen, his eyes soft, Sadie knew before Jim said a word that Lothario Bean had died.

"Smashed his skull. Bled internally. Didn't last long."

Erma cried quietly. Dorothy shook her head, brought a box of tissues to her, said it was a pity. That dear man was the salt of the earth, and what would that poor widow do? And those beautiful daughters? Sadie cried for the little Mexican. She was glad he was a Christian. She imagined his great enjoyment in this wonderful place called heaven. He had been such a loving man.

When Mark came home from work, he found Sadie curled on the recliner, still numb, her eyes red from crying. There was no supper on the table, the house was dark and cold, the laundry still hung on the rack stiff and dry. Sadie was beyond caring. If he wanted to go ahead and muddle around in his black fog of silence and self-pity, he could. She was not going to apologize if she didn't do anything wrong. So she turned her face away and did not say one word. If he wanted to know something, he could ask.

She heard him go outside. Wearily, stiff with cold, she got up, made her way to the bathroom, then soaked in a long, hot bath, shampooing her hair over and over. Wrapped in a heavy robe, she took two Tylenol for her pounding headache and laid back on the recliner.

It was 8:00 before Mark came in. He stood awkwardly by the table, his arms at his side, watching her. He turned to go to the refrigerator, then changed his mind, going to the pantry, and emerging with a box of cereal.

His shoulders were as wide as ever, bent over the dish, as he hungrily shoveled the food into his mouth. His dark hair was disheveled, in need of a good wash.

She would have to tell him about Lothario Bean. If she waited for him to speak first, they'd grow old like this. It was ridiculous. She would have to be the one to make amends, innocent or not. She knew better now. See what works. See what don't. Learn by it.

Slowly, she let down the footrest of the recliner. Mark turned, a question in his eyes.

"Lothario Bean was kicked by a horse at the ranch. He's dead."

"No!" Mark's voice was incredulous, filled with raw disbelief. Then, "Aw, the poor man."

He came over, scooped her out of the chair as if she was a child, then held her on his lap as he kissed her, gently, tenderly, murmuring words of endearment. Sadie told him she was sorry about the quirt, and he said it was okay, he was acting childish as well. All of Sadie's happiness came back multiplied by 10.

Chapter 7

THEY ALL ATTENDED LOTHARIO BEAN'S CATHOLIC funeral service, Richard Caldwell and his wife, Barbara, seated with the many Latino relatives. Mark and Sadie were amazed at the similarities to the Amish, the close sense of community, the caring love shown for each other by these dark-skinned people from Mexico. Lothario Bean's daughters surrounded their mother, who was dressed in traditional black, a veil over her face. Bravely his wife received condolences from the many people he had encountered in his life.

Afterward at the ranch, they had a memorial service of sorts, seated informally in the dining room, eating pulled pork sandwiches and scalding hot bean soup, coffee, and Erma's banana cream pies, filled with sliced bananas and piled high with genuine whipped cream. They reminisced about past events, Lothario Bean's eagerness to please, the humility he possessed, his outstanding love and support for his wife and daughters. A new sense of closeness enveloped them. This mixture of cultures, all human beings now, wrapped in a sense of loss felt so strongly that it was touchable, a thing to be cherished.

Sadie never wanted to quit her job at the ranch, knowing she had an extended family in all of them. Mark told her she could work as long as she wanted. They didn't need the money now, but if that's what she wanted to do, she should.

Richard Caldwell hired an Amish man to replace Lothario Bean. He had just moved into the area from Indiana. Richard Caldwell asked Sadie if she knew him at all. She didn't.

"He says he's worked with horses since he's three years old, which I think is a bit unlikely, but you never know. Check him out for me tomorrow morning, okay?"

So when breakfast was served, she lingered, wrapping silverware, filling the ice bin, observing from the background as the ranch hands filed in. She heard him before she actually saw him. He had a deep, hearty laugh, which seemed to never stop. It rolled out of him after every sentence, each of which was punctuated by what could only be described as enthusiastic listening. He had to be a great personality.

His hair was longish in the back, which was good, helping to balance the long neck, the beaked nose, and the dark rimmed glasses he pushed up or down on his nose, depending who or what he wanted to examine. Clearly this man was a great lover of life. No beard. Single.

The cogs in Cupid's wheel were matching perfectly. Sadie wrapped her arms around her waist and held very still, listening, observing, and then fairly skipped through the swinging oak doors to the kitchen.

"Where's Erma?"

"Upstairs," Dorothy said, from her sink full of dishes.

Grabbing her apron strings, Sadie pulled her in the direction of the dining room.

"You have to see this. The perfect man for Erma Keim!" Pushing her through the doors, Sadie stepped back, giggling, waiting for Dorothy's return.

"I ain't never endorsing no man for that giraffe. I told you!" Dorothy exploded the minute she was back in the kitchen.

"Dorothy!" Sadie wailed, her disappointment keen.

"I mean it. He's much too nice lookin' for her. She'd completely make his life miserable. The poor man. I ain't sayin' a word, and you better not, either. I'm serious."

When Erma came back to the kitchen for a Diet Pepsi, she popped the top, took a long swig, and spilled a rivulet of the freezing soda down the front of her dress. She snorted with impatience before lifting the can to repeat the process again, running to the sink for a clean, wet cloth to dab at her dress front, her hair and covering a hopeless mess. Sadie decided to obey Dorothy. Perhaps it was for the best.

Goodness, that Erma Keim was a sight. They had helped her with her covering and showed her how to use hairspray at the time of Sadie's wedding, which evidently was all lost. Dorothy shook her head, wiping her hands on a clean dish towel.

"See, she can't even drink a soda properly. Now I ain't Amish, but there's a big difference in your hair and that white thing on your head. Hers looks as if she was in a hurricane."

Sadie laughed, agreeing, and decided to drop the subject.

Spring breezes did their best to lift everyone's winter blahs. New green weeds poked their way through brown, dead growth, but the patches of snow and the cold rains were persistent into April.

Mark and Sadie were on their way to church, the cold spring rain splattering the windows of the buggy, leaking through the small rectangles cut into the window frame to allow the reins to pass through. The top of the glove compartment got wet. Mark wiped it off with a clean rag whenever he thought about it. Truman's hooves splashed through the puddled water, the wheels slicing through it, but everything was dry and cozy inside the buggy, with a light, plaid blanket across their legs just to keep the chill off.

Sadie pinned a black wool shawl securely around her shoulders, and she wore a black bonnet on her head. The shawl was usually only worn to church. At council meeting they were encouraged to wear the garment wherever they went, but very few of the young women did. It was cumbersome, knocking things off shelves, and not very suitable for shopping. But it was warm and perfectly suited to a chilly Sunday morning buggy ride.

Mark looked so handsome, his new beard in perfect symmetry, his jaw line in sharp relief against the whiteness of his shirt collar. He was in a quiet mood, which was normal and comfortable when not accompanied by the blackness and anger that devastated Sadie.

They had forgiven, forgotten. Life was smooth and so good.

"A penny for your thoughts."

Mark smiled. "You don't want to know."

"Mm-hm. Yes, I do."

"I'm thinking of my mother's dying wish. She wants me to find my siblings. Do I want to honor that? Or wouldn't you do it?"

"You won't have any closure, rest, whatever you want to call it, if you don't."

"I know. But...I'm scared."

"You have reason to be."

✠ ✠ ✠

The best part of attending church services was seeing her family. Her excitement at seeing all of them lent wings to her feet. She walked swiftly to the washhouse door.

All the joy of her morning evaporated when she saw Anna, a wan reed, her complexion blue-white, her eyes enormous in a face almost skeletal, sagging weakly against the wall, her feet propped against the cement floor as if to keep her standing erect.

Summoning all her strength, Sadie desperately tried to appear normal. Anna's smile was mocking, a pulling away of her mouth setting her teeth free. Her eyes were hard, boring into Sadie's, a challenge.

"How are you, Anna?"

"Good."

A thousand questions screamed in her mind. Where was Mam? Dat? Her sisters? Why was no one trying to help? Surely this was evident to the entire community. It was so different and yet so similar to Mam's illness. These things could be hereditary.

When Neal Hershberger walked in, his hair cut in the English style, chewing and popping his gum, his eyes brazenly searching the girl's bench, a hot anger welled up in Sadie's throat, a bile threatening to choke her.

Oh, my. Dear God, I have forgotten to pray. Wrapped in my own problems, I am not being watchful. Am I my sister's keeper? Please answer me. She bent her head to hide her tears from the men and boys facing them.

When she saw Neil Hershberger openly flirting with Suzanne Stutzman, saw Anna cringe backward in desperation, Dat sitting sound asleep in the front row as the young preacher droned on, she felt as if she had to do something.

Dat and Mam were so dear. Sadie's love for her parents had only increased with her absence, but they were by all means sticking their heads in the proverbial sand, either unwilling to face the disaster that was Anna, or just tired and optimistic, hoping it would all get better soon. She had to do something. Anything. She bet Anna weighed a hundred pounds, if that.

Asking Mark's permission after services, she invited her parents, sisters, and Reuben for Sunday supper, especially including Anna.

"I can't. I'm going away," she countered.

"Where?"

"The supper crowd."

"Can't you skip? This once?"

"No."

Anna wouldn't budge. Sadie gave in, glad to have her parents and Reuben even though her sisters were with the other young people. Mark was jovial, talkative, keeping Dat entertained, while Sadie prepared meat loaf, scalloped potatoes, and a salad of lettuce, bacon, sliced hard-boiled eggs, thinly sliced onion, and shredded carrots, with a homemade mayonnaise dressing.

After the meal as they sat around the table, full and content, Sadie braved the subject of Anna, a forbidden one, she knew. Her desperation, her only strength, grabbed at straws of reassurance.

"Dat?"

"Hmm?"

She had his attention; his eyes were kindly upon her.

"Does Anna even weigh a hundred pounds anymore?" she asked, her eyes giving away her fear.

Mam looked startled.

"Oh, of course. She isn't that thin."

"Do you realize she is sick, Mam? She needs help. Someone should at least talk to her about her... Mam, now come on, you can't tell me otherwise. She is definitely going through an eating disorder."

Dat burst out, quite uncharacteristically.

"That eating disorder you're talking about is named Neil Hershberger!"

Reuben was eating his second slice of chocolate layer cake, soaked with milk and shoveled with a small tablespoon into his mouth, which was opened wide to accommodate the entire mountain of cake. He chewed, swallowed, and shook his head up and down.

"That's for sure."

"Anna is completely obsessed with him," Dat continued. "I hardly know how to handle it. I'm afraid if we get too strict, she'll do something... completely crazy."

Mark nodded.

Sadie shook her head. "She's way, way too thin. Do you think she'd come live with us for awhile? I think I could at least get her to talk to me. She's pathetic."

"I'll come live with you," Reuben shouted, waving his empty spoon before digging into the soaked cake for another round.

"Nothing wrong with you!" Mark said, laughing.

"Nothing cake can't fix," Reuben grinned.

✩ ☆ ✩

After much coaxing, begging, pleading, and numerous phone calls, plus the promise of going to the mall in Chesterfield, Anna relented a few weeks later and agreed to stay with Sadie for awhile. Sadie welcomed her with open arms, fighting tears as she gathered the skeletal frame against her body. Leah and Rebekah accompanied her, turning the day into a sisters' day, helping Sadie houseclean the kitchen cupboards. Leah was dating Kevin, with plans of becoming his wife in the future, and Rebekah had just begun dating Jonathan Mast, a shy personable young man of 22.

As Sadie knew she would, Anna stayed in the background, listening, very rarely taking part in the conversation. She ate almost nothing all day, maybe a half of an apple, a few bites of cracker, a few sips of water. When Leah and Rebekah hitched up Charlie, waving their way out the driveway, Anna turned to Sadie.

"So start right away. Start lecturing me. That's all you want me here for, anyway. You want me to tell you something, Sadie? I'm just here because Neil can pick me up in his car. Mam and Dat won't let me go away with him. I sneak out. So get used to it, sister dear. I'm going away with Neil."

If Sadie would have acted on impulse, she would have smacked her sister's sneering face. Sadie's anger boiled, but not to the point she couldn't control it. So to bide her time, she kicked at a pile of dirt, absentmindedly extracting small rocks.

"What makes you think I'm going to lecture you, other than your guilt?" she ground out evenly.

"I'm not guilty," Anna said, pushing one hip out impatiently.

"Okay."

Sadie pretended to lose interest, changed the subject, and walked back to the house. Chattering about mundane subjects now, she put clean sheets on the guest bed upstairs, helping Anna hang her brilliant array of dresses in the closet. They did chores together and fed Wolf, who Anna seemed to bond with immediately, throwing a small stick for him to retrieve over and over, a thin color showing in her wan cheek from the exertion.

"He is so cool!" she cried, her eyes alight.

Quite clearly Anna adored Mark, his dog, his horses, his barn, everything. That was a good thing, Sadie decided, keeping her happy to be here. She even got Anna to try on the trousers she always wore to ride Paris. When Anna couldn't walk in them without losing them to a puddle around her ankles, Sadie looked genuinely surprised.

"But ... "

She looked up, floundering now.

"You're not fat," she said, completely bewildered.

"No, I'm not."

Sadie decided to leave it at that.

Anna had her dress tucked under her chin, bent over, unable to grasp the fact that she would not be able to keep the trousers from sliding down over her hips.

"But I'm not ... I'm not this skinny."

"Yes, you are, Anna."

"Well, good! Neil loves skinny girls. He doesn't like fat."

"Who is Neil?"

"Neil Hershberger."

"Oh. Him." Then, "Are you dating?"

"No, not really. Well, we go out."

"You go out. Where do you go?"

"I'd rather not say."

Sadie walked out the door, down to the barn, with Anna following in silence. It was one of those spring evenings in Montana that was achingly beautiful, every slope and plane of the land in contrast with the majestic sky, the colors so vivid, it made you want to fling your arms out and take off running, the way six-year-olds did quite regularly. Anna helped Sadie saddle up, brushing Paris's long mane and tail, her thin, white face pensive.

"Do you have any idea how much I wanted to be you already?" she asked suddenly, angrily.

Sadie stopped, eyeing her sister closely before returning her answer.

"Why does it make you angry to want to be me?"

"It doesn't. I'm not angry. Just forget I said that."

Sadie bit off the words of rebuke, knowing there was no sense pushing her point of view. Shrugging her shoulders, she turned to throw the saddle blanket across Paris's back, followed by the well-polished saddle. There was just something about throwing a saddle on a horse's back that made the horse lower herself ever so slightly, without actually seeming to do it. A certain readiness, a locking of her knees, perhaps. As if she knew the weight of it would settle solidly on her back and was prepared.

Nothing was said as Sadie tightened the girth, then tightened it again after Paris let out the air she had used to stretch her stomach, the way she always did. As she slipped the bit into her mouth, with that satisfying chunk that meant it had slipped between Paris's teeth, adjusted the leather strap over her ears, buckled the chin strap and threw the reins across her neck, Sadie ground her teeth to keep from spewing unwelcome words at her sister.

She was as delicate as a spiderweb and as strong as one. If you took a hose with the nozzle turned to jet and squirted a fragile-looking spiderweb, you still could not loosen it from the object to which it was attached. You just couldn't.

How to help her? That was the thing. Force was certainly not going to do it. Or was there a time coming when force would be the only way?

Love would be the answer. Build up her character, bolster her self-esteem, slowly allowing her to see herself as she really was. Who knew?

"Okay, Anna! Up you go!" The words were spoken brightly, with too much enthusiasm, her thoughts cloudy with distraction.

"I'm not riding." With that, Anna stalked off, her shoulders squared.

"And just why not, after all the trouble I went to, saddling her up?" Sadie yelled after her.

"I can't ride," Anna called back, breaking into a run.

Her mouth pressed into a straight line boding no good, Sadie threw the reins over the hitching rail, jerked them into a knot, and raced after her sister, her feet sliding in the watery slush in the driveway. She soon caught up, jerking Anna backwards by her shoulders, bringing her to a stop. She was appalled to see how fast Anna was breathing after that short sprint.

"Oh, no, you don't, Anna. You're not going to manipulate me with your moods. You are going riding."

"I don't want to. You can't make me."

"Yes, you are. You wanted to go riding, now we're going."

"No!"

"Yes!"

"Why?"

"Because."

Anna sighed, dropped her shoulders, relented, handed over her resistance.

"Good. C'mon."

She saddled Duke, swallowing her misgivings about him. He lifted his head obnoxiously, making Sadie stand on her tiptoes to attempt an entry with the shining steel bit. Instead of losing her temper, she went to the cupboard where the harness was kept, extracting a box of sugar cubes and a carrot, offering them on an open palm, stroking his neck, crooning to him, rubbing his face. Anna watched, her arms crossed tightly around her middle.

"Boy. I'd never go through that to get him to put the bit in his mouth," she observed dryly.

"Only thing that works."

After letting Duke savor the carrot, allowing him to nuzzle her hand, Sadie made another attempt at inserting the bit. After a moment's hesitation, he willingly took it.

With Anna on Paris and Duke beneath her, hopping, sidestepping, doing anything he could to make it hard for Sadie, she had to concentrate on keeping her seat, trying to control him as best she could. He lifted himself off the ground, his front feet flailing the air, then came down crow-hopping, bouncing sideways as Sadie tried desperately to perceive her next move. He was a handful.

"He's gonna buck you right off of there," Anna shouted.

"I hope not!" Sadie yelled back.

After he settled down, they rode together, Paris walking sedately as if to remind Duke what a loser he was and to show him how it really was done. The pasture was green and brown, with the only patches of snow on the north side of dips and hollows or beneath low spreading pine trees. The ground was wet, the earth still absorbing the piles of winter snows, so they rode slowly, carefully. The smell of the earth and sky, the woods, the wet rotting leaves, the calls of the jays, the mockingbirds' warbles of mimicry all lifted Sadie's mood. Anything was possible on an evening like this.

Sadie looked over at Anna. Her face was set in stone, her mouth grim, her eyes darting from Paris's ears to the ground below, alternating between pulling back on the reins and holding the saddle horn. She was afraid! So very afraid! Oh, my goodness! Is that why she never rode? She was terrified.

The trail across the pasture took a steep downturn, wound around a grove of trees, the shadows looming long and black. Anna's eyes opened wide as she grabbed the saddle horn, bracing herself for the descent, her face whiter.

"I'm not going down there," she said softly.

"Come on, Anna. Paris is used to it."

Sadie led the way, Duke prancing and sidestepping, unwilling to be completely controlled.

Paris followed daintily, Anna's expression inscrutable. When the trail evened out, Anna breathed a notable sigh of relief. Sadie grinned at her.

"That wasn't so bad, was it? You're doing great. Straighten your back now. Relax. You're doing great."

"I am?"

"Of course."

They rode on, the horses' hooves making a dull, sucking sound in the mud. Then, suddenly, Anna spoke.

"Sadie?"

"Hmm?"

"Does...does it mean a...a...boy, a guy, loves you if he wants to take you out in his car?"

"His car? A vehicle?"

"Yes."

"You're surely not seeing an English boy? Guy?" Sadie mimicked, smiling genuinely.

"No. But...Neil...you know. Neil Hershberger bought a car. He doesn't want to be Amish. He...sort of hates his dad. He says I don't love him if I don't ride with him in his car."

Oh, boy. Problem number 162, Sadie thought wryly. How to answer?

"You really like Neil, don't you?"

Anna nodded, her expression containing so much pain, it was like a contortion of her features, a clouding over.

"Why?"

She shrugged. "He's cute."

"He definitely is that," Sadie agreed.

Chapter 8

"He's wild, but ... I think he'll change. Once we start dating, he'll ... change. He just says ... I think if I agree to go places with him in his car, he'll ask me for a date, because that will show him that I love him, right?"

Oh, boy. Literally walking on eggshells now. How to correct her without tearing down the frail stepping-stone they had placed so inefficiently a few minutes before?

"Well...," Sadie breathed. She was at a loss for the correct words now.

"I think he loves me," Anna blurted out, her voice abrasive in its desperation.

Paris whooshed air through her nostrils, lowering her head. Duke responded with a snort of his own. They came to a knoll, a sort of elevation, between two lines of trees. The rolling Montana landscape unfolded before them, dressed in the dull greens and browns of the time between winter and spring. Sadie knew a few weeks of sunshine would make all the difference, coloring the earth in those wonderful shades of green, like an artist who decides his palette is depressing sets about correcting the dullness with broad, bold, tumultuous strokes.

"Look, Anna!" Sadie said, pointing.

"What?"

"How beautiful it is!"

"Oh, yeah. But, Sadie, if I refuse to go with him, he'll tell me off. Our friendship would be over before it even got started."

Her words ended on a wail of wretchedness, a sound so deep and primal, Sadie knew she had to respond the only way she knew, telling her the hard truth, letting her deal with it.

"It's the best thing that could happen."

The words were blunt, clear, flung into the cold, Montana air. Anna's head came up, her eyebrows lowered, her face twisted into a mask of anger.

"You sound just like Mam. See? You're all against me! Every last one of you. Even that goody two-shoes Reuben! I hate you!"

With that, she jerked on Paris's rein, surprising the horse. Sadie saw the confusion in her eyes, her bearing before Anna dug in her heels, leaning forward, goading Paris with the power of her terrible rebellion. Paris ran then. At a speed much too fast for an inexperienced rider.

Wheeling Duke, Sadie screamed, "Stop! Paris, whoa! Stop! Anna!"

Paris was confused, frightened as she had been that day hitched to the spring wagon with Daniel beside her. The only instinct she knew was to get home as fast as she could. But with Anna sliding and flopping around on the saddle, they'd never make it.

Leaning forward, Sadie urged Duke, who was just waiting for the order to run. His feet gathered beneath him, his haunches lowered, as power surged through his magnificent legs. His neck stretched out, his head moved up and down, for a moment Sadie thrilled to his power and speed in spite of the dread that wrapped itself around her senses, a claustrophobic tentacle squeezing the breath from her body.

Oh, dear God! Keep Anna on her horse! she begged. That turn around the alders! At this rate, they'd never make it.

"Whoa, Paris!" Sadie screamed again, screamed over and over till her voice was hoarse and inconsistent.

Still they pushed on. Then it was over so fast. It only takes a second for a very thin person like Anna to be flung from a fast-moving horse's back. She looked like a limp rag doll with barely any stuffing inside the fabric of her arms and legs. She flew through the air and hit the muddy ground, folding in on herself, the arms, legs, the black of her coat, the brilliance of the dress. A sickening, mud-filled clunk. A little pile of muddy clothes.

Was Sadie screaming? Or was it Anna? She had to haul back on the reins with every ounce of strength. Duke wanted to follow Paris, who had already disappeared around the corner of the alders, heading home, with or without her rider.

Sadie didn't remember dismounting. She just knew her knees were shaking so badly she had to concentrate on every step to reach her sister, whose face was turned away. She was lying on her side, her legs flung out, her arms drawn in. How badly was she injured?

A low moan was the first thing she heard. She was alive. That was all that mattered. Praise God! Another moan.

"Anna!"

There was no coherent answer, only another moan. Never move an injured person. Sadie called Anna's name over and over, moaning sounds the only response. Wildly,

Sadie looked about her, then hurled herself into the saddle, urging Duke without meaning it, an unnecessary thing done out of habit.

When they slid into the barnyard, Mark came racing down the path from the house, waving his arms.

"Sadie! What is wrong with you? Riding like that? Duke? Why Duke?" he yelled, his agitation an engine of words tumbling over each other.

"It's Anna! Is Paris here? Did you see her run home?"

As she spoke, she dismounted, running through the forebay opening, then slumped visibly, relieved to see Paris outlined against the water partitions.

"Oh, Mark! She's here!"

"What happened?"

Mark shook his head in disbelief as she quickly related her story. Then he ordered her back on Duke, quickly leaping up behind her. As long as she lived, she would never cease to be amazed at Mark's ability to leap onto the back of a horse, cat-like, springing up as if it required no effort on his part. She remembered the first time she had seen him springing, no, bouncing off the truck that day on the snowy road.

Duke took off, Mark's weight holding him back, his gait a fraction slower. They found Anna, still moaning, her breath coming in painful jerks. Mark bent over her, calling her name.

"Anna! Anna!"

She began crying then. Whispering how much it hurt. She couldn't breathe. It hurt. Was she going to die? In the end, Sadie stayed with her while Mark rode to the phone. Anna was so cold. Why did it hurt so badly?

"I think you have a few broken ribs, Anna. Or worse."

"It hu...urts." She could only gasp in broken whispers.

Birds twittered their good-evening calls. The cold settled like a harsh blanket as the sun slid behind the mountain, a warm kindness that bade them farewell. Why did it take them so long? Then she heard it. The wail of an ambulance. Shivers chased themselves up her back as quick tears sprang to her eyes. Help was on the way.

With Mark's direction, the ambulance drove as far as they were able to across the muddy pasture, driving slowly, a red and yellow beacon of hope as Anna continued gasping for breath, crying out in pain. Two men carried a stretcher. Her shrieks of agony began when they poked and prodded, then carefully slid the stretcher beneath her battered body.

Sadie let the telephone ring and ring and ring, repeatedly pressing the redial button. Reality suddenly hit. How much would her poor Mam and Dat be able to take? Now Anna. And Sadie just home from her own ordeal. *God chasteneth whom he loveth.* Yes, this was true. But, like children, there was no chastening if they behaved themselves. Must be God saw plenty wrong with them, or he wouldn't try to fix them the way he did.

Please answer! If they didn't, she'd have to send a driver to tell them to come to the hospital. Then, sure enough, Reuben.

"Hello?"

"Reuben? Oh, I'm so glad you answered."

"I just got home from work."

That gruff voice! Reuben was growing into a young adult right before everyone's unseeing eyes.

"Listen. Anna was thrown from Paris. She was taken to the hospital. Get yourselves over there as fast as you can."

"Is she...is she, okay?"

"Well, yes. As okay as she can be. See you, Reuben."

✿ ✪ ✿

Anna had three broken ribs, her right lung was punctured, she was battered and bruised, but there were no life-threatening injuries other than her emaciated state. That awful thinness from years of depriving herself of good, wholesome food.

Dat and Mam, of course, were visibly distressed, but so glad to find their daughter alive and responding to the doctor's care. It was an attribute to their Amish upbringing, this receiving of bad news with grace and dignity borne with calm acceptance. Stoic was the best description, Anna thought, as she watched Mam clasp Anna's forearm, her eyes wet with unshed tears, her face a harbor of love, a safe, sound place for her battered Anna.

"*Siss kenn fa-shtandt.*" Mam's usual exclamation.

They asked many questions. Nodded their heads. Leah and Rebekah came in, their eyes wide with questions. Reuben had his say, then, his love for Anna fueling the jet stream of his words.

"Sadie, I think it's time you took a lesson from this. You are always in some sort of trouble with this crazy horse business with Paris. It's okay, but one of these days, someone's going to get killed. You had to have your own special horse, and look at all the troubles she brought us. It's about time you retire from.... Well, just slow down and take it easy for once."

After that, he became self-conscious, kicking the toe of his sneaker against the footboard of Anna's bed until Dat made him stop.

Mam nodded. "My mother's favorite saying was, 'What most we long and sigh for, might only bring us sorrow.'"

"But, Mam!" Sadie burst out.

Mark put his arm protectively around her shoulders, his presence letting her know he was on her side, as she told her mother Paris had brought so much more than sorrow. Mam remained adamant, Dat backing her. Reuben glared at Mam. Leah and Rebekah's faces were inscrutable.

"But...but..." she floundered.

"You need to be more careful, Sadie. Horses can be a source of danger, as you should be aware of by now, surely," Dat said firmly. "It's a wonder you're not dead."

Reuben's words were blunt, but sort of like one of those squishy things you throw against a wall and they slowly slide off, although they leave a sticky residue. Sadie considered them, but only a small part. Paris was a part of her life, like Mark, her beloved house beneath the trees, the ranch, Dorothy. She couldn't imagine life without any of them.

Anna moved home and was kept like a queen in a hospital bed as she healed. The doctors diagnosed her anorexia and prescribed medication. The family set up an appointment for counseling.

Sadie visited often. Mam firmly took matters into her own hands, deciding Sadie was part of Anna's problem, and asserted herself. Late one Saturday morning she made a pot of coffee, then opened the oven door to reveal a large pan of homemade sweet rolls, the spirals of brown sugar and cinnamon tantalizingly curled among the puffs of sweet dough baked to a golden brown. She poured a soft caramel frosting over the warm rolls before serving them on pretty plates, accompanied by a breakfast pizza, which consisted of potatoes, eggs, cheese, and sausage.

Sadie sighed happily. "Dear Mam. I can't imagine being happier than I am at this moment. Your food!"

That voice of appreciation made it harder for Mam, but she remained strong, a matriarch of wisdom, knowing her oldest daughter needed to be lovingly rearranged, put in place. The conversation drifted to a quiet lull, allowing Mam to open the subject of Anna's disease, the dreaded anorexia.

"You know, Sadie, you are the oldest daughter, and you do have a way with Anna. I'm grateful for everything you've done so far. She needs building up now. I think…"

Here Mam hesitated, searched Rebekah's face, then Leah's, as if seeking approval.

"You can't help being you, Sadie. You are beautiful, you have a gift of riding, a way with horses, and now you have Mark, your kind and handsome husband. But to view yourself through Anna's eyes…"

Here Mam stopped again, then reached out to put a hand on Sadie's arm.

"Believe me when I say you are blessed, and being you is not what makes Anna what she is. But I don't think you realize the depth of Anna's self-loathing. She has always looked to you as a sort of idol. An *opp-Gott* almost. To attain your height was the despair of her life. And Sadie, this is not your fault. But…we need to understand how frail she is. She's like the Bible verse where the house is built on sand, not the rock of Jesus."

Sadie gasped.

"You mean…you actually mean Anna doesn't have Jesus in her heart?"

"Does she?"

Mam searched Sadie's eyes, and Sadie's lowered first.

"She needs the Lord. But we can't do that for her. She needs to let him into her heart, so we'll just be here for her. And Sadie... just back off a little. Don't lecture, or... how can I say this in the right way?"

At first Sadie reeled from Mam's judgment of her. Slowly, though, as time went on, the truth became apparent. She was always the fixer in the family, the one who always got it right, the queen, the oldest. Yes, Mam was right. The experience brought a new humility over the coming weeks.

She visited Anna, telling her of Mark's dark moods, her own insecurities, the socks she ruined by soaking them in pure Clorox, the sausage gravy she burnt to a crisp at the ranch. And all the time Anna was recovering, with all the friends she received, the bouquets of flowers, the cards, the gifts, not once did Neil Hershberger as much as try and contact her in any way. There were no messages on the telephone's voice mail, no cards, no flowers. She searched feverishly through each envelope, but each day there was nothing.

One evening, when the light of a spring day lingered into that softness that is so beautiful you can hardly stand it, Sadie sat on her parents' porch swing, rocking gently with Reuben beside her. Anna lowered herself painfully into the wooden porch rocker by their side.

"Ouch. Everything hurts!" she exploded impatiently.

Sadie laughed. "It will for awhile yet, my dear."

Dat and Mark had gone to the end-of-the-year school meeting, so Sadie stayed with Mam and the girls, an event that never failed to bring her joy.

When the distant, shrill ring of the phone began, Reuben leaped off the swing and raced to the shanty. It was a dash of desperation to catch the caller before the voice mail came on and before they left their phone shanty, because no matter how many times you called back, they were gone and you never found out what they wanted. It was one of those minor annoyances of Amish life, like searching for a lighter that was always to be kept in a small basket at the base of the propane lamp, yet someone always took off with it. Some folks tied a lighter to the propane lamp. But it looked so ridiculous, that brightly colored plastic lighter hanging in midair by the black carpet string, that Sadie never bothered. She just kept a large box of long matches in a drawer that no one, not even Mark, knew about. It worked.

Reuben raced back, threw himself on the swing and announced there was a group of Amish friends coming with pizza.

"Who?" Anna asked, her face leaking its color like a deflating balloon.

She was visibly afraid. Sadie could see her chest heaving, her heart beating thick and loud. It was Neil, she knew. Would he be with them? It was too painful, this complete obsession.

Sadie helped her shower and comb her hair, laughing and joking, trying to keep the atmosphere lively, upbeat. She remembered Mam's words, remembered to let Anna choose her own dress, nodding approval. She was so pretty. But in her own eyes, so ugly. A pitiable caricature of her true self.

Neil Hershberger, of course, was not among them. Lydia, Suzanna, Ruth Ann, and Esther. Her best friends, bearing a stack of steaming pizzas from the best pizzeria in town. Followed by Melvin, Michael, Jerry, her cousin Danny, and Merv Bontrager.

Merv Bontrager! Oh, my goodness. He was at least three years older than Anna. It was as if he stepped out of the surrounding shadows and into the illuminating light of Sadie's knowledge. Why not? Goose bumps roused the fine hairs on her arms as she thrilled to this new prospect. Why not? He was perfect for Anna. He had enough confidence to keep them both afloat, that was sure. She would not say a word to anyone.

She watched Merv from the background, watched him like a hawk. He ate lots of pizza, laughed and talked, but his eyes rarely left Anna. When she spoke to him, it was like a queen extending her royal scepter, he was so honored. But—how to get Neil out of her head?

The group of youth around the table was quite boisterous, enjoying themselves, the bantering, the youthful zest for life. They were at an age Sadie had almost forgotten. It seemed so long ago that she was one of them. But, oh, the sweetness of this! She had forgotten the simplicity, the innocence.

When the school meeting was over and Mark returned, Sadie did not want to leave, glad to see Mark sit down and help himself to a large slice of cold pizza, turning his attention to Merv, who responded to Mark's questions politely. Yes, he was busy. Yeah, it was a bit hard to start his own roofing business, but that was only in the beginning. Yeah, there was a real need for roofers. Tear-offs, for sure.

His brown hair was cut neatly, his blue eyes alive with pleasure when Anna spoke to him. His white short-sleeved shirt was open at the collar. He was relaxed, at ease, able to maneuver his way in a conversation so well. Oh, the possibilities!

Anna said she was thirsty, so Merv was instantly on his feet, getting ice from the freezer, filling a tall glass with cold water, then bringing it to her, totally devoid of self-consciousness. Handing the glass to Anna, their hands touched, his eyes a caress on hers. Was that a blush spreading across her too-pale cheek? Their eyes held, stayed.

Sadie was fairly bouncing up and down on the buggy seat the whole way home, grabbing Mark's arm, squeezing it with both hands to get her point across. He laughed easily, held her close, and told her to calm down.

Mark said the school meeting dragged on longer than necessary in his opinion, shaking his head at the audacity of Fred Troyer. They needed another schoolhouse built, and David Detweiler offered a piece of ground, a nice, central location, but Fred had to throw a monkey wrench into the works and put in his two cents, saying the school should be built a few miles to the north. His grandchildren wouldn't have to pay transportation then; that was the only reason, everyone knew.

"He's as bad as his wife," Mark finished.

Sadie instantly changed the subject. "But, Mark, you know what? If Neil would just stay away now, I think Merv would have a chance. But I'm afraid when Anna is better, she'll return to the youth's events, the singings and suppers, and then what? Huh?"

"Oh, don't worry yourself about it. As I said, that Fred and Ketty are something else. But, you know how *goot-manich* that David Detweiler is? Of course, he said it's all right with him, they voted on it, and old Fred got his way. Sure would have liked to see it go the other way, but who am I to say? We don't have any children yet, so, of course, it's all right. Whatever the older men decide."

"And, Mark, you know what? If someone could put a bug in Merv's ear, he could just ask her for a date. Anna, you know, she might say yes. She just might. Neil isn't going to ask her. Do you think Neil will ask her out? I mean, for a real date?"

"I don't know, Sadie. But the thing that gets me, look how many families will have to pay transportation now. Even at five or six dollars a day for each family, at 130 days, that's over a thousand dollars. Fred should have thought of that. I wouldn't be a bit surprised if we have another meeting."

"Probably. Why do you think Neil doesn't come visit Anna?"

"Likely because he drives that old clunker around."

When they turned into the driveway, the deep barking of Wolf welcomed them, a sound Sadie had grown to cherish. He was such a good, faithful dog, so devoted to Mark, easily adopting Sadie as his second master.

Sadie hopped off the buggy and went to say good night to Paris, after helping Mark unhitch Truman. He had a nasty habit of running out of the shafts before the britchment snap was released, which could result in a bucking horse and broken shafts, among other things.

Where was Paris?

"Hey, Paris. Are you lying down already?"

Sadie walked to her stall, peering through the vertical, steel railing, certain of seeing Paris standing in the darkened area. Only the headlights gleaming through the door illuminated the forebay, but it was enough light for Mark to unharness his horse and put him in his stall.

"Paris?" The fear began in the pit of her stomach, taking her breath away. No. It couldn't be. The horse thieves were caught. It was all over. This could not be.

Chapter 9

But it was. Paris had been taken out of her stall, the door closed and latched behind her. But what really broke Sadie's heart was imagining how obedient Paris would have been, her large eyes questioning, unsure but obedient. She was gone. No amount of consolation did any good. Absolutely none.

The next day Mark went to work weary from a restless night, the endless searching, Sadie's questioning, his inability to make this right for his beloved wife. They called the police, of course, but were received with a sort of tired disbelief, as if this surely had to be a joke, which made Mark angry. Banging the receiver down into its cradle and stalking about the phone shanty muttering to himself brought a fresh onslaught of tears from his stricken wife.

✵ ✵ ✵

In time Sadie accepted it, gave herself up to it, in the Amish way. Paris was gone. The neighboring community kept an eye out, watched their own horses, but knew she was an extremely valuable horse, and perhaps it wasn't the will of God that Sadie had her at all.

Hadn't Sam Detweiler preached last Sunday about where our treasures are, there will our hearts be also? Sadie better watch out; that palomino horse was taking the place of God. This the grandmothers discussed at the quiltings without malice, certainly not wishing any evil on Mark Sadie, just stating a fact. She surely had a streak of bad luck, that girl and her horse. They felt so sorry for poor Mark Sadie. But you know, she'll be in the family way before long, and then what good will the horse do her? All these discussions of wisdom, wise in the ways of life, were spoken out of love and concern for Sadie's safety.

Sadie persuaded Mark to till the soil so she could start a garden. He thought the ground was too wet, but Sadie remained adamant, remarking that Mam already had planted her peas and onions. So Truman pulled the plow, and they evened the ground with a harrow and an old bedspring, which worked just great. Sadie was ecstatic. Mark put in stakes attached to a heavy string, and she planted a pound of peas in perfectly aligned rows.

They bent side by side, poking the papery, yellow onion sets into the damp soil, covering them loosely with the hoes they had been given as wedding gifts. When Sadie insisted on planting the red beets as well, Mark gave in, shaking his head in disagreement, saying it was too early. They would need them pickled, preserved in quart jars for church services at their house.

"Oh, imagine, Mark! We're an old married couple. We'll have church services at our house. The deacon will announce in services that church will be at Mark Peight's, and all the women will offer to bring something!"

Mark grinned. "We'll have to have church in the basement."

"I figured."

☆ ✡ ☆

She told Dorothy that sometimes she heard Paris
whinny from the barn and ran down to see if she was
back, but she never was. Dorothy shook her head.

"I'm tellin' you, though, yer better off. That Paris is a
peck o' trouble. Ya don't need her."

Not even Erma Keim understood. "Why a horse? Why
trouble yourself? She's gone. Good riddance. You're still
alive, and, you know, you could be dead."

Dorothy said Erma didn't have a very nice way with
words after she went out to rake the lawn of its winter
debris.

"I mean, she has about as much tact as a steam engine.
It's why she don't have no husband. Imagine the poor
guy's life?"

"I know."

Sadie was snapping green beans to cook with new
potatoes and ham. She sat by the window, watching
Erma's long, powerful strokes of the rake, her red hair a
veritable flame in the strong sunlight, her covering blowing off repeatedly, which she dashed after and pinned
back on her head.

Sadie was almost finished when a dark figure approaching Erma Keim from the barn caught her attention. He
wasn't wearing a hat, which wasn't unusual in the Montana wind, which caught hats in its grasp and whirled
them away without warning, tore off coverings, and
made a complete mockery of hairspray.

Steven Weaver! The man from Indiana!

"Oh, my word! Come here, Dorothy!" Sadie hissed excitedly.

"Can't!" Dorothy called, stirring her famous white sauce for baked macaroni and cheese.

"Turn the burner off!"

Dorothy complied, walking heavily to stand by Sadie's chair. Slowly she breathed in, then out. Steven walked up to Erma, stuck out his hand, a broad grin on his friendly face. Erma looked at him, then brought her arm back, her elbow protruding under the sleeve of her red dress and met his hand with a solid smack.

Sadie winced, and Dorothy shook with a deep belly laugh.

"What a giraffe! She don't even know how to shake hands! Especially with a man."

When Steven dropped his hand, it didn't look as if he minded how firm her handshake had been. He looked delighted, if anything. Their tall forms stood in the middle of the lawn, talking, the wind whipping his hair and the legs of his trousers, her skirt twisting and flapping and her red hair a complete disaster, the pins sliding out yet again.

She was laughing when her covering went flying off. She grabbed desperately for it but could not catch the elusive object. Just then Reuben came dashing by at his usual unsafe speed on the riding mower, caught sight of the rolling white object and slammed on the brakes, leaned back, his arms stiff as a board to the steering wheel, as he brought the mower to a halt, inches from the white covering. Reuben swung his legs over, hopped off, grabbed the covering, and brought it to Erma.

Steven was bent at the waist, slapping his knee with pure merriment, watching intently as Erma tried to pin it back on, taking extra pins from her belt. She had to turn her back to Steven, the wind coming in that direction, as she struggled to pin it in place.

"Come here!" Sadie hissed.

Dorothy had been on her way back to her cream sauce, but she turned immediately, peering eagerly through the window just as Steven reached up to hold her covering in place so Erma could pin it.

"Oh, my lands!" Dorothy breathed.

Sadie watched, spellbound, when she saw how flustered Erma became, picking up her rake, catching her covering strings, looking down to her shoes, then to Reuben, who stood observing them both with innocent curiosity. He said something, and Erma slapped his back so hard he took a few steps forward, then laughed.

"Oh my, she must be really worked up," Sadie said. "She almost knocked Reuben on his face!"

"What'd I tell you? If that Indiana chap knows his good, he'll hightail it right back to his home state. She'll make his life miserable. Mark my words! Miserable!"

But she had a light in her eyes and was humming a silly little love song when she returned to her cream sauce, dipping and waving her spoon in time to her song.

Sadie's life remained completely peaceful, except for the ache in her heart about Paris, who had disappeared that night leaving no trace, much the same as so many horses before her. The sun gently drew the seeds into sprouts that pushed their way up through the hard, wet soil in late spring. The nights were still crisp and cold, the air brisk and snappy when Sadie hung laundry on the line in the early morning, that unceasing Montana wind tugging at the heavy towels and dresses as she pinned them securely, sometimes needing more than one clothespin on each corner to ensure her peace of mind while she was at work down at the ranch.

Erma Keim remained a constant source of entertainment, spicing her days with a dash of peppery comments, clashing with Dorothy's bristling wit like a bad summer thunderstorm.

In the evening Mark would lean back and howl with laughter when Sadie related an especially bizarre incident, but of late he had become increasingly withdrawn yet again. It was always the same. First she would blame herself. Scouring the past days, even weeks, for a certain thing she had said or done, enabling the black cloud to hover over his head, raining down the sadness, the dissociation, that extracting of himself to another, darker place. She dreaded it.

She prattled senselessly, as incapable of changing the descending cloud as changing the horizon or the order of nature. Still she tried to bring him back, knowing it wouldn't work, then went about her work with a lump in her throat, knowing she had let him down yet again.

It was especially bad this time. He slept on the couch, his face to the back, his knees drawn up almost to his chin. His dirty work clothes reeked of barns, horse manure, and other scents that Sadie could only describe as dirty.

No amount of wheedling would make one stitch of difference. First, after her shower, she sat on the space where his knees left an indentation and put an arm across his wide back. Slowly she began a relaxing massage, asking him softly if he felt ill, or if his head hurt, willing him to break the silence and tell her what had happened to bring this on. A rude shrugging of the shoulders, a grunt, a burrowing into the couch cushions, followed by a long drawn-out sigh was her only answer.

So she got up, went to the bedroom, groped around till she felt her box of long matches, struck one along the side of the box harder than was necessary, took off the glass lamp chimney, turned up the wick, and lit it. Tears dropped onto the surface of the nightstand. Replacing the chimney, she pulled back the quilt and top sheet and slid into bed with her book of the week. Swiping viciously at her eyes, she opened the book, but all the words swam together, a black-and-white blurb of unreadable nonsense that only made her cry harder.

Was it the lack of a good, hot supper on Thursday? Had she become too snippy about leaving his soiled boots beside the stove on Wednesday? That was likely what it was. She would have to remember next time. Place a rug along the back of the stove for his boots, then shake out the accumulation that hardened on the soles afterward. She'd have to be more careful.

Having reached a reasonable conclusion for herself made all the difference, so she laid her book down, blew out the lamp, and soon fell asleep. You just had to know how to work at these things. Didn't even the experts say marriage wasn't easy?

When Mark disappeared on Saturday morning, she presumed he went to town, or forgot to tell her he had a few horses to shoe, or went out back to chop more firewood. She cleaned her house all morning, starting in the back, throwing open every bedroom window, allowing the spring breezes to enter, filling the room with the sweet smell of new growth, rain-washed earth, and spring flowers. She swept the wide-plank oak floors with the soft broom she had just purchased at Fred Ketty's new dry goods store. All Amish women had to have a Soft Sweep broom. Inexpensive, the bristles so soft and pliable, it allowed a much cleaner sweep than those stiff bristled ones at Walmart.

The thing was, English women used vacuum cleaners, which whirred across the floor and sucked up the dirt and dust and household accumulation of questionable things, like pet hair and dander and bugs and spiders. When she cleaned at the ranch, she dusted first, then ran the powerful vacuum cleaner across the carpeting or hardwood floors.

At home she swept first, raising little puffs of dust and woolies from under the bed, making a pile outside the bedroom door before collecting it in a dustpan, then liberally spraying her cloth with Pledge furniture polish. She removed the candles, lamp, tray of lotions and colognes and worked the cloth energetically across the surface. When everything was replaced, she used the Swiffer, picking up any dirt and dust the broom had missed.

There. Now for the bathroom.

At the ranch, she had to dry the huge garden tub, then spray it with Tilex. Never anything else. Barbara Caldwell considered it the best product, so Sadie used it and never said a word. It was Barbara's bathroom, and if she was happy with the result of her cleaner, it was good.

But at home Sadie used cheap old Comet. The dry stuff you shook out of a tall green container, wet a cloth, and scrubbed away. It never scratched anything she knew of and had a cleaner, smoother finish. No water spots.

She was on her hands and knees, scrubbing happily away at her new white bathtub, the water running, when she thought she heard someone calling her name. Quickly, she yanked down on the lever, stopping the flow of water. She stepped outside the door, looked left and right, but couldn't see anyone. Wolf hadn't barked, had he?

"Sadie!" There. Someone was calling.

Wiping her hands on her apron, she hurried to the front door and was gratified to see Mark standing by the barn door, waving a piece of paper.

"What?" she called, so glad he was talking to her.

"I'm going to the ranch."

"Okay."

She stepped back, eager to finish cleaning the bathtub. Why did he let her know now? He had been gone all morning without letting her know of his whereabouts. Pushing back the resentment, she tried to think of more pleasant subjects. She wished he'd finish the porch steps so she could wrap up her landscaping project. She could hardly wait to plant shrubs and flowers, especially since Dorothy had offered to take her to Rhinesville to a huge nursery and greenhouse combination. She promised the use of Jim's truck so she could buy anything she wanted, even trees.

The thought of Dorothy weaving that rusted pickup truck in and out of traffic, her short legs and arms barely able to reach the pedals or the steering wheel, driving the same way she did everything else—as fast as possible— talking all the while, definitely caused Sadie a few misgivings. If only she wouldn't maneuver the turns like that— seemingly on two wheels, sometimes spinning gravel from under the tires when her foot hit the gas pedal too firmly. But still, it was a free trip.

That was an awful bunch of dust and woolies on her broom. Stepping outside, she whacked it down on the porch railing to loosen them, and after a distinct crack, was left holding half a handle, the remainder of her broom lying in the mud below. Oh, no. That was the only broom she had except a porch broom, and she certainly did not want to use that. So she decided she needed a few dresses for summer, and she'd hitch up Truman and drive to Fred Ketty's store. The cleaning would have to wait till she returned.

Smoothing back her hair, she pinned on a clean, white covering, grabbed her purse, and was out the door.

The loss of Paris was always worse at the barn. She hated going there and struggled to keep her eyes from wandering to the empty stall. The currycomb still contained honey-colored hair from Paris's coat. She raked it out with her fingers, savored the softness as she sifted it between her thumb and forefinger, slowly letting it fall to the concrete floor of the forebay. Setting her mouth determinedly, she brushed Truman hard, willing the dark brown horsehair to drive away the endless longing for Paris.

She knew, now, that Paris was a very valuable horse, so perhaps it was for the best. She'd be in good hands, likely making some rancher wealthy with that bloodline of her past. She'd have to give up. Wasn't that the way of it? What you couldn't change, you had to accept.

Throwing the harness across Truman's back, she adjusted it, fastened all the snaps and buckles, the collar riding well on his thick neck. Leading him to the buggy, she told him to stay, then hurried back to lift the shafts. There was always that small space of time when you were never sure if the horse you were hitching up would stand obediently until the shafts were lifted. Even then, if he had a mind to, he could have gone running and kicking, free of doing his duty of pulling the buggy. Truman was well trained and, with a slight tug of the britchment strap and a command of "Back," he responded, stepping back lightly, fitting between the shafts neatly.

Truman was in high spirits, and Sadie's arms felt as if they had quite a workout by the time Fred Ketty's store came into view.

That Fred. Sadie smiled to herself as she noticed the gray siding on one side of the building, white on another, and beige-colored siding on the front. Likely he'd been scavenging the local lumberyard to build his wife her dry goods store. The dubious-looking stainless steel chimney poked its way out of the black shingled room, a thin, white column of smoke whirling away on the breeze. Why a fire in the stove? Sadie barely needed her sweater. The door stuck, so Sadie shoved harder, entering the store with a bang and two quick steps.

"Sadie!" Ketty boomed.

"H...hello, Ketty," Sadie said, floundering a bit, grabbing for composure.

"Welcome to my store!"

"It's nice!"

"Really nice, isn't it? My Fred is something. Never saw anyone that can put up a nicer building for less than 2000 dollars."

"Really?"

Ketty nodded proudly, then lowered herself around the cash register to whisper confidentially that Fred is good buddies with Jack from the lumberyard. Gave him stuff he can't sell anymore.

"That's good," Sadie said, smiling.

It had to be close to a hundred degrees in the place. Sadie took off her sweater, asking if she could put it by the cash register.

"You too warm? Well, I got a bunch of cheap apples from the fruit man, and we don't eat so many apples, me and Fred. I hate to see them go to waste, so I told Fred if he starts me a wood fire, I'd cook down the apples for *loddveig*. Nothing better than *loddveig* on a warm dinner roll, *gel*, Sadie?"

Sadie nodded, smiled, said all the appropriate things, her eyes looking for the right shade of blue, her fingers searching for a good, lightweight, sturdy fabric. She scratched her head, then wiped her forehead with a clean handkerchief. This was absolutely miserable. What was wrong with this woman? Why didn't she open a window? Perspiration beading her forehead, she quickly made her purchase, steering clear of the red-hot, potbellied stove snapping and crackling in one corner, a heavy pot of apples bubbling and steaming on the top.

"Three yards of this, please."

"Sure."

Fred Ketty made a sweeping motion with her arms, a grandiose gesture of the experienced store owner, one who would become quite well-to-do the minute she had sold Sadie her fabric.

Sadie looked behind Ketty to the plush recliner, the cup of coffee, the heavy book. What had she been reading? On a Saturday? This early in the morning? A half-eaten cinnamon roll lay haphazardly across the Saran-wrap-covered plate that contained five more.

War and Peace? Fred Ketty was reading *War and Peace*? Sadie looked sharply at Fred Ketty as if seeing her for the first time. Was she a genuine intellectual? People said she was way smarter than she looked, which was a blunt statement, but honest.

She imagined Fred Ketty with her hair down, dressed in English clothes. She was tall, statuesque, actually, her eyebrows quite regal-looking. If she wasn't wearing the rumpled dress, the too-small glasses, the lopsided covering, she could probably look quite distinguished. A lawyer?

Sadie imagined Fred Ketty walking the streets of New York City, wearing a black belted trench coat and large, dark glasses, carrying a designer briefcase, four-inch heels coming down on the paved sidewalk. She bet she could do it if she hadn't been born Amish. But here was Fred Ketty, her keen eyes looking at the world through her plain glasses, perfectly happy, avidly curious about the world's goings on, about history, especially World War II. It was an innocent outlet for a mind that could have been taught so much more. It was the way of it. No sadness in this birdlike happiness.

"How's marriage treating you?" Fred Ketty asked, folding a three-yard length, her bright eyes looking straight through her.

Sadie opened her mouth to say, "Fine," but instead, ended up with a catch in her throat, her mouth wobbling. She sat behind the counter with Fred Ketty for an hour, eating the softest, most wonderful cinnamon rolls with cream cheese frosting and drinking chai tea, which Fred Ketty said was good for the sinuses, among other things.

She told her about Mark, and Fred Ketty clapped a warm hand on her shoulder and said that boy had a rough start. How in the world could she ever figure it wouldn't show up sometimes? The human spirit could only take so much and not more, and he was likely doing the best he could, and she'd always said that Mark had married exactly the right girl, as strong as Sadie was. She was the perfect helpmate for a guy like him, and if he went into a depression like that, she'd have to detach herself and go on with her life and know she couldn't change him. And if it got too bad, she could come over and sit in her store and eat sticky buns and drink chai tea.

She laughed so deeply and genuinely when Sadie told her about Mark sleeping on the couch, that it rolled between them and caught Sadie infectiously until her whole world looked better and better.

"It's called marriage, Sadie dear!" she gasped, lifting her too small glasses to wipe her eyes, and Sadie was so glad Fred Ketty was here in her cheap little store and not a lawyer in New York City.

Chapter 10

"WHY DID YOU NOT TELL ME, MARK?"

Sadie's words were ripe with frustration. "Why? Why put me through all these days of silence, the months of not knowing what in the world is eating you, and suddenly, bingo, you let me in on your wonderful secret, which you had absolutely no right to hide from me at all?"

Mark leaped up, pushed back his kitchen chair, and slammed the door behind him as he left the house, giving Sadie no answer. She was so angry.

It was sweltering. Dry, hot wind tugged at the curtains, stirring the thick, tepid air but giving no real relief. In Montana the summer was not as unendurable as in Ohio, but there were always a few uncomfortable weeks, and this year had been no different.

Absentmindedly, she stirred the cold soup, that sweet concoction the Amish still considered a good, refreshing alternative to cookies on days when no one was comfortable. A large amount of fresh blueberries in the bottom of a generous pottery serving bowl, a liberal amount of sugar, a few slices of heavy homemade bread broken on top, and ice-cold milk poured over everything. *Kalte sup.*

It was so good. Sweet and creamy and fruity. Dorothy shivered to think about it, which made Sadie smile.

Wearily she began gathering knives, spoons, and forks, heading for the sink. Why had he done this on his own? Searching, going to the library, asking Duane Ashland, of all people, to use the computer. *Genealogy*. The word was hostile somehow. Against her. So now, out of the clear blue sky, he announced he had contacted his brother Timothy, and they planned to meet. He lived in Oregon. He was going, and did she want to go?

What about the months of wondering if she'd actually made a mistake? Marrying him the way she had, thinking her whole life would be one long day of love and adoration. She felt angry, bitter, and betrayed by his secrecy. So angry, in fact, that he was going to know it. She was absolutely not letting him get away with blithely skipping over these past months of hurt and disappointment.

She rattled the dishes as loudly as she could, somehow taking delight in banging them. She jerked the dish towel off its rack, snapped it into the air, and began drying dishes as if her life depended on exactly how dry they would become. To punish him, she wouldn't go. He could go by himself. He could pack his own suitcase, too.

Being all alone in one's kitchen, letting anger and bitterness eat away at your soul like battery acid, was not the thing to do. It was plain to her after a miserable evening. Something would have to give.

Dear Father in heaven, I am so mad. I am such a complete mess. I can't forgive Mark. I can't stand him, even. You know my heart. All my horrible hatred and bitterness. Cleanse me now. Let my sins be washed away. Give me a new start.

So she prayed, swinging back and forth on the porch

swing, the new porch steps beside her a tribute to Mark's hard work. She turned her head to listen. A buggy? Yes, a horse and buggy was traveling down Atkin's Ridge, coming in their direction. Oh, she hoped it was someone from her family. She missed them all so much. It had been too long since she had been back home with Mam and her sisters.

Listening eagerly now, she stopped the swing. The crunch of gravel on steel wheels was gratifying. It was Reuben and Anna! Leaping up, she began waving long before they reached the house, then ran down the steps and across the yard to greet them.

"Check out my new buggy!"

Reuben was 16 years old now and was still eager to tell Sadie everything he knew, blurting out the good news without as much as a hello.

"Wow! Sharp!" Sadie burst out.

Anna was grinning widely, and Reuben tried hard to maintain his air of grave manliness, but he couldn't hide his little-boy delight.

"Look at this! Gray and red! The carpeting is black and gray!"

"The glove compartment is very nice, too! Wow! Dat paid a lot for this rig!" Sadie said.

Mark came up from the barn and duly exclaimed about the new buggy, the harness, and where did he get the horse?

"It's Charlie!" Reuben crowed.

It was Charlie, a bathed and currycombed one. Even his mane and tail were clipped.

"Go tie Charlie and come in," Mark ordered.

They needed no second invitation, quickly gathering on the porch in the hot, still evening. Reuben seemed almost shy about the fact that he had turned 16. There was always a big fuss when one of the girls reached that age, which he never understood, displaying plenty of disbelief in the entire ritual. But when it was his own turn, he soaked up the attention like a dry sponge.

"So now Anna has a ride to the suppers and singings, right?" Sadie asked, smiling appreciatively at Reuben.

"I guess so," he said gruffly.

Anna winked broadly.

"How's life treating you, Anna?"

"Okay, I guess."

The usual noncommittal answer from Anna.

"No Neil Hershberger yet?"

A look of pain crossed Anna's face, and she bent her head.

"I guess not. He's dating Sheryl."

"He's what?"

Sadie was clearly disturbed.

"Sheryl?"

Anna nodded.

"Why?"

Anna shrugged her shoulders, her eyes downcast, biting her lip. Reuben shushed her with his eyes, drawing his eyebrows down with a slight shake of his head, rolling his eyes in Anna's direction. Sadie nodded slightly, then changed the subject.

Mark suggested they go fishing. He was hungry for some fresh trout, and with Danner's Creek this low, they'd have a good chance at a few fat ones. Reuben jumped up, clearly beside himself at the opportunity to show Mark his fly-fishing skills, which left Sadie with Anna for another hour or so before darkness folded itself across the land.

Sadie went to the kitchen, bringing back tall glasses of lemonade, the fresh-squeezed kind that Mark loved so much. Anna sipped daintily at hers, making a face afterward.

"Sour," she commented.

"It's the way Mark likes it."

"I'm never getting married," Anna said bluntly.

"I wouldn't."

Anna's head came up, and a smile crinkled her eyes at the corners. Her face was still gaunt, but not as angular, not quite as skeletal as it had been in the spring. The belt on her apron was tied loosely, so she still had the appearance of being painfully thin.

"Why do you say that?"

Sadie shrugged. "We just aren't... It's been a difficult summer. He finally came out and told me today, today, mind you, what has been so heavy on his mind."

Sadie told Anna the story, coming to a close with a frustrated, palms-up, arms-outspread jerk of her arms.

"Go figure! Go around leaving me in the dark."

Anna nodded. "I know how he feels."

"You do not."

"I do. I know exactly."

"Tell me."

Anna was quiet, sipping her drink, alternately making horrible faces till Sadie laughed, asking why she put herself through all that misery drinking that lemonade.

"I don't know how to explain it, but I know how he feels."

"Please, Anna."

"Well, you don't talk as if you're afraid people will think you're dumb if you say what you think."

"Can you say that differently?"

"I'm not a good talker. Like now, I can't.... Often the words don't come out right. Then if I do say ... say how

I feel, I imagine you … all my sisters think I'm dumb. So I don't talk."

"Why would we think that?"

"You do. Often I am dumb."

"Anna!"

"Well, all my older sisters are beautiful and smart … and … and someone. If you love others a lot, look up to them, it's pretty scary. Because if you do give an opinion, they'll think it's stupid. I am not smart like the rest of you. So I stay quiet."

"And then you don't eat because it's something you can control?"

Anna shrugged, sipped her lemonade, and pursed her lips, which Sadie saw but was thinking too deeply to notice. What were the right words?

"So you think Mark feels the same way?"

"Probably."

"He was afraid I'd laugh at him for looking for his brother? But we had talked about it before!" Sadie burst out.

Anna nodded. "Still, think about it. He's afraid of you, in a way."

Anna looked off across the lawn, her eyes softer than Sadie had seen them in a long time. "He's afraid you'll laugh at him. Think he's *bupp-lich*."

Sadie shook her head in disbelief.

"Ask him," Anna finished.

She told Sadie, then, about her return to the youth's events, how Neil acted as if nothing ever happened and that their friendship would continue, begging her to go out with him in his car. She had gone, of course, she would always go with him, so glad he wanted her back, telling herself he was too shy to meet her parents or ask her for a real date. How she loved him! Sadie nodded, understanding.

Then one night about a month ago, she realized he had no good intentions toward her and, selfishly, wanted her to leave her family and the Amish community for good. How he had pleaded. He said if she loved him she'd prove herself and go away with him. She almost went. She hadn't told anyone, knowing they would think she was foolish.

One night she dreamed Neil was leading her with a rope, the rope tightening around her neck, and she woke up screaming and screaming, choking and crying.

Mam had mentioned Anna's nightmares to Sadie. They had both agreed it was only normal after her accident. But this?

After she told Neil she would not leave the community, he had retaliated by dating Sheryl, a good five years his senior, and certainly a pitiful choice, leaving only a trail of heartache.

Anna finished miserably, "Now, he's trying to prove to me that he's staying Amish, obeying his parents, only not doing it for me."

"You don't care, do you?"

Anna shrugged her thin shoulders.

"Are you eating?"

"Better."

"Good girl, Anna. I'm so glad to hear you say that."

Anna smiled, a small timid lifting of her lips, but a smile nevertheless.

The following Saturday, Dorothy insisted they were going to the nursery. The summer was almost gone, and early fall was a good time to plant evergreens. She wanted a white pine of her own.

Sadie had hoped she would forget about it, especially when she remembered the steering wheel of the old pickup being stubborn at certain times. With Dorothy, though, there was no forgetting. Erma Keim could cook by herself, she said, since she knew how to make everything better than Dorothy did, anyway.

So Sadie dressed in her lightweight blue dress, combed her dark hair carefully, spraying it liberally with hair spray and pinning her covering with extra pins. She knew that with the lack of air conditioning and Dorothy's love of a strong breeze, the windows would be lowered the whole way down, as they hit speeds nearing 75 miles an hour if there was a good highway.

Mark watched her pin her covering and laughed.

"I can only guess what you'll look like coming back."

"If I come back!" Sadie laughed.

Mark sobered, then walked over and put his hands on her shoulders, bending his head to kiss her deeply before holding her tenderly against his body.

"Please be careful. I couldn't live without you. You are my life, the reason for my existence. Nothing else makes any sense."

Sadie clung to her husband, turned her face away, and felt the bitterness, the sadness, the impending sense of failure, leave a trail of debris as it was ushered out the door of her heart. When she cleared her throat, the debris followed, leaving a clean, white trail, sparkling with stardust, accompanied by the strains of angel harps.

Forgiveness, then, was incredibly important when two people became one, united in holy matrimony, as the minister had said. Sometimes their union had certainly not been holy. Or sacred. Why didn't someone write a manual about *after* your wedding day? A complete list of how-to's in every situation.

Well, for now, on this wonderful, glad morning, hope sprang up, completely new, stronger than ever.

"I love you, Mark," she whispered.

"I love you, too," he answered, taking a deep breath.

It's one of life's greatest mysteries. No matter what, you simply were not happy if you were angry with your husband. Even if you had more than enough reason to be. Even if you believed yourself to be a victim of his selfishness, his manners, you still did not have the all-consuming happiness that came with forgiveness. She felt like skipping out to the truck when it ground to a halt at the end of the new walkway Mark had finished.

"Good morning, Dorothy!"

"Don't you look nice, Honey?" Dorothy said, her way of greeting.

"Thank you!"

She slid the truck perfectly into drive, shifting gears much better than her husband ever did, her short arms and round fingers finding the gears as expertly as any truck driver. They wound their way along the rural roads, the morning air cool enough to keep the windows closed except for an inch or so at the top and still be comfortable.

"Where are we going, Dorothy?"

"To Rhinesville."

"How far away is it?"

"'Bout an hour."

"So, we get on 26?"

"Yeah."

Sadie glanced over at Dorothy, quite suddenly looking shorter and older, her arms outstretched, her small feet barely reaching the gas pedal or the brake. Sadie thought of the big rigs passing them from behind, with their furious speeds, and swallowed.

"Are you used to driving this truck?" she asked, quietly.

"Who? Me? 'Course I can drive this truck. I drove it for years. 'Fore I worked at the ranch."

"Oh."

"Don't you worry, yer in good hands. You wanna stop at the Dollar General? They have a big one in Rhinesville. Clorox is a dollar a gallon. It's up to a dollar and 29 cents at Walmart. See what I mean? You can't beat the Dollar General. You know their off-brand a' Ritz Crackers? They're a dollar sixty-nine. Mind you, real Ritz at Walmart's up to two ninety-eight. It's a sin. How 'n the world do they expect a person to pay their bills? Now nobody needs three bucks for them crackers. I ain't buyin' 'em."

Sadie nodded in agreement.

"I told Louise the other day, there ain't no way I'm packin' their school lunches no more. I give 'em three dollars, and they get a hot lunch at school. Bless their hearts, those kids is so good. So sweet. Sadie, the Lord smiled on me the day those kids came into my life. I'd give 'em everything I got. So would Jim. Love 'em to death, so we do."

She leaned over to check her mirror.

"Somepin' comin'?"

"No," Sadie said.

"Well, here we go, then."

With that, Sadie was introduced to the wildest ride she had ever encountered, with Dorothy pressing her foot on the gas, clutching the steering wheel with both

hands, passing anything in her path. They shot past tractor trailers, wove in and out of all the traffic, hardly ever
going below 75 or 80 miles an hour. Sadie chewed on
her lower lip, watching the mirror on her side and then
the smaller cars ahead. The scenery was beautiful, with
yellow beech trees, dark green pines, large horse farms,
and cattle ranches dotting the countryside. Sadie sincerely
hoped she'd reach Rhinesville safely and be able to return
home without too much anxiety.

The nursery and greenhouses were worth every tense
mile. Acres of land were covered with healthy looking
shrubs, perennials, trees, and evergreens, as well as greenhouses containing the last of the season's flowers. Dorothy
walked tirelessly in and out of rows of flowering shrubs
and bushes before purchasing a small white pine for $9.99.

"It's not so dear," she commented. "And when I'm
dead and gone, this tree will remind Louise and Marcelona of their foster mother, now won't it?"

Sadie nodded agreement, settling for two arborvitae,
two blue junipers, some ivy, day lilies, and hardy sage.
She enjoyed her time at the nursery so much, she was
reluctant to leave, buying a birdhouse for her porch at
the last minute, Dorothy scolding and shaking her head.

"Now what's that gonna do you good? Ain't no bird
gonna build a nest in that teensy hole."

"They might. You never know."

She couldn't tell Dorothy the birdhouse was simply
"for nice"—for display. She would never get over that,
bringing it up every day for a month. That was just how
Dorothy was, and Sadie had learned a long time ago not
to tell her things she wouldn't approve of.

"You know Mark coulda made you that birdhouse
fer nothin'?"

"He doesn't have time."

"Why not? He has to run around shoeing horses as fast as he can so's you kin spend it all on birdhouses?"

"I guess so."

Dorothy shook her head. Sadie was almost splitting her face to keep from laughing. If anyone else would have said that, Sadie likely would have been offended, but not Dorothy. She didn't have a mean bone in her body; she just felt it was her Christian duty to warn Sadie.

They traveled slowly through the town, looking for the Dollar General. It was beside a McDonald's, which left Dorothy fairly hopping up and down with glee. She parked the truck with a lurch, reached down and got her imitation brown leather purse, and dug, pulling out two coupons.

"Which one do you want? McDonald's or Burger King?"

"It's your call, Dorothy."

"I like McDonald's. I like their sundaes. Hot fudge. Maybe we better go to the Dollar Store first, make sure our money lasts. Nothin' else, we don't have to splurge. Eating out is so dear, you know. We can get a bag o' chips at the Dollar Store."

She almost ran across the parking lot, her green polyester shorts slapping about her knees, her white blouse embroidered in a rich teal thread around the neckline.

"Here, Sadie. Here's the carts. You better get one out here. This is a popular store. Never any carts. Never. We're lucky we got one this time, so we are. Mark my words, the Dollar Store's gonna put a hurtin' on Walmart. One o' these days, we'll read it in the paper."

Dorothy's hair was sticking straight up, completely electric with excitement, when she discovered the shoes were only $17.99, on sale from $24. She bought two pairs, saying she'd really have to explain it to Jim, but likely they'd last till she was about ready to retire.

She bought and bought and bought. She exclaimed loudly about every price, stocking up on Clorox, Ritz Crackers, chocolate sandwich cookies, saltines, handkerchiefs for Jim, socks for the children, until her cart was full to overflowing with various useful items.

At lunch, Dorothy ate a Big Mac with the dressing squeezing out from beneath the sandwich, spreading it across her face and completely unaware of it, talking between bites, saying this was the funnest day she had since she was 50.

And when she backed into a utility pole, giving Sadie's head quite a lurch, she got out to check the back bumper and said Jim could whack it out. She'd tell him someone hit her. They had. "They" was the utility pole. Why'd they put a pole at such a busy place? People didn't think, that's what. That's why the world was the way it was. Nobody thought.

They roared down the highway, the yellow Dollar General bags flapping and waving, the shrubs and bushes tilting this way and then the other, depending which way Dorothy turned in or out of traffic. Sadie prayed they wouldn't blow a tire. When they wheezed up the driveway and came to a skidding stop, Sadie leaned back and sighed, only not loud enough for Dorothy to hear.

Dorothy waved away the proffered gas money, saying Jim would fill it up, he had nothin' else to do with his money except go to the fire hall an' play Bingo, and she'd a' liked if he didn't do that. He was better off at home. Her Jim was a good-looking man. You never knew.

Chapter 11

WHEN THE BREEZES TURNED COOLER, THEN COLD, Mark said it was time to go. His work had slowed enough to allow him to plan the much-thought-about trip to Oregon. He became withdrawn, pensive, but not sullen or angry. He talked again of his past, the times he remembered Timothy. They discussed the reason his dying mother carried so much grief for him, if she barely mentioned the others.

Sadie could tell Mark was in an agony of indecision, even after the tickets had been procured, all the necessary arrangements made, and he had talked to Timothy on the phone. Still he wavered. Would it be for the best?

Timothy would try and contact his siblings, but hadn't elaborated if he had accomplished this. They were simply stepping out into the unknown, having no reason to believe any good would come from it.

Sadie could ask questions, but more often than not, she would receive a shrug of the shoulders, or a denial, an "I don't know," or words to that effect.

Sadie had decided to go along. Reuben and Anna would take care of Wolf and the horses. Leah would fill in for Sadie at the ranch. She was Erma Keim's good friend, so Sadie figured if things got too rocky, Leah could always tell Erma to back off. Mam made a new coat for Mark and a nice one made of wool for Sadie. They bought new shoes, a few shirts for Mark, packed their suitcase, and waited nervously for the driver to take them to the Amtrak station.

"At least no one is terminally ill this time," Sadie quipped, trying to bolster Mark's mood.

"Yeah."

"It'll be okay. You might be surprised how normal everyone is. If you feel no bonding, no connection, then just come back home and continue living your life without them. Nothing will change."

"But what will they think of me? My being Amish. I'm sure they think I'm just one big joke. A loser, who isn't even nearly as good as he thinks he is."

"We'll see, Mark. Don't be so hard on yourself."

He went to the refrigerator, helping himself to a slice of deer bologna, followed by the jar of bread and butter pickles. He folded a slice of Swiss cheese into the bologna, piled on a generous amount of pickles, and crunched all of it between his teeth.

"Mm, that's good! Those pickles are the best thing ever."

"Give me a bite."

Sadie jumped up, eagerly reaching for the bologna combination, only to be slapped away playfully.

"Come on, Mark!"

Elaborately, he dropped the last bite into his open mouth, then hunched his back as Sadie rained blows on his arm.

"Ow! Ow!"

"You need to learn how to share!"

Just as he had made another roll, the driver stopped at the end of the walks, with Sadie chewing a great mouthful on her way out. Her garden had yielded well for a brand new one. But then came the tedious job of peeling those gigantic cucumbers, cutting them in halves, scooping out the seeds, cutting them in long spears, and making banana pickles out of them. They were called that because of their resemblance to bananas: long, yellow, and curved, till they were all packed in the jar properly, standing upright, with the turmeric, that orange spice that turned everything yellow (including fingertips and countertops and wooden spoons), making them a beautiful color. Banana pickles were often served in church, fitting perfectly inside a roll of ham or eaten with cheese. Or like now, wrapped inside a roll of Swiss cheese and bologna, creating a burst of sweet and sour in Sadie's mouth.

The driver, Tom Nelson, the oldest, most dependable driver, with an impeccable driving record, having driven a huge 18-wheeler for "40-some" years, was in a sour mood, grunting a surly hello, throwing his cigarette reluctantly out the window when they got into the 15-passenger van.

"Whyn't ya tell me there was only the two of you? Woulda brought the truck."

"I thought I did," Sadie offered.

That was greeted by another grunt. "Gonna cost ya more."

Mark said nothing, so Sadie kept her peace. Observing Tom from the seat behind the driver, she decided he'd likely be in a better mood if he shaved and got a haircut. That gray hair looked itchy and uncomfortable, growing in stubbles all over his face that way. His glasses could have done with a good cleaning as well.

Sadie grimaced as he reached for his ever-present bottle of warm Coke, twisting the red cap off and draining it in a few gulps before returning it to the cup holder, wiping his mouth and belching softly, as he scratched the plaid flannel fabric of the shirt stretched across his stomach.

"So where we goin'?" he rasped.

"Oregon," Mark answered.

"What?"

The beady brown eyes peered at Mark, the head elevated slightly to see him better, his eyes adjusted to the bifocals in his glasses. Mark laughed.

Tom bent over his steering wheel, pulling himself into a more comfortable sitting position before saying, "You better be pulling my leg!"

Mark was still laughing when he told him about the train tickets, which seemed to put him in a better mood, caught up in Mark's good humor.

He drove well, the way these retired truckers did, watching for wildlife, his head constantly swiveling from side to side. "Eagle," he pointed out. Or, "Mule deer." Sadie would never quite figure out how he kept the van on the road while spotting all the wildlife. Mark wasn't driving, and he didn't find all the interesting things Tom did. Sadie guessed if you logged as many miles as this driver did over the span of 40 years, with uncountable hours spent behind the steering wheel, it all came automatically and you didn't even think about it. Sort of like frying an egg or hanging out laundry for an Amish housewife, repetitive things you never thought about on most days as you did these mundane tasks.

"I told Thelma, some of these cats is gonna hafta go.

I can't take it. I'm allergic to 'em. Hackin' and coughin,' you'd think she'd listen to me. I'm the one has the hairball in my throat, not them cats, she says. Says, I quit smokin' these cigarettes, I quit coughin'. She says it ain't the cats. Sure it's them cats. Hair floatin' all over th' trailer, so it does. Cats on my table, cats in my bathroom, on my recliner, all over the house. Shouldn't a' got married that second time, that's what. She told me she had a few cats, she didn't tell me they'd have little 'uns. Wouldn't a married her, I'da known."

Sadie smiled to herself, wondering how often she had heard this very same story. Who had put in the new pet doors? Or bought the electric water cooler type cat dish that kept their water fresh?

"How many cats do you have?" Sadie asked, same as she always did just because she enjoyed hearing these cat stories so much.

"I dunno. Big gray bruiser named Rex. A dog's name, ya ask me. Rex is big. That cat weights 30 pounds, I bet. We got Lulu, she's a smart one. Won't drink out a' the cat dish. Opens the spigot in the bathroom. Jes' sits there batting at the handle until she gets it open."

One by one, he ticked off the cats' names, their attributes, as proud as any father with his family. When Sadie told him this, he denied it so vehemently she was actually afraid she had offended him. She was relieved when he changed the subject to something more interesting, in his opinion.

Trains are funny things. You sit quietly and don't really know you're moving until you feel a faint shudder and the buildings beside you start moving of their own accord, or so it seems. Sadie had been looking forward to the ride, remembering well the long, quiet, time they had spent prior to their marriage going to stay with his dying mother in North Dakota. There was just something soothing about sitting close to Mark, relaxed, knowing she was doing something for him, something he cared about deeply, a service she did gladly. Enjoying the sights, the sounds, and rhythm of a train, the atmosphere of togetherness where people of all ages, names, backgrounds, sat together in a common bond of traveling, all depending on the power of the wheels beneath them to take them to their destinations. There were always talkative folks, friendly, inquisitive, and those who ignored you, pretending you didn't exist, which was okay with Sadie either way.

Mark was quiet, falling asleep an hour after the train began moving. Sadie traced the soft line of the black hair growing along his jaw line with the tip of her finger, watched the way the thick eyelashes fluttered as she did so, and smiled to herself. So big and so strong, shoeing horses, building houses and barns, wielding a chain saw, swinging an ax, and yet so vulnerable when it came down to it. Victim of a puzzling past, he was now hurtling through the state of Montana, across Idaho, and into an unknown city in Oregon to find a brother he had never known, perhaps to uncover another painful, long-buried incident and face down yet more demons of his complex nature. Well, if it was too difficult, they'd leave. Sadie would not allow it to become a situation that would only make his life harder.

She smoothed his blue shirt collar, flicked off a piece of thread from the sleeve of his new gray coat, then adjusted her own seat to a more comfortable position before closing her eyes. But she was too excited to sleep, so she sat up and looked around her.

A portly gentleman was unwrapping a cupcake. Sadie's mouth watered as she watched him unwrap the entire cake and fold the creased paper carefully before holding it up to the light for closer inspection. It had to be carrot cake, according to its orange color. The tiny white flecks were undoubtedly coconut, the heavy frosting applied so liberally it had to be cream cheese. When he inserted it into his mouth, easily biting off half of it, she had to restrain herself from reaching forward and extracting a tantalizing morsel for herself.

When the complete cupcake disappeared entirely with one more wide-open chomp, and he leaned down to rummage in a small box, his face growing quite florid with his efforts, he produced another one as big as the first. He proceeded to unwrap as precisely as before, licking his fingers carefully before folding the paper perfectly. Sadie swallowed. She was really hungry.

She wondered what a person had to do to acquire some food. She blushed when the portly gentleman caught her eye and smiled. Surely he couldn't read her thoughts? Had she appeared as beggarly as she felt?

The ring of white hair around his red face reminded Sadie of a white bottle brush bent in a V-shape and Super-glued to his bald head. She wondered if his hair was like Mam's, each new white hair having a will of its own, in her words. He was just as round as a bowling pin, his shirt front gleaming with buttons, his little round knees protruding not too far away from his rotund stomach. To her embarrassment, he caught her eye again, chuckling out loud now. Quickly, she turned her head, desperately hoping he hadn't seen her close observation.

"You know, if looks alone could get one of these cupcakes, they'd be flying across the aisle," he chortled, reaching below the seat with a grimace and a grunt, producing a plastic container.

"Will you do me the honor of sharing my dessert? Compliments of Sir Walter Bartlett."

His little blue eyes were diamonds of merriment, topped by a shelf of bristling white eyebrows, small bottle brushes to match the one around his head. His nose was so small and red it almost eluded the observer, his mouth wide, hid by his sagging bulbous cheeks, filled to capacity with his dessert.

"If you want, I'll allow you one!"

"Oh, no! I couldn't. They're yours." Sadie said demurely.

"Of course not. I bring these on the train to share. Last time it was cherry croissants, which, I believe, are the lesser dessert, according to my way of judgment. But you know, never take a treat for granted, and the bakery on Second Street has a vast array. A vast array of yet untried possibilities."

He laughed so happily at the thought, a gurgle of laughter welled up in Sadie's own throat. Leaning across the aisle, he offered the box of cupcakes with a flourish and a sweeping motion that reminded Sadie of an orchestra conductor.

"Please accept my humble gift," he chortled.

Sadie chose one, then thanked him politely. "You shouldn't have offered them," she concluded.

"And why not? It only increases my pleasure of a fabulous dessert to be able to share it with such beauty as yours. Are you Hutterite? Or perhaps Mennonite?" he asked as quickly.

Sadie shook her head. "Neither. We're Amish."

Completely flummoxed, he shook his head in confusion. "Never heard of 'em."

Sadie barely heard his reply as she bit into the sweetness of the richly textured cupcake. She had never tasted better. She closed her eyes in appreciation to find Mr. Walter Bartlett leaning eagerly across the aisle in anticipation of her evaluation of his gift.

"Simply the best carrot cake I've ever tasted," she told him honestly.

Waving a short, puffy finger delightedly, he bent forward at the waist, then sat back, still waving his finger. "Aren't they? Aren't they, though? If I compare them to the pumpkin, however, I do remain a bit indecisive for the reason of the frosting. I believe the maple-flavored icing on the pumpkin cupcakes complements the pumpkin better than the cream cheese does justice to the carrot, pineapple, and coconut. Then there's always the question of the lack of raisins. I have yet to find a single raisin that I feel would elevate the essence of the carrot and pineapple so splendidly."

Suddenly a genuine sadness, almost grief, pulled down his happy features until he appeared unusually morose. "But, oh, the day they pulled the German chocolate! That was a hard day, indeed. I walked home that day, opened my umbrella to the pouring rain, so fitting to my loss, and I thought, Where? Where in all the world will they bake those little Dutch chocolate cakes topped with the brown sugar, coconut, and pecan topping? Since, however, I have come to grips with the lack of my favorite cake, substituting the coconut-covered devil's-food ones. In a way, they are a sad replacement, but it's all right. I'm no longer grieving."

He took a deep breath and sat up straight, squaring his shoulders in a brave and manly fashion, then turned to her with martyred eyes. "So hard, sometimes," he said quietly then.

Sadie nodded her sympathy, which brought a sniff of resignation. Mark stirred beside her, and Sadie turned instinctively, but he resumed breathing deeply, lost in his slumber.

"Husband?" Walter asked politely.

"Yes," Sadie nodded.

"May I ask your destination?"

"Barre, Oregon?"

"So far?"

Sadie nodded. "We're going to find my husband's brother, or siblings, we don't know how many will be there. His family was broken when the children were small, so he's trying to reunite."

Walter nodded happily. "Very good. Very good. Genealogy is such a wonderful thing. With computers now, you just Google everything. So easy." He nodded companionably.

Sadie could have told him about her lack of computer knowledge, but decided not to, the Amish and their ways being such a complete mystery. Besides, he had plenty of hardship in life with the baker pulling the German chocolate cakes from the shelves, therefore exposing poor Walter to such deprivation. Dear little round man. Sadie wanted to go home and find a good recipe and bake him two dozen cupcakes and present them to him warm from the oven.

God made such a wonderful variety of people, all so different and all so special. God must love people like Walter very much, their friendliness, their guilelessness. Likely that's what one of the disciples looked like when Jesus saw him beneath the olive tree, "and there was no guile in him." There was no deceit. No cunning. No sly behavior. That was the sort of person Jesus needed to follow him. The honest, the loving, the ones you could just hug and hug, like Dorothy. She was so full of fussing, spitting, complaining, but she was as guileless as this man. This rotund little Walter whose worst vice in life was the sweet desserts on a baker's shelf, who handed out compliments, wished everyone well minutes after he met them, and seemed unaware of life's darker side. He was much too busy being Walter Bartlett. Sir Walter Bartlett.

Sadie was sorry to see him weave his way down the aisle, clutching his plastic box of cupcakes, waving his fat little hand in her direction. She'd never see him again. But that was okay. He had touched her life with one wonderful carrot cupcake, a fat little fairy that touched her with his magical wand, filling her train ride with happiness.

Leaning over, she kissed Mark's cheek, waking him in the process.

"You smell like...?" he said softly. "What were you eating?"

Sadie giggled and kissed her husband. She loved him when he woke up with that sleepy "little boy" crease on his forehead.

"Oh, a fairy gave me a carrot cupcake with cream cheese icing."

They reached their destination with surprising swiftness, the hours on the train clicking by as quickly as the clicking of the rails. When they emerged with the flow of passengers, standing inside the station, awed at the city lights, the height of the skyscrapers, the smallness of two people alone in a foreign (or so it seemed) place, Sadie clutched Mark's hand as he called a taxi, then relaxed when the taxi arrived only a moment later.

Mark had a conversation with the driver, and they were whisked through rain-slick, light-filled streets, a kaleidoscope of brilliance and energy, honking horns, strains of music, shouting pedestrians, and people just moving, moving, moving. Into a hotel lobby, their steps muted on deep, plush carpeting. A few words to the man at the desk, while Sadie looked around at the gigantic green plants growing up toward the windowed ceiling. Was it just a glass ceiling?

The lights were low and people spoke softly. The women wore high heels, and she felt like the country mouse in the city, which she knew she was, though she sort of enjoyed the privilege, smiling back at inquisitive faces, holding Mark's hand, glad she was the wife of this tall, dark man who received his share of appreciative glances.

Sadie felt the hotel room was too costly. Was it really right to spend so much money on one night's sleep? This seriously bothered her conscience until Mark put it to rest, saying they could sleep in a motel for half the price, but, for safety's sake, he was not about to go looking for the seedy section of town with the cheap motels.

"We are Amish and look just different enough to attract attention, so I feel safer right here where folks don't need my wallet."

After that, Sadie relaxed and enjoyed her stay at the beautiful opulent hotel. The fixtures in the bathroom were gold, so she touched them tentatively, carefully, and wiped them clean after her shower just because she felt guilty leaving them water-stained. They weren't real gold, were they? She asked Mark, and he laughed for a long time, saying no, they didn't live in King Pharaoh's time. Sadie felt like a country mouse all over again and told him so. He laughed again and said that was a part of his attraction to her: her childish honesty, the way she spoke her mind.

"Even when I tell you cabinetmakers are good at their trade?" she asked eyeing him sharply.

A dark cloud passed over his face, covering his features, then left again when he took a deep breath. "Just forget it, Sadie," he said gruffly.

So she did and went to the window, pulling the braided, gold cord to draw the heavy brown drapes aside. She stood, her hands on the wide windowsill, and leaned her forehead on the cold glass, peering down on the streets below, all glossy and golden with light. How did men build a skyscraper? Who ever had enough audacity to attempt it, even? It was amazing. But she guessed as long as there were human beings on the earth, God would impart the wisdom to enable civilization to do whatever was good and necessary.

"Look at the Egyptians," she muttered softly without realizing she had said anything at all.

"What?" Mark asked from his pillows on the bed.

"Oh, I was just thinking about building skyscrapers. They always did. The Egyptians built those pyramids. A bunch of other things. How could they without equipment? It all seems so brave and...well, who thinks this stuff will even work? Who knows if the concrete and rods and bolts and stuff will hold? It's the same way with bridges. How can they go ahead and do this awesome amount of work and know it will work?"

Mark smiled. "It's called courage and faith. It's what I need in great quantities for tomorrow. Think about it, Sadie. Our tomorrow is not so different. We planned this, we're going through with it. We're hoping what we're doing will work. No going back now. With a bit of faith and well...let's not be afraid. It'll be a spiritual bridge or skyscraper or whatever we want it to be. Imagine, Sadie the possibilities are so...promising. And yet...I'm so terribly afraid. Come to bed. You're my number one support in this bridge-building project."

Chapter 12

IN THE MORNING, MARK WAS QUIET, HIS FACE TAUT with apprehension. He did not want a hearty breakfast so they had bagels and coffee brought to their room. Sadie noticed Mark's untouched bagel and the tremor in his hand when he reached for his coffee mug.

She held her peace, however, knowing he did not like any display of weakness, especially for her to notice and bring it to his attention. This she had learned the hard way, having her feelings hurt repetitively by blurting out a few unmasked words. The silence was broken only by the soft sound of lifted coffee mugs, swallowing, or a clearing of the throat, a napkin dabbed.

Finally Sadie asked, "You have the address?"

Mark nodded.

"So all we need is a taxi, right?"

"Right. Ready?"

There was no smile, no affirmation of his love, only a rapid thrust of his arms into his coat sleeves, a shrugging of his shoulders, and a quick pull on the gold door handle, stepping back, his eyebrows raised with impatience as she shrugged into her own wool coat.

The taxi driver was skilled, talkative, and knew the streets well. Before they had a chance to wonder how far it was, the taxi pulled to a fluid halt, the driver assuring them this was the proper address.

They peered out the right window, taking in the old brownstone, the Georgian façade, the enormous front door, the huge windows flanked by heavy wooden shutters. The stone on the exterior was aged to perfection, three stories in perfect symmetry, an old, sturdily built home kept well with loving care, standing the test of time.

The boxwoods surrounding the low windows were trimmed to precision, the inlaid stone walkway and steps leading to the front door a tribute to skilled masons.

A copper-plated sign by the post beside the stone walkway read "Jackson Peight, MD."

"He's…he's a doctor?" Sadie whispered.

Mark said nothing. Then, "Let's just leave."

Sadie shook her head. "Does he know you're coming?"

"Of course."

"Then we're going."

Sadie opened the door, stepped out of the cab, and breathed deeply. The smell of cold winter air mixed with city odors of traffic and asphalt, that indistinguishable no-name aroma that cloaked all cities. It was not offensive; it was a smell of energetic people and vehicles and food and grass and trees.

Mark followed and the taxi moved off, leaving them standing on the sidewalk looking up at the house as if it might swallow them alive. Sadie shivered, shaking off the foreboding that threatened to envelop her with its tentacles.

Mark's face was ashen. "I can't do this Sadie. Please. I'm nothing. He's an English man. A doctor. He's so much more than me. He'll laugh in my face."

Sadie turned, her hands going to his coat front, giving him a small tug the way she would to a child as a way of slight rebuke.

"Stop it. Those feelings are of the devil, in Mam's words. Don't listen to them. Come."

It was Sadie who led the way, who pressed her finger decisively to the ornate doorbell, who rocked back on her heels, lifted her chin, and smiled a much wider, braver smile than she felt.

A few seconds and the door opened, swung wide. A replica of Mark stood aside. An English replica, his black hair cut short, but the same eyes, the perfect mouth, a plaid button-down shirt tucked into relaxed jeans.

"Come in. You must be Mark."

Mark nodded, his eyes flat, expressionless. He offered his hand and received a firm grip of welcome.

"Jackson."

"Mark." Then, "Do you remember anything about me?"

"Oh, yes."

Mark introduced Sadie. Their coats and luggage were quickly whisked away by an older person Sadie could only guess was the housekeeper. They were led to a room with a fireplace crackling on the far side, facing beige and white chairs and sofas. Tables and various antique dressers holding tastefully displayed vintage items sat atop expensive rugs strewn across the worn oak flooring. Candles flickered on the mantle, lamps gave off a yellow pool of light, illuminating the room in small circles, as if they were a helpmeet to the stripes of sunlight stealing through the heavy wooden slats of the venetian blinds.

It was a lovely room. The touch of old decor mixed with new required an expert's eye. Jackson was a year younger than Mark, or was it two? How had he acquired so much at this young age?

Sadie smiled at appropriate times, answered questions, but was so involved in her assessment of the room, she feared she'd be impolite.

Jackson was effusive in his welcome, and Sadie could tell Mark was responding, the hooded, evasive light in his eye replaced by a spark of interest, a small smile that wouldn't be reined in too much longer.

They were joined by a heavy-set woman who floated into the room on waves of cologne, her dress swirling about her buxom figure in swirls of red. Her hair was dark, cut to just below her chin, her face wide with curiosity, taking an interest in everything surrounding her.

"Hi! I'm Jane. Just plain Jane," she laughed.

Introductions followed, Jackson pulling her large form against him closely. He introduced her as his wife of exactly six months and a few days, Jane dipping and beaming, exclaiming at the likeness of the two brothers.

They were all seated and served coffee and tea before Jackson settled in for a serious talk.

"Yes, Mark, I do remember. Not everything, likely, the way you do, but I remember the bad times probably just as distinctly as you. The thing, the one single thing, that's hardest for me is—how could she? How could our mother leave us hungry, uncared for, and simply drive away with that man? You know, it's funny, but I don't remember him at all. Can't imagine his face, his features. That act of a mother abandoning her children is one of the biggest hurdles of my life."

Mark nodded. "You feel as if there was something you did wrong. Like, perhaps if we had been better children, or we had done more, or looked better, she wouldn't have done it. Like *we* failed *her*."

Jackson watched Mark's face, incredulous. Finally he shook his head. "I find it unbelievable to hear you say that. I thought I was the only one who wrestled with that demon of my past."

Jane clucked her tongue, then laid her head reassuringly on her husband's shoulder and was instantly gathered into the safety of his arm.

Jackson continued. "It was tough. Still is. I allow, though, it's as tough as we let our past control us. The reason I studied medicine...it was a sort of block. The more I buried myself in my studies, the better I was. I was ravenous to learn, to move up the ladder, to excel, to prove myself worthy. I was far ahead in my classes, always. But it really was my saving grace. To stay busy, challenged, immerse myself—it just worked well. My foster parents had the money to put me through college, so I was very fortunate, I realize that. My dad is a surgeon. My mom is the greatest person on the face of the earth. I'm serious. I don't know why the Lord smiled on me the way he did the day I was put in the foster system, but he did. They are my parents, my stronghold. It's amazing to this day."

Jane nodded, her eyes wide with emotion.

Sadie shrank inwardly when Mark cleared his throat and said gruffly, "Yeah, well."

There was a space of silence where Sadie watched nervously, knowing Mark was fighting that internal battle of feeling worthless. He drank coffee, ran a hand across the knee of his trousers, fought to rise up against the tide of black nothingness his mother had pitched him into the day she left.

Then Mark lifted his ravaged eyes. "Yeah, well, you're lucky."

"I know that," Jackson responded sincerely.

Then Mark launched into his own tale of the foster care system. The abuse, the existence of a loveless world, the hunger for stability, the batting around from home to home, unwanted, used, the drugs, the alcohol, and finally, his grandfather, the reason he became a member of the Old Order Amish church.

Jane got up and extracted a box of Kleenex from a heavy holder, dabbed her eyes daintily, clucked, and gasped, shaking her pretty head from side to side as Mark related his story.

"Wow," Jackson breathed, finally. "What kept you sane?"

"I know what it's like to walk on the edge, let me tell you," Mark said, with a harsh laugh.

"Have you gone for counseling?"

"Oh, yes. A lot of good, positive feelings about myself and my past have come to light through counseling. It's a good thing. God imparts wisdom to those people, I don't doubt. I probably would not have made it through my early twenties if it wouldn't have been for counseling."

Sadie nodded.

"And Sadie."

Sadie turned to Mark, a glad light in her eyes, met his own, ignited, but as was the Amish custom, they remained seated apart, awkward and ill at ease with any public display of affection.

"I'll have to tell you how we met," Sadie offered. She began a colorful account of the wintery day with Nevaeh lying in the snow, desperately flagging down the cattle truck that had been moving too fast to begin with. Mark laughingly explaining when you drive a rural Montana roadway, you do not expect to meet a half-dead horse and a very pretty girl in the middle of a snowstorm.

Jackson and Jane were delighted, and the conversation took a lighter turn for awhile, until Mark related the demise of their mother, the dark valley of guilt that finally brought her to her knees, the peace she had before meeting her Savior.

Jackson kept shaking his head, repeating, "Unbelievable. Absolutely." The brothers struggled to restrain their emotions, then got up and left the room together, Jackson turning to Jane, saying thickly, "We'll be back. Why don't you show Sadie the rest of the house?"

Jane was just the most lovely personality, Sadie soon decided. She was bubbly without being overbearing, humble in showing Sadie her home, and genuinely interested in Sadie's upbringing, her family, and the Amish culture.

They ended up in the surprisingly small kitchen, lined with tall dark cupboards and a bar with comfortable bar stools. Sadie perched while Jane served her another cup of ginger tea and made grilled roast beef and goat cheese sandwiches with spicy mustard and olives.

"I love these sandwiches," she announced happily.

"I probably should have waited till dinner, but, oh, well. You knew Timothy was coming, didn't you? We're all going out to dinner later today."

When the doorbell rang late that afternoon, the talking still had not ceased. Like the floodgates of a dam built into a levee, the river of words burst through and continued to flow, surrounding the two brothers with a sense of stability, closure, and certainly memories, both unpleasant and downright absurd, coming to light. Each was examined with a blood brother's viewpoint and discarded or put away, leaving in its wake a new kind of peace, threaded with uncertainty, perhaps, but a peace, nevertheless.

As the afternoon wore on, shoes came off, feet were elevated on stools, pillows put behind backs, accompanied by a sense of brotherhood swirling about both of them, infusing their laughter, discovering how much alike they really were. They both loved fresh-squeezed lemonade without too much sugar, slept on their stomachs, had huge appetites, and had a cowlick on the left side of their foreheads.

Finally Jackson looked at the clock. "He said he'd be … be here around 4:00."

"How much do you know about him?" Mark asked.

"Not much. He's the only one who responded. You know Beaulah was killed in a car accident, in November of '08?"

"Really?"

"Yes. She was hit by a fuel truck when she pulled out of a street in town. She lived in Ohio somewhere. She was 24 years old. Not married. I know very little about any of the others. I don't know, maybe it's just as well."

"I agree. So, you never feel as if you're being sucked into a giant whirlpool?" Mark asked suddenly with urgency, as if he needed to clear this with Jackson before Timothy arrived.

Jackson looked up sharply. "Why would I?"

"I mean, don't you have days when you feel everyone is against you, and it's just a matter of time until you can't take another day of battling these feelings of inadequacy? Of not being enough?"

For a long while, Jackson said nothing, leaning forward, his elbows on his knees, staring at the floor between his feet. Then, "I guess I do."

"Jackson!" Jane exclaimed.

"No, nothing serious, my darling," Jackson said, sitting up and rubbing her soft shoulder with affection.

"It's just that, yes, I know what you're talking about. When that empty feeling does threaten, which is less and less, now, I put on my shoes and go running. I run for as many as seven or eight miles. It's wonderful therapy."

Mark nodded in perfect agreement. "I ran a lot."

There was a distinct bell-like tone, and they all looked at each other.

"Timothy."

Jackson nodded, went to the door.

Involuntarily, Jane touched up her hair, sat straight, while Sadie tucked a few stray hairs behind her white covering. What would Timothy say?

Jackson returned, followed by a strapping youth, his long, unkempt, dirty-blond hair hanging over his eyes, his ears, and well down into the hood of his gray sweatshirt. Loose jeans hung sloppily below the waistline of his boxers, the hem torn and scuffed, the threads gray from contact with the ground.

His eyes weren't visible at first glance, until he picked up a hand and pushed his hair back, then everyone could see that they were as dark brown as his two brothers'. He had the same perfect mouth, but his teeth were brown and crooked, decay spreading across the neglected grayish-white objects in his mouth.

His cheeks were packed with deep scars where acne had taken its toll, the worst of it gone now that the teen years were behind him. He smiled an unsteady smile, an unsure separating of his lips that had nothing to do with his eyes.

"Hey."

He shook hands limply, a mere sliding of a sweated palm against his two brothers', a nodding in Jane's and Sadie's direction, his eyes glancing nervously at his feet, a small cough, a sniffling sound before tossing his hair to the side again.

"How y' doin?" he muttered in the general direction of the women.

"Good. Good. It's nice to meet you!" Jane said effusively.

Sadie murmured something, she wasn't sure what, her throat swelling with the same emotion she felt that day when Nevaeh stumbled out of the woods, down the embankment, and crumpled her pitiful body onto the road, surrounded by that cold unrelenting snow.

Here was a youth surround by a cold, unforgiving, joyless existence. Sadie sensed in him the same hopelessness, the same victim of circumstances that had shaped his life so much beyond his control. She bit down on her lower lip, averted her eyes as goose bumps raced up her arms and across her back.

"Sit down, Timothy," Jackson offered.

"It's Tim."

The words were spoken defensively, that self-conscious sniff following the words, as if the sniff sent the words out and supported them.

"Okay, Tim. So … you came. That's good."

"Yeah, well. I ain't staying."

"But you will have dinner with us?"

"Yeah."

The first awkward silence of the day followed.

"So, you … want to tell us about yourself?"

"No."

Mark said that was all right, he'd go first, and proceeded to tell Tim his life's story. He got as far as the Amish uncle, when Tim lifted his head, the anger creating dark, brown fury, turning his eyes into blazing outlets of raw anger.

"I hate him."

Mark's eyes opened wide. "You know who I'm talking about?"

"Yeah."

"Were you raised Amish?"

"Yeah."

"Surely not by him."

"No, but I know what he did to you."

"How?"

"Word gets around."

"Who raised you?"

"Aunt Hannah. The old maid. Till I turned 16. Then I left. Went to New York City. Big mistake. Came back. Hannah was dead. Heart attack. I stayed in the area among the Amish but never really went back. Guess I'm half-Amish. Remember all of it. It's good, in a way."

He shrugged his shoulders, picked at the hole in his jeans, pulled at a thread, then rolled it between his thumb and forefinger, unsure of what to do with it before straightening his back to put it in his pocket, blinking with a terrible embarrassment. As he lowered his head, the curtain of long hair obliterated him into the safety of his shell.

Sadie had to restrain herself from going to him, peering under that hair and telling him he was just fine exactly the way he was.

"So, what do you do?" Mark asked.

"I'm a roofer."

With that he actually straightened up, flipped his hair back, and looked directly at Mark, a tiny spark of pride passing quickly through his brown eyes.

"In Illinois?"

Tim nodded. "I'm a good one. Boss said."

Again he lowered his face, picked at a scab on his arm.

"I'm sure you are, you've got some shoulders on you for a...What are you? Twenty? Twenty-one?" Jackson asked.

"Twenty-two, I guess. You know they never found my birth certificate. Had a...mess when I applied for my driver's license."

In the course of the evening, they found out Timothy had a steady job, but that was the only stability in his life. He lived from one paycheck to the next and ran with a questionable group of friends who led him from one bad habit to another. But they were the only real form of love and friendship he knew.

Sadie listened, watched, and observed his total lack of support, his free-floating existence, before sitting beside him on the sofa, reaching out a hand, placing it tentatively on his gray sweatshirt.

"Tim, did you ever consider returning to your roots? You know when your mother passed away, you were the only one of her children she really worried about. She mentioned you so many times, asking us to find you. It was her dying wish. I think of all the deep regrets she carried with her, you were the worst. In her own way, she loved you the most."

Tim shrugged, sniffed. "Yeah. Well, Hannah loved me. Sort of. She died. My mother's dead. So that's as far as that goes. Poof!"

He illustrated with a rapid opening of his fingers, a short, derisive laugh, followed by a backward movement of his shoulders, and then he slumped against the back of the sofa, his long legs splayed in front of him, tapping his feet in time to remembered music.

Well, he was up and on his feet, Sadie thought. Sick and thin and maybe dying, yes, but on his feet! He had, in his own way, admitted that his real love was Aunt Hannah, his substitute mother, and not in the sort of life he led.

"Would you allow Mark and me to try?" Sadie asked, turning to look at Mark as she spoke.

Mark's mouth literally fell open. He stared at Sadie in a way she knew was without total comprehension.

"You're not my mom."

"I'm your sister-in-law."

There. She had reached out and stroked Nevaeh under the unkempt mane, where her poor neck was so thin and scrawny, the hairs so matted and pitiful. Now she had reached out to Tim, offering her love.

Was it too much? Too soon? Would she drive him away?

The foot kept tapping. The hands were jammed deep into the pocket of his sweatshirt. His shoulders hunched. He sniffed, then coughed. He scratched his stomach, smoothed the sweatshirt, then looked at Sadie. Really looked at her.

Then he smiled, a small one, but a smile, no matter what he would choose to call it. Sadie could feel the leaning of Nevaeh, a sort of turning her neck in her direction, as if to let her know she appreciated the gesture of affection.

"I guess you are."

His voice was small, stripped of its coolness, the mask of bravado he wore every day, leaving his words as vulnerable as a newborn baby, completely dependent on someone else's care. Babies did best on their mother's breast, but if that wasn't possible, they could thrive easily on a substitute of another human being feeding them a good formula.

"Mark is your real brother. You were raised Amish. We are your family. Your real family," Sadie went on.

Jackson and Jane exchanged a knowing look, a smart doctor who could see the miracle unfolding before his eyes. He also knew Sadie had gone far enough; this would take time.

As if on cue, Sadie backed off. "Well, Tim, you know where we live. If you decide to change your life, you know where we are."

Tim nodded, a strange melancholy landing on his features, clarifying the desperate sadness in his brown eyes.

"Yeah, well I'm...guess you'd say caught in a spider web of my own making. I'll go back home. I'll let you know. Give you my cell phone number."

He sniffed again, self-consciously, and Sadie lifted triumphant eyes to Mark.

Chapter 13

When they left the brownstone on River Drive, Sadie could tell Mark had left a sizable chunk of his worst childhood baggage behind, hopefully buried beneath the city streets, never to be picked up again. His step was light, he was ravenously hungry, he teased Sadie with a new lighthearted attitude she had never seen before. They ate sandwiches at the train station, they ate on the train, and they ate when the train arrived at the station in Montana. As Sadie watched her husband, she could only guess at the price he had paid to make that visit into the unknown, reminding herself yet again that he didn't have that strong system of support from a normal home life the way she did.

When their life resumed its usual rhythm, Sadie thanked God they had gone, returned, and met Timothy and Jackson. Doing so had instilled a sense of worth in Mark. Was it because Mark had filled Timothy's bottle with Jell-o water? Had helped Jackson eat his oatmeal? Had found a new sense of having done something right? In that time of darkness and pain, had he somehow found that in all situations some good can come of it? Surely he had.

This spring in his step, this light in his eye was a miracle. Sadie had been afraid that Jackson being a doctor would intimidate Mark, lowering his fragile self-esteem, but it had worked the opposite way. Mark was so proud of Jackson and so concerned about Timothy, a new sense of purpose surrounded him.

The winter came early, its harshness arriving along with it. The cold was mind-numbing, the thermometer hovering below zero every night in spite of the sun's feeble rays during the day. Snow enveloped everything. It clung to pines and firs, placing a huge burden on the sturdy limbs with its weight. It was not unusual to be awakened during the night by the sound of a gunshot, jolting Sadie out of a deep sleep, before realizing it was only the sound of branches snapping beneath the snow's weight. Mark said ice and snow were nature's pruner, something Sadie had never thought about. She guessed they were.

Dorothy was not doing well at work, which caused Sadie a few moments of anxiety. Her hip was bothering her quite a bit, and her usual quick movements turned into painful hobbles, her mouth a tight line of determination. Erma Keim accosted her at every turn, telling Dorothy to go to the chiropractor, which, of course, was like igniting dry tinders.

"That quack ain't touchin' this hip. Let him crack backs and collect his 30 dollars. He ain't gittin' a red cent off'n me."

And that was that. Erma told Sadie if that thick-headed old lady wanted to be that way, then she'd just have to live in her pain. She guaranteed that Dorothy's hip and pelvis were out of line, and if Doctor Tresore was allowed to take an X-ray and adjust her a few times, she'd be so much better. Sadie nodded agreement, but added that maybe Dorothy's hip joint was actually deteriorating and she needed a replacement, which gave Erma so much hope of running the ranch kitchen all by herself that she immediately stopped harassing Dorothy about the chiropractor, leaving an aura of peace in the ranch kitchen.

Richard Caldwell was getting ready to host the annual Christmas banquet, as usual, spending more time in the kitchen, Barbara joining him as they pored over recipe books. He watched Dorothy limping between the refrigerator and the pantry before putting an elbow to his wife's side. When she looked up at him, he shoved his jaw in Dorothy's direction, shaking his head in concern.

"Your hip bothering you, Dorothy?" he boomed.

The sound of his voice alarmed Dorothy to the extent that she dropped a five-pound block of Colby Jack cheese on the linoleum, then snorted impatiently.

"Now look what you made me do, Richard Caldwell! No, my hip ain't bothering me at all."

Erma pursed her lips and raised her eyebrows, a hand going to her unruly red hair, leaving a trail of flour and bits of pie crust in its wake as she returned to crimping her apples pies. Sadie stirred brown sugar into the baby carrots and said nothing.

Later that evening when she was getting her coat and scarf from the hook on the wall, Dorothy approached her after Erma had gone to talk to Barbara about a Jell-o dessert. Dorothy's eyes were mirrors of humility, tears brimming on her lower lashes.

"Sadie, if'n I tell you what's bothering me, you ain't gonna tell anyone, right? Least-ways not Erma."

"Of course not, Dorothy. I'm just afraid you're going to have to go to the hospital and have surgery."

"No, no, no. It's not my hip."

Dorothy raised herself on her tiptoes and held a short hand to her mouth. Sadie bent her head slightly to receive the long-awaited secret.

"It's corns. I got them corns all over my toes. I bin using them little adhesive tapes, you know. Those Dr. Scholl's. They don't help a bit. I got 'em so bad, I can hardly walk. The Dollar General is letting me down so bad. You know, if them shoes were worth what I say they are, I wouldn't get corns, would I?"

"Oh, my, Dorothy. Corns are extremely painful. I know just what to do. You can have them removed at the doctor's office, or you can use tea tree oil. Just dab it on with a Q-tip for a few weeks."

Dorothy nodded, her eyes downcast.

"It's heartbreaking. The Dollar General is letting me down so bad. I can't buy any more shoes there. In fact, I'm not sure them Ritz crackers is fit to make my choco-late-coated crackers anymore."

Her withdrawal from Dollar General was obviously quite painful, so Sadie assured her it was okay to change stores. Suddenly she had a great idea, assessing Doro-thy's round stature and small feet. Those Crocs everyone wore! The perfect footwear for Dorothy. Sturdy, wide, slip-proof.

"Dorothy! I have the perfect idea for you. Crocs! I'll go to town with you, and we'll fit you into a completely trouble-free pair of shoes. Your corns won't be touching anything and will heal in no time at all."

It was love at first sight. Dorothy slid her poor, corn-addled feet into a pair of sturdy Crocs, stood up, and began walking down the aisle of the local shoe store, her head bent, concentrating on the placement of each foot, so much like a small child. Slowly a beatific grin spread across her face as she stopped, turned, and walked back to Sadie.

"It's like walkin' on air. An' I don't have to bend down and tie 'em. Oh, it's a miracle, Sadie. The Lord heard my prayers and took mercy on me and…" She lowered her voice and hissed behind a palm, "…my corns!"

Sadie nodded happily. There were no brown or black ones for Dorothy. She was undecided between bright pink or lime green, then settled for a furious shade of purple.

"Next time I'll get the lime green."

When she opened her wallet to hand over a crisp 20 and a 10, she pursed her lips, but told Sadie quietly that wasn't so dear if you counted the comfort. And when they drove steadily past the Dollar General without stopping, Dorothy shook her head with great sadness and wisdom.

"See, that's what the world's coming to. You pay for a cheap product, that's what you get. And you know what else I thought about? They sell them Dr. Scholl's corn adhesives *right beside* them shoes. They know whoever buys them shoes will return for corn thingys."

She arrived at the ranch the following morning, no limp in sight, her purple Crocs flashing with each step. Erma asked what happened to her limp. Dorothy said she went to the chiropractor, winking broadly at Sadie behind Erma's back. Dorothy's gait was new and refreshing, rocking slightly from side to side, the shape of her Crocs making her appear so much more like a lovable little duck.

✿ ✪ ✿

There was no phone call, no warning, not even a letter. Just the sound of an aging motor driving an old Jeep up the driveway, making its way steadily through the deep snow. And then, nothing. The rusting Jeep just sat at the end of the walkway. No doors opened, no lights blinked or horn blared.

Mark went to the washhouse, slipped into his boots, and shrugged his coat on quickly before making his way down the walks. Sadie watched behind the half-drawn curtains as he bent his tall form to peer through the window. The interior light was too dim for Sadie to see who the person was, so when the washhouse door slammed shut and she heard Mark speaking to someone, she immediately put down the book she was reading and watched the door to the kitchen. It was Timothy.

"Here's Tim!" Mark announced.

Tim stood just inside the door beside the refrigerator, a timid smile playing across his features. Sadie closed the space between them, hoping he would extend a hand, but there was no move to do anything at all. Definitely no hug. Not a handshake.

"Hey."

That was all. That noncommittal "Hey."

"Hello, Tim."

She bit off the last part of his name just in time and sighed with relief, watching his face, the way he sagged at the hips, a certain lowering of himself as if to convey his feelings of inadequacy. Well, here he was. All six feet of complexity. The challenge was staggering.

Too cheerily, Mark asked, "So? What's up? You here for a visit? Are you here to stay? Did you drive that Jeep the whole way?"

Tim actually smiled, revealing all the crowded decaying teeth, then quickly put up a hand, painfully aware of his teeth.

He said, "I'm just here. Work's slow. Thought I'd come check out where you guys live."

Sadie nodded, smiled. "*Kannsht doo Amish schwetsa?*" (Can you speak Dutch?)

Tim smiled only with his eyes, his hand going up to cover his mouth. "*Ya, ich kann.*" (Yes I can.)

"*Alles?*" (Everything?)

Again, a smile with his eyes, a nod.

So the conversation switched easily to the Dutch language. Sadie put on the coffeepot, then brought out the square Tupperware container of molasses cookies.

"Did you have supper?" she asked.

He shook his head, swallowed as he eyed the molasses cookies. He was obviously very hungry.

Quickly Sadie moved from the stove to the refrigerator and back again, heating the leftover chili from their evening meal. She placed a few squares of cornbread on the stoneware plate, put aluminum foil over it, and turned the oven on. She brought out some saltines, applesauce, and slices of dill pickles, arranging them on the table with a glass of cold water. Conversation lagged as he lowered his head and ate ravenously, refilling his bowl, crumbling more saltines, spreading the cornbread liberally with soft butter.

"Didn't have time to stop to get something to eat," he murmured.

Sadie knew he had more than likely been penniless, unable to pay for even a single meal. She said nothing, just shook her head with understanding. All they really got out of him that first evening was that he'd be there for awhile, check out the land, see if he liked the people.

"You mean, the Amish or the English?" Mark asked.

The question caught him by surprise, so he gave no real answer. After eating almost everything on the table, he could not stay awake after driving so many hours. Mark showed him to the guest room, the upstairs bathroom that was almost finished except for the trim work, and helped him adjust the wick on the kerosene lamp, providing a lighter for him.

"Don't need a lighter. I have one."

"If you smoke, Tim, we expect you to quit if you want to stay with us, okay?"

Mark said it quietly but firmly. Tim nodded but said nothing.

Sadie was cleaning up the few dishes when Mark came back down, a light in his eyes.

"Well, Sadie, my love, he's here! Are you sure you're going to be okay with this?"

Sadie stopped rinsing the chili bowl and said quietly, "I am, Mark. I may not always be, but, yes, I'm willing to give it a try."

"We may be in for the roughest ride of our life."

"You think so?"

"I know so. This young man is ... well, this will take a lot of effort, a lot of wisdom, and whatever else we can scratch together to help him straighten out his life."

Sadie nodded soberly.

Since they both had to leave for work the following morning, Sadie left a note and hoped they could trust him with Wolf and the horses.

When Jim's pickup bounced up the drive in the evening, the Jeep was gone, and Sadie raced into the house, becoming breathless in the process, looking for Tim, calling his name, but he was nowhere to be found.

They were deeply disappointed, eating their evening

meal in near silence, wondering why he had stayed, only to leave again. There was not a trace, no clothes, no duffel bag, the bed made neatly, the quilt tucked beneath the pillows as if Sadie had made the bed herself.

Mark sighed, then told Sadie what he had said about his smoking. "Do you suppose that was the reason? Like I just said too much too soon. I didn't want to appear like some holier-than-thou, but still…I don't want him here with any of his old habits."

Sadie nodded. "It's tough. And we're so young. We certainly don't have any experience raising teenagers. We're barely out of that stage ourselves."

"I am!"

"Well, yes, you're ancient. Going on 30, which is alarming."

That was as close to lighthearted banter as they could manage, wondering all evening where Tim had gone and why. They discussed his teeth, and Mark said there was no doubt in his mind that poor boy did not have the proper nutrition he so badly needed as a small child.

"I can't imagine how he ever became as tall and well built as he is," he concluded.

"Aunt Hannah."

Mark nodded.

That night they both lay sleepless and restless, wondering what had happened. The next morning Sadie stayed home from the ranch to make candy and cookies for Christmas, it being only a few weeks away.

Mark loved chocolate-coated "anything," which had become a private joke between them. She had acquired plenty of coating chocolate, and with a song of Christmas in her heart, set about melting it in a large stainless steel bowl on top of a pot of boiling water, noting carefully

Mam's handwritten warning on the directions: *Don't leave on burner after water has been boiling for a few minutes. Overheated chocolate will become clumpy.*

"A few minutes"? Typical Mam. Not two minutes or five minutes. Who knew what "a few" meant?

Should she wait until Mam arrived? She had promised to spend the forenoon with Sadie, bringing Anna, the only sister who had off work. She sighed her disappointment when she saw the horse and buggy pull into the driveway and only Anna hopped off, pulling the reins through the silver ring and knotting them expertly.

Sadie ran to the door, yelling to her sister. "Need help, Anna?"

"No, I'm fine."

Sadie shivered, closed the door, heated the coffee, and waited eagerly for Anna to arrive at the house. When the washhouse door banged closed, she greeted her eagerly, inquiring about Mam.

"She never comes over here when she says she will," Sadie moaned.

"She said to tell you she's sorry, but Fred Ketty's having a quilting for the teacher's quilt, and it has to be done by Christmas. She said Abe Marian started the whole project back in October, but with those five little ones, she can't accomplish much in a week. Don't know why she took it on. Why doesn't she let the older women tackle it?"

Sadie shook her head, a wry grin spreading across her features. "That's Abe Marian."

That was the way of it, the Amish community woven together with its intricate ways, personalities, individualities carefully held together by the Master's hand. Each one was known by the others, accepted, loved, sometimes talked about or clucked over, but forgiven in spite of small blunders and, often, large ones.

Anna was looking so pale, her skin was translucent, narrow blue veins threading their way up past the delicate skin around her beautiful eyes, the dark shadows beneath them a grayish-white. When she turned to go into the kitchen after hanging up her coat, her waist was alarmingly narrow, her dress folds hanging limply over her nonexistent hips. She folded her angular form into a kitchen chair, a mere whisper of her former self.

"Anna."

"What?"

Her dark eyes looked to Sadie, bearing defiance, guilt, fear, and what else? Desperation? Acknowledgment of starving herself?

"You ... you're not looking well."

A shrugging of the shoulders. A waving of the hand. A dismissal.

"Are you eating okay? Throwing up?"

No use hiding anything. Sadie had nothing to lose this morning, this ghost of Anna's former self seated at her kitchen table.

"Oh, be quiet, Sadie. I'm here for two seconds and you're already starting in on me."

"Somebody has to. Mam and Dat won't say a word about anything. Neither will Leah and Rebekah. Everyone at home just lets you go right ahead killing yourself."

Sadie's words were pointed, harsh, spoken loudly, the words coming slowly and thickly like a predator stalking prey already caught in a steel-jawed trap.

"Shut up!" Anna screamed suddenly, lunging at Sadie, pummeling her with weak, white fists, propelled only by her anxious fury. It took Sadie completely by surprise.

The blows rained on her shoulders, her arms, her back, Anna's face a twisted caricature of her normal features.

"Anna! Please don't."

She closed her eyes, cringed, turned her back. Somewhere she heard a door opening, as if in the distance. The blows stopped.

"Hey, hey, what's goin' on here?"

Timothy! He had an arm around Anna's waist, pinning the stick-thin arms to her wasted body as she tried weakly to escape.

"Sadie, help me! Let me go! Get away from me!" Even her cries were weak and pitiful, the meowing sounds of a starved kitten begging for its mother.

Sadie adjusted her apron, smoothed back her hair, and told Timothy to release her. Anna slumped onto a chair, bent over, and sobbed, her head in her trembling white hands. Timothy stood, his hands in his pockets, his shoulders squared, and looked at Anna with an expression as raw and vulnerable as Sadie had ever seen. It was pity, pure and simple. He understood. He met Sadie's eyes, raised his eyebrows in question. She shook her head, raised her own. Suddenly Timothy was on his knees, holding Anna's fluttering, blue-veined hands in his own, murmuring, stilling them.

"It can't be that bad. Nothing could happen that makes you want to beat up … "

He lifted questioning eyes to Sadie. "Your sister?"

Sadie nodded, grimacing.

Timothy gave Anna's hands a small tug. "Give her a break. It can't be that bad."

Shuddering sobs were the only answer. Tim stood, stepped back, and shrugged his shoulders.

"*Voss iss letts mitt ess?*" (What is wrong with her?)

"She's … anorexic. Bulimic." Sadie mouthed the words.

Tim understood. His eyes opened wide, his eyebrows lifted, he puckered his mouth into a low whistle, shaking his head as if he realized the sad significance of it. Slowly he rolled his eyes to the melting chocolate, the shadow of a grin reaching his features. Sadie looked, caught his meaning, held a hand to her mouth to stifle the smile beginning there, her eyes betraying her merriment. Their eyes caught, the humor a piece of shared chocolate, a bond acknowledged, accepted, a trust crackling to life.

Tim became self-conscious, then, shuffled to the recliner and sat in it, staring out the window. Sadie went to the light stand, pulled at two tissues and handed them to Anna, who grabbed them and blew her nose without lifting her head. Finally she raised herself, her eyes brimming, averting them from Sadie before looking in Timothy's direction, the anger consuming her again.

"Who is he?" she croaked.

"Mark's brother, Tim. Timothy Peight."

Tim cleared his throat.

"Tim, this is my sister Anna."

Tim stood up as Anna lifted her eyes to his face. "Hello, Anna, I'm pleased to meet you."

Anna said nothing, her glare the only response. Sadie bit back words of rebuke, but they rushed to the surface again when Anna blurted out, "Oh, go brush your teeth."

Chapter 14

AND SO BEGAN SADIE'S STRANGE DAY, AS SHE called it later to Mark. Timothy closed his mouth, went back to the recliner and stayed there, a piece of furniture that could not be moved about and just about as talkative. Anna refused to talk as well, so Sadie prattled on about nothing. Becoming flustered, she coated pretzels, peanut-buttered Ritz crackers, raisins, Cheerios, and anything she could think of to keep her hands occupied and to alleviate the abysmal silence, the air rife with resentment. All her cookie sheets and jelly roll pans were filled. The parchment paper ran out, and still she coated food. Finally, when Sadie thought she would turn into a remote-controlled car, zipping from point to point, driven by the earlier outburst, Anna suddenly broke the silence. Tim was asleep. Good.

"Sadie, I…didn't mean to hurt you. I don't know what got into me. My life is so plain down weird, I can't handle it. I was doing much better, felt like eating, and didn't hate myself quite as much. Then Sheryl broke up with Neil. Now I'm back to where I started. Square one."

Sadie said nothing. Waited.

"See, Merv... You know Merv?"

Sadie nodded.

"He's really a nice guy. I prayed and prayed for God's will. I know he will ask me, eventually, and I would do well to become his wife. But... "

"It's Neil." It wasn't a question; Sadie only filled in the obvious.

Miserably, Anna nodded. "I can't control Neil, I can't control my future. The only thing I can control is my figure. And, I am finally thin enough now. I no longer feel fat."

Sadie shook her head. Slowly, Anna's hand crept out, one finger unfolded, the tip coming down on a speck of chocolate. Lifting it, she held it to her tongue, then closed her mouth, tucking her hands below her armpits as if to keep them from straying for more chocolate.

Sadie watched her, lifted a chocolate-covered pretzel, still warm and a bit sticky, to her mouth.

"Mmm," she said, closing her eyes.

Anna swallowed.

"Go ahead, Anna. Eat one. Eat the whole cookie-sheet full."

Anna laughed, a small, hard, sound.

"So is Neil paying attention to you?"

Miserable eyes, then a miserable voice, talking, talking. It was all a matter of time. He would, eventually, come around. He would settle down. She could help him by dating him, just being with him. But he....

Her voice trailed off into a state so abjectly pitiful, Sadie stopped all movement and strained to hear the whispered words.

She thought he.... In whispered words, the root of her trouble was spilled over the table, the horror curdling Sadie's stomach with its wrongness.

"No!" The plastic spatula she was holding sliced through the air and smacked the table with a resounding splat.

"Oh, no, you don't, Anna. Believe me when I say this. It's not what he wants. It's not what you want. He means you nothing good. You have *got* to get rid of this guy, this Neil."

Tim stirred, sat up, the recliner rocking as he released the handle. Quietly, with Mark's cat-like grace, he came to the kitchen, went to the sink, and helped himself to a large tumbler of water. Anna's eyes went to Timothy, assessing the long, dirty-blond hair, the tall, lean figure, the loose jeans. Did she notice his scarred cheeks? His decaying teeth? The teeth, definitely, she thought. Her face was unreadable.

Tim came to the table, folded himself into a chair, raised his eyes to Sadie's, and asked if he could help himself. She nodded, still watching Anna's face. Tim threw a whole chocolate-covered Ritz cracker into his mouth, chewed twice, and swallowed, reached for another, then another. Anna swallowed, watching him. He ate six, then asked if they had plenty of milk. Sadie nodded, and he moved to the refrigerator to fill his large glass with milk, guzzling all of it in five or six large gulps, promptly reaching for more crackers coated with chocolate.

"I hope you're going to pay rent," Anna remarked sourly.

"Think I should?" Tim asked, meeting her gaze squarely, challenging her. Infuriating her, Sadie observed.

"Yes, I think you should," Anna said.

"You know, it's absolutely none of your business."

Sadie winced. Touché. Immediately she changed the subject to something trivial, her words tumbling over each other in her need to smooth things over, but was rewarded by the lack of even a single comment. Tim ate a chocolate-covered pretzel, then tried the raisins, Anna watching him with an increasingly nauseated expression.

"You know," Tim said, slowly putting Anna on the edge of her seat, bristling with defense at the mere sound of his voice. "Couldn't help overhearing your little conversation there. Looks like you got some guy trouble."

He paused. "Is it true, Anna?"

Anna's face flamed, and she ignored the use of her name.

"Like I said, Anna. I couldn't help overhearing. Sounds as if you have some problems. Bill. His name Bill?"

Anna could not have been more contemptuous, her eyes flashing as she faced him squarely. "I wouldn't say anything if I couldn't hear."

Tim laughed easily, then, his hand going to his mouth to cover the offending teeth. "Oh, I can hear all right. You just weren't speaking very plainly."

"I was, too!"

Tim shook his head.

Where did he come up with this sort of audacity? Sadie wondered. This poor self-conscious individual who could barely lift his head when they first met. With Anna he was at ease, completely in control with a sort of teasing banality. Was it Anna's vulnerability? She was a scarred, troubled creature like himself. Whatever it was, Sadie realized he enjoyed Anna's company or he would have left. Or perhaps he suspected he knew how to help her.

"As I was saying, you can't have this Bill guy..."

"Not Bill. Neil," she broke in, quickly.

"Believe me, this guy does not want you. Not in the right way. I know. I've been there. You don't want him.

He's no good."

"What do you know about him? Nothing. Why don't you just stay out of it?"

"Okay, I will."

And he took down his coat and went outside, leaving Anna peering out the window, turning her head to watch as he slipped and slid down the sidewalks to the barn, his arms waving wildly to keep his balance.

"Now where's he going?"

"I have no clue."

Sadie smiled to herself, watching Anna. She was clearly frustrated but curious now. They ate a lunch of turkey, tomato, onion, and lettuce sandwiches on Kaiser rolls, with mustard, of course. Sadie knew Anna would not touch the sandwiches if there was as much as a speck of mayonnaise on them, the fat-laden condiment containing the ability to put 10 pounds on her.

After she had actually eaten half of a sandwich, Anna's mood shifted. She became lighthearted, talkative. She related incidents of her weekends, who was dating whom, the pitiful creature that Sheryl had become after breaking up with Neil, hardly ever coming to the Sunday evening singings, how cute Reuben was, so certain the whole world was his, driving Charlie and that brand new buggy. When Sadie wondered at the ability of Charlie to keep up with the youth's horses, Anna laughed, telling her old Charlie could still kick up his heels with the best of them. They were laughing when Tim came back into the house, but stopped when they saw his expression.

"Hey, Sadie, I hate to trouble you, but I had the barn door open, decided to clean out the stable, and this...this yellow...sort of yellow...horse came stumbling into the barn. Do you have a horse loose somewhere? He acted as if he's been around the barn."

Sadie dropped her spoon, heard it clatter to the floor as her mouth opened in disbelief.

"Y...Yellow?"

"Sort of."

With a cry, Sadie ran to get her coat, pulled her boots on, tied her head scarf as she ran, slipping and falling the whole way to the barn, propelled by one single thought—Paris.

At first, she thought it was Paris. Then she thought it wasn't. But when the dirty, unkempt, horse turned its head and nickered, she knew without a doubt it was her horse who had found its way back. She was thin, her coat was coarse and long, but it was Paris. Sadie was unaware of anyone or anything other than throwing her arms around the thin neck and staying there. She cried and whispered to Paris, told her of the times she missed her most, then stepped back to assess the damage that had been done to her beloved horse.

She appeared to have lost weight but was in better health than Nevaeh had been. She didn't stand on the right hind foot. No matter, she'd heal everything up. Crying sometimes, then laughing to herself and talking, she was unaware of Tim's and Anna's presence until Tim cleared his throat self-consciously, the way he sniffed when he was ill at ease.

"I guess you know the horse" he said, finally.

"Yes, Tim, I do."

Anna, completely forgetting her former animosity toward this stranger, filled him in with the details about Paris, the enduring relationship through all the trials. And now, after Sadie had given her up completely, she had come back. Tim's face was an open book as Anna spoke.

He watched her large eyes, the shadows of deprived nutrition beneath them, the thin, white hands gesticulating. They watched as Sadie continued stroking Paris before going to the wooden cupboard and taking down a currycomb.

Slowly, lovingly, she worked, cleaning the mane, the burrs and dirt falling on the cement floor of the forebay. Anna offered to help, but Sadie waved her away, so Tim told her she could help him clean the stable for Paris.

Anna looked at Tim, the pitchfork he held toward her, back at the stable, and then at Tim again. She wrinkled her nose and wrapped her coat tightly around herself, rocking back on her heels.

"I don't know if I'm strong enough."

"You would be if you'd eat normally."

"Define normal!"

Tim laughed uproariously and admitted he was on the other end of what was considered normal. But she sure was on the extreme opposite. So which one was the healthiest? Sadie could tell that Anna knew the answer, but the younger sister went right ahead cleaning Paris's coat as if she hadn't heard.

Supper was not ready when Mark came home. The house was dark, chocolate-covered food all over everything. The fire burned low, but surprisingly, a bright light shone from the barn window. When he stepped inside, he couldn't fathom the horse Sadie was still grooming, applying antiseptic to scratches and open wounds, while Tim swept the loose hay in a pile and fed it to Truman and Duke.

With a cry, Sadie dropped the antiseptic and ran to his waiting arms, hysterical with the joy of Paris's return. Mark held her, soothed her, and held back his own emotion. He shook his head in disbelief, the only way he could convey his feelings.

When Tim joined them, Mark smiled at him and said he was genuinely glad Tim was back. Mark asked where he'd been. Tim looked down, scuffed the cement floor with the toe of his shoe.

"I had some business to take care of."

"Okay," was all Mark said, asking no questions.

Anna had taken her leave, declining Tim's offer of assistance, obviously very uncomfortable under his watch. He said something, Anna replied, and she was off down the drive, turning to the left at an unsafe speed.

Paris had been sufficiently groomed, cleaned, and her wounds treated. Sadie returned Paris to her stall, which had been strewn with clean shavings as well as a large portion of oats, corn, molasses, and two blocks of good hay. Sadie finally turned to leave the barn, joining Mark who was patiently waiting by the door, the lantern in his hand creating a circle of yellow light around him. They walked to the house together, followed by Tim with a hand on Wolf's collar, throwing a snowball for him before entering the house with them.

Sadie was starved, her stomach rumbling as she scooped up the chocolate candies and stacked them neatly in Tupperware containers, popping the seal to assure the airtight quality. Turning to Mark, she asked if it was all right to make "*toste brode, millich und oya*" (toast, milk and eggs).

"Sure, you know how much I like that," Mark said grinning.

Timothy nodded. "Aunt Hannah made it."

Heating a large saucepan, Sadie poured a generous amount of milk into it, then cracked open and deposited the insides of a dozen eggs, leaving them to poach. Opening the broiler of the gas stove, she carefully laid six slices of thick, homemade bread on the broiler rack, then stood up, closing it with her foot. Hurriedly, she set the table with a clean tablecloth, three soup plates, utensils, a bowl of applesauce, some leftover red beets, and half a chocolate cake. When the eggs were soft-poached, the milk almost to the boiling point, the toast dark and crispy, Sadie put two slices of the toast in each bowl, set the eggs and milk on a hot pad in the middle of the table, then poured the cold water in each glass.

It seemed as if Tim's self-consciousness became more noticeable when he was expected to bow his head for a silent prayer before mealtime. He never made eye contact, his sniffing became more frequent, and he shuffled his feet uncomfortably when Mark said it was time for "Patties down," the Amish term, in child's language, for silent prayer.

Tim helped himself to six of the eggs, as Sadie had expected, politely asking if she and Mark had all they wanted. He ladled enough milk over everything to fill the soup bowl to brimming, then added a liberal amount of salt and pepper before digging in. He ate all the red beets and half the applesauce, accompanied by a chunk of chocolate cake so large Sadie could not believe he ate it all in less than six bites.

They talked of Tim getting a job, of his offer to pay rent, and whether he was thinking of returning to the Amish. Mark did not set any rules, but by that first warning about not smoking, Tim knew about what was expected of him.

After Sadie washed dishes, Tim asked her what really was wrong with Anna. He spoke in a quiet, nervous manner that completely won Sadie over. As accurately as she could, she related Anna's sad story about her obsession with Neil. But Tim said nothing at all when she finished. He made his way to the stairs with an abrupt "good night" before closing the door quite firmly.

Richard Caldwell had a fit, as did Jim Sevarr and the ranch hands who knew Sadie and Paris's story. Richard Caldwell slapped his knees, gleeful in his exclamations, chortling about the rotten luck of the horse thieves or the tattered remains of the ones that had slipped between the cracks of the law.

"Good for 'em!" he yelled, his *Schadenfreude* completely consuming him. "For all they put you through," he shouted, "good for 'em!"

Dorothy shook her head and said no good could come of it. She thought they were done with that cursed palomino once and for all. Sadie became so insulted she had to blink back tears.

"She ain't a blessing, that's sure, unless you figure every time Sadie got out of her scrapes alive was one. Ain't no blessing to me, so she ain't."

Erma became completely defensive and said that palomino was not cursed and that was an awful term to use. Her face got red and she opened her mouth for her usual fiery retort. Sadie held a hand over her own mouth and shook her head, her eyes begging her to keep her peace. She knew Dorothy meant well; it was just her way of protecting Sadie.

They were into the Christmas season at the ranch, baking extra pies, dozens of cookies, and huge fruit cakes, besides the everyday cooking. The ranch was prospering; the price of beef spurred Richard Caldwell into acquiring more land, more cattle, as well as more horses and equipment. The usual 20 cowhands that ate in the huge dining room often doubled, especially for the evening meal.

Dorothy, who was in her element, barking orders, wearing the brilliant purple Crocs, would have to admit defeat around three or four o'clock every afternoon, succumbing to the pain in her lower back or a cramp in her leg. That was usually when the pressure was on to have the huge evening meal ready and waiting on the steam table, with napkins and utensils, everything clean and in perfect order.

So in the middle of everyone scurrying around in the usual manner, Dorothy sat, her one leg elevated on the seat of a kitchen chair, holding a bowl of macaroni and cheese and one of chocolate pudding. Erma's baked beans had turned out a bit dry, so she was adding some warm water, leaning over the hot oven door, her brilliant red hair only a shade brighter than her face. Dorothy chewed with great enjoyment, savoring a too-large mouthful of macaroni and cheese, watching the heat rise in Erma's face.

"Told you to do them in the electric roaster."

Too slowly, Erma replaced the lid, shoved back the oven rack, and closed the door, adjusting the knob in front. She watched Dorothy slurp her coffee before spooning up more of the cheesy concoction, Erma's eyes mere slits in her red face.

"I'm not used to electric roasters at home, Dorothy. And besides, they're slow."

"No, they ain't."

"Yes, they are."

"No, they ain't. I know that for a fact."

"You better not eat all that chocolate pudding," Erma said with concern, changing the subject as abruptly as she could.

"An' jes' why ever not?"

"I'd get terrible heartburn. Coffee, chocolate pudding, and macaroni and cheese." Erma visibly shivered.

"Don't know what heartburn is."

"That's good," Erma said, rolling her eyes in Sadie's direction. Sadie was slicing a roast of beef, the meat falling away under the direction of her knife.

"Is the gravy made?" Sadie asked curtly. Sometimes these stupid little spats just irked her, and today, patience was in short supply.

"Ain't no hurry," Dorothy said around her macaroni before slurping yet more coffee.

The kitchen door opened slowly. Steven Weaver poked his head through the opening and asked if they wanted a few bushels of Rome apples, leftover from the market in town.

"The guy said I can have 'em, but I have no use for 'em."

Erma almost cried in her haste to fix her hair and covering, desperately spitting on her hands and smoothing the wayward tendrils, making her look like a skinny, wet cat. Oh, dear. Sadie cringed when Erma wiped her hands after washing them, then charged through the bathroom door, her elbow already pulled back like a bowstring, ready to fire. She literally slapped her hand into Steven's, accompanied by her loud, jovial yell.

"Where you been, stranger? Haven't seen hide nor hair of you in a coon's age!"

Dorothy stopped chewing, her mouth a straight line,

her cheeks bulging, as she opened her eyes wide, her eyebrows shooting straight up. And when Steven Weaver met Erma's hand halfway and they laughed great guffaws of pure merriment together, it was obvious they were so happy to see each other. Sadie realized God had surely sent the perfect match for Erma Keim. Who else but Steven would enjoy a cymbal-crashing greeting like that? It was enough to send a half-dozen other men running for cover.

When Erma accompanied Steven to the door, offering to bring the apples in, Steven waved her away. But she charged straight through the door anyway, following him like a devoted puppy. When 10 minutes passed and no Erma or apples followed, Sadie smiled to herself. You go, Erma.

Sadie found Dorothy rattling bottles and mumbling to herself in the bathroom, the door of the medicine cabinet ajar. She just closed the door quietly and continued whipping potatoes.

That Sunday in church, Erma looked a bit crestfallen, for her. Her hair was slicked back tighter than usual with less *shtrubles*, her covering pulled forward well over her ears. Her usual effusiveness was dampened to a gentle, "How are you, Sadie? Nice dress."

Sadie walked into the kitchen to stand with the women and noticed Erma following her, a wistful expression on her face. Sadie shook hands with her usual friends and family, noticing Mam's new covering, then accepted everyone's sincere congratulations on the return of her beloved horse. She acknowledged it humbly, her eyes shining nevertheless, the days of missing her horse gone now, reveling in the pleasure of seeing her, touching her.

When she watched the boys file in and Steven Weaver was not at the head of the line, she swallowed her disappointment. Surely he had not returned to Indiana, leaving Erma without hope! During the service Sadie prayed for her friend, for the strength she would need to rise above this, if, in fact, he had decided to return. Erma was such a dear person. So genuine, so human. Seemingly imperfect, but so unselfish, and above all, sincerely caring about everyone in the community, English people as well as her Amish. Surely God would not be so cruel.

So often, though, this happened. Young men were lured to the west by the breathtaking scenery, the hunting, the adventure, but then yearned for their home folks, their busy way of life, and sooner or later, returned to their home state. The minister expounded the wisdom of Solomon, but Sadie was only half-listening, watching Erma Keim's display of emotions across her face. Poor dear.

Chapter 15

THEY WENT HOME TO DAT AND MAM'S FOR SUPPER, a time of renewal, the scents of Mam's kitchen bringing a lump of emotion to her throat. Mam was frying chicken, Mark's favorite, and had a casserole of scalloped potatoes in the oven. Leah was tossing a salad and Rebekah was setting the table, both of them dressed in their Sunday best, waiting until Kevin and Junior came to pick them up. They talked as fast as they could about Tim, and about Anna's meltdown, Mam staring in disbelief as Sadie related the whole incident.

"It's that Neil," she whispered. "I had no idea." Helplessly, she looked at Rebekah. "I thought you said she liked Merv."

"I thought she did!"

"Somebody is not communicating," Sadie said firmly.

Mam turned the chicken, hissing and snapping in the pan, before turning to Sadie.

"And just how do you communicate with a rock? How? If I ask her questions, I get no answer. Only a shrug of her shoulders. It's just as if she's another girl. I know how skinny she is. I know, too, that the more I say, the worse it gets. It's just a vicious circle, and as long as that Neil is in the picture, it's not going to change."

Mam choked back tears bravely, a matriarch over petty emotions, a strong pillar of the family, having overcome so much adversity herself. Mothers were like that. When the storms of life blew in, creating chaos, uprooting younger people as they struggled to understand situations in life that were beyond their control, talking, talking, restlessly trying to figure out situations, mothers wisely knew there was no use. God was up in his heaven and knew everything, including the reasons, something mortals did not have to know. That's what faith was for, no doubt about it. Same as Dat. Except Dat was perhaps more of a disciplinarian. So parents were a wonderful thing, when it all came down to it.

Dat teased Sadie about changing Paris's name to Lassie, that it was just like the old classic story of a dog finding its way home. Sadie smiled and smiled, she was so glad to be at home with her family, thinking of Paris in the barn, safe, warm, and secure.

Timothy would not accompany them to Sadie's parents, so they left him at home.

Sadie asked Dat about Tim, what would be the best way to approach him to make the decision to come back to the Amish.

Dat shook his head. "It's going to be tough."

Mark disagreed, saying he had his share of wild days and was thoroughly sick of the whole scene. He had been sick of it even before he came to meet Jackson.

"I think he's just too shy to tell anyone how he feels. To change back into Amish clothes, to make all new friends, feel at home in the community. It's a big mountain to scale for a person as bashful as Tim."

"Bring him sometime," Dat said. "Christmas would be as good a time as any."

Sadie looked at Mark, raised her eyebrows in question. Yes, they would bring him. Or try to.

Mam's fried chicken, as usual, was outstanding. And as usual, Sadie could not resist that second piece, followed by a large slice of homemade butterscotch pie. The coffee was perfect. Reuben came dashing in at the last minute just to say Hi, being otherwise occupied, in his words. Two of his friends were waiting in the buggy, so he grabbed a piece of chicken on the run, Mam calling after him about taking one for his friends, and he yelled back they didn't need any, which made Mark laugh and Dat smile and drink his coffee.

The atmosphere was so cozy, so homey with Mark beside her, his wide shoulders leaning back in his chair, at ease, happy to be here, confident in Sadie's love, a place to call his own, a reason for living after the overwhelming ordeal that had been his childhood.

"Only forward." Sadie seemed to hear the words, and yet there was no voice. I bet God just put those words in my head, she thought, looking around to see if anyone else had heard them. Just keep our eyes on the finish line, run the Christian race with Jesus Christ our Savior by our sides, and we won't go wrong. Thankfulness washed over her, along with a deep sense of purpose where Tim was concerned. There was so much good in Tim.

At work on Monday morning, Erma Keim walked quietly, even sedately through the door, unbuttoning her coat as she went, hanging her scarf neatly on the hook. Turning, she smiled, wished them a good morning, then turned to look at herself in the mirror. Sadie looked at Dorothy, and they both raised their eyebrows. What was going on? Sadie's heart sank, her sadness for Erma slowly churning in her stomach.

Dear God, she prayed, please give her the strength. Tears were close to the surface as she begged God to help Erma Keim through this time of trial.

Erma's hair was again combed back severely, her covering forward, well over her ears. She walked softly, rocking her feet from toe to heel, then asked Dorothy if she needed help with the bacon.

"I...guess," Dorothy stammered in disbelief.

Serenely, quietly, Erma placed bacon on the hot griddle, averting her eyes. Sadie put water on for the grits, sliced oranges, arranged the apple and pineapple for the fruit compartment, her heart heavy. Should she approach Erma? Offer condolence? Ask her outright whether Steven had returned to Indiana? After they served breakfast and filled their mugs of coffee, Sadie slid an arm around Erma's narrow waist, laying her cheek on her upper arm.

"Erma, tell me what's troubling you. Please feel free to confide in me. I pitied you so much when you looked so sad in church yesterday. You're just not yourself at all this morning, either. Is it Steven? Did you two...sort of have something going? It..."

She raced on, feeling as if she was sinking, unable to bring any happiness to Erma this way.

"Did he...he return to Indiana?" she blurted out, ready to accept Erma's sad fate.

Erma slid a long, thin arm around Sadie's waist, then released her, stepped back, and laid her large hands on her shoulders.

"Oh, Sadie, you are a dear. It's nothing like that." Bending her head, looking over her shoulder, then at Dorothy, she whispered, "I have a date."

The breath seemed to leave Sadie's body, she had no voice or air to start her words after that. She remembered Dorothy's look of disbelief, then her peal of laughter ringing through the kitchen, slapping her knees, her elbow catching the handle of her cup, dangerously rocking it, spilling a small amount of the steaming liquid on her sleeve.

"Who with? That long-nosed Mr. Weaver that comes in here?" she screeched.

Erma smiled, an angelic version of her usual rich-throated guffaws.

"Yes, him."

That was all she said, smiling sweetly at Sadie before turning to her coffee. Sadie squealed, congratulated her, then begged her to be herself.

"You don't have to change, Erma. Seriously. We love you just the way you are. Evidently, so does Steven!"

Erma looked confused, a bit sad, even. Looking around, making sure no one would hear her, she whispered, "I don't want to wreck my blessing!"

Christmas was a time of heightened activity in the Amish community. Hymn singings, school programs, Christmas dinners, caroling, shopping, gift exchanges, baking and cooking among the most important events. So Mark and Sadie had very little time to spend with Tim or fret about Anna's problems.

Paris remained lame in the hind right foot in spite of Mark's expertise, removing the shoe, cleaning the hoof, telling Sadie it may be the start of laminitis, which was like an arrow to Sadie's heart. They soaked the foot in warm water, applied the secret home remedy, that strong black salve that was a miracle cure for most horse hoof ailments. Still the reddened, infected tissue remained.

On Christmas morning, a storm blew in. The sun appeared for only a short time, cloaking the valley in shades of lavender and orange, only to disappear behind a heavy gray bank of clouds swollen with churning winds. Icy snow fragments began pelting the earth just as Mark and Sadie tucked themselves into the buggy, the presents and chocolate treats placed under the back seat.

Truman was a handful, crow-hopping, shaking his head to dislodge the bit in his mouth, pulling on the reins, wanting to break free and run too fast, putting the light shafts connecting him to the buggy in decided jeopardy, the way he was carrying on.

This was a serious storm, Sadie decided, when Mark opened the window and clicked it fast to the holder on the ceiling. "Can't see," he murmured, as he squinted into the steadily increasing snow.

Sadie wrapped her black, woolen shawl tightly around her shoulders, her gloved hands holding the fringes to keep it in place. Shivers chased each other up her back, and she let go of the shawl to pull the heavy lap robe up over her shoulder on the right side.

"Cold?"

Sadie nodded, relieved to see him reach up and unhook the window, letting it slam into place, then adjust the reins through the small rectangular holes in the frame.

The buggy swayed, slid, then righted itself as Mark slowed Truman, hanging on to the reins with both arms stretched out. Sadie could feel the weight of the buggy being pulled partly by Truman's mouth and his determination to run at breakneck speed, propelling them along, winding uphill over Atkin's Ridge.

The house on the side of the hill was the most welcome sight, the yellow glow of the gas lantern a friendly

beacon through the whirling, biting, whiteness. Home
was always an anticipated pleasure, but at Christmas, a
horse just couldn't go fast enough. Sadie hopped eagerly
off the buggy before Mark had time to pull the reins
through the window.

Even with the long uphill run, Truman wasn't winded.
Steam rose from his body, some hairs on his flanks were
frosted from the moisture, his breathing accelerated only
slightly as he tossed his head up and down, his way of
asking Mark to hurry up and loosen the neck rein so he
could lower his head.

Mam greeted Sadie at the door with a quick hug,
taking the presents, then Dat shook hands warmly as
he shrugged his coat on, going to help Mark with his
horse. Leah and Rebekah were helping in the kitchen,
rosy-cheeked, smiling, so happy to see her. Reuben was
sprawled across the recliner, dressed in his "good" trousers and red Christmas shirt. He was definitely turning
into a nice-looking young man, an air of confidence in his
manner, and a wide, teasing grin. He slapped the footrest
of the recliner down before bouncing to his feet to greet
Sadie.

"Hey, Sis! Where's Tim?"

Sadie shook her head. "Couldn't persuade him to
come."

"Why not?"

"Claimed he had nothing to wear."

"I'll hitch up Charlie and go pick him up."

Sadie shrugged her shoulders. "Good luck!" she said
soundly, meaning there was hardly a chance he could be
persuaded.

When Anna came down the stairs, Sadie had to fight
the rising panic in her throat. Dear God in heaven. The

prayer began before she was even aware of it, automatically switching to a plea for higher help.

Huge dark circles lay like harbingers of death below each eye. Her cheekbones were prominent, the white skin taut over them. Even her teeth seemed to protrude from the pale lips, the square jaw containing only a hint of flesh. Her eyes were enormous, filled with fear. Did she know she was being controlled by something she could no longer handle?

"Hello, Anna! Merry Christmas!"

Her voice came out cracked, high, breathless. When Anna smiled, it was only a parting of those pale lips. The eyes remained flat, afraid. She gripped the back of a chair, then slid into it, folding her skeletal frame weakly against it.

Reuben scurried through the kitchen, pulling on his beanie, his coat buttoned against the cold on his way to collect Tim, as he put it, grinning assuredly at Sadie. Numbly, she went about the kitchen, grating cabbage, washing dishes, putting whipped cream on the coconut cream pie, watching Anna from the corner of her eye. She sat in her chair, her breathing coming in short gasps, then actually reached down for support, her long, thin fingers gripping the sides for a prop, her shoulders sagging weakly when she let go.

Instantly, Sadie was by her side. "Anna."

There was no answer.

"Anna, do you hear me?"

Anna stared ahead, her eyes seemingly locked.

Suddenly, very afraid, Sadie shook her by the shoulders. "Anna! Talk to me!"

As soon as Sadie's hands left her shoulders, Anna began to slide in slow motion, her head outweighing her neck and shoulders with no strength to hold it, like a sack half-full of feed sliding along the back of the chair before crumpling to the floor. They were all around her then, Dat lifting her to take her outside to revive her from her faint, Mam hovering over them, her face ashen, Leah and Rebekah angry, then crying, Reuben running from the barn, his eyes wide.

Grimly, Sadie heated milk in a saucepan, added sugar, then chocolate syrup. Likely her blood sugar was so slow it wasn't even readable, or else she hadn't eaten in days. Or—she had eaten too much and then purged the food from her body. How had things gotten so out of control? Catching Mark's eye, Sadie shook her head.

When Anna came out of her unconscious state, she lay weakly on the sofa, her eyes dry, still terrified. There were no tears, just this dry-eyed lethargy, coupled with the wide eyes of fear. Sadie brought the hot chocolate and asked her to drink it, which of course, Anna refused.

"I'll be fine. I have the flu," she croaked, her voice edged with panic.

"Drink it!" Sadie hissed.

Anna remained adamant, her lips compressed into a straight, thin line of determination. Sighing, Sadie got up from her crouched position, sighed, dumped the hot chocolate down the sink drain. The light of Christmas was only a flicker, tossed by a harsh wind of fear and doubt, for the remainder of the forenoon. The ham was carved, the pineapple sauce falling away with each slice, the mashed potatoes were piled high, browned butter dripping from each cavity. No one wanted to eat, but, like robots, they went through the motions, their eyes sliding to Anna, a mere bump under the quilt she had pulled over herself.

As Sadie helped wash dishes, she formed a plan: There would be no presents until the family held a conference, a no-holds-barred meeting about Anna. Reuben still had not returned, and if Tim showed up with him, he'd just have to sit in. Something had to be done, Christmas Day or not.

How to approach Mam was the next problem, but when she came to dry dishes while Sadie washed, she plunged right in, grateful for Mam's understanding. With tear-filled eyes, she nodded in agreement. Dat remained aloof but finally gave his consent. So they seated themselves around the still form on the couch, her eyes closed, as still as death itself. Just as Sadie was about to ask Anna the first question, a buggy flashed past the window.

Charlie! Reuben had returned. Would he bring Tim along in?

It was Tim all right, dressed in Mark's clothes, sniffing self-consciously, throwing his hair out of his eyes. He was wearing black trousers low on his hips, a beige shirt with the sleeves rolled halfway up his forearms, a black vest hanging open, appearing relaxed, completely at home in his Amish clothes. Reuben was jubilant, proudly producing Tim to his family as if he had discovered him all by himself.

"Look it!" he beamed.

Tim tried to shake it off, but the huge grin on his face gave away his true feelings.

"Does this mean ... ?" Mark stammered.

Sadie put a hand on his arm, steadying him as Reuben yelped gleefully, "What does it look like?"

Anna's head rolled to one side, and she fixed her large-eyed gaze on Tim, her expression as vague as the thin body under the quilt.

All Tim said was, "Guess I'll try it; see how deep my roots go."

Mark lowered his head as tears rose to the surface, and Sadie slipped her arm through his.

Mam went to set the warmed food on one end of the table, stooping low to talk to Reuben as Tim strained to hear her words. They ate hungrily, bending their heads to the delicious food the way growing young men do when they can't fill themselves up fast enough. After they finished, the family opened the subject of Anna's sickness, confronting her with the sad facts of her slide into the delusional state she was in. Dat and Mam both talked to her, asking her if she was willing to go for help.

Anna shook her head from side to side. "I only have the flu."

She kept insisting. No amount of coaxing would change her. Leah promised her a new rug for her room. Rebekah pleaded with her for Mam and Dat's sake, but nothing changed. Reuben finally became quite frustrated and told her he hoped she was happy now, ruining everyone's Christmas this way. Sadie saw Tim wince. She saw his eyes as he watched her, listened to the family's pleading without comment, shifting uncomfortably in his chair. A few times he looked at Mark, opened his mouth slightly as if to speak, then shut it. Finally he walked over to the couch and placed his hand on Anna's forehead.

"Yeah, you are running a temperature. I think you do have the flu."

Turning, he addressed the family, saying she did have a fever, then looked at Anna and asked if she wanted some chicken soup, a cup of tea? Anna's eyes were fixed on Tim's face, as if a savior had indeed presented himself.

"Soup, I'll have soup."

"I'll get it."

Mam followed him to the kitchen, flitted about like a nervous bird, emptying a can of Campbell's chicken noodle, filling a mug with tea. Anna insisted on coming to the kitchen, the quilt wrapped around her shoulders, then sat at the table, bent her head, lifted the spoon methodically to her mouth, until it was all gone, then started busily slurping the hot, sugary tea. Tim sat with her, saying nothing. The color in her cheeks slowly returned. Sadie wanted to go to her so badly, but Mark shook his head no.

They began to talk. Mam suggested they begin opening gifts, which they did, fully aware of the miracle taking place in the kitchen. Dat was presented with a very expensive fly-fishing rod, the product of everyone chipping in, leaving him wide-eyed, exclaiming over and over about his wonderful gift.

"He'll never go to work now," Reuben chortled, leaning way out of his chair to watch the progress Tim was making in the kitchen. Sadie grabbed his shirt sleeve and hauled him back.

Mam was given a new canner and a cultivator for her garden, both items to make her life easier, which she exclaimed about in great detail, saying she had no idea anyone would spend so much money just for her. For Reuben there was a huge package, containing a brand new black leather saddle with a bridle to match. There was a moon inscribed on both, in memory of his horse named Moon, which he accepted with a quiet, controlled coolness, but Sadie could tell inside he was jumping up and down with pure glee. The girls had their usual dress fabrics, decorative items for their rooms, harmonicas, which Rebekah promptly began to play, getting Tim's and Anna's attention.

Anna smiled weakly, then came in to sit on the couch, Tim following to sit cross-legged on the floor by her side.

Rebekah was good. She played a rendering of "Silent Night," followed by "What Child is This?"

Sadie opened her package, a new bathroom set, the rugs reversible, something she had wanted ever since she had her own bathroom. The rubber-backed bathroom rugs never lasted very long, having to be put through the wringer of the washing machine. They were suitable for awhile, but eventually the rubber backing became pinched between the covers of the wringer, resulting in a tear, then bit by bit the rug deteriorated. These reversible ones would be much more serviceable, much easier to wash.

Mark received a German-English dictionary, which Tim promptly tried out to see if he remembered any German from his school days. Every Amish student learned German but spoke Pennsylvania Dutch, a sort of pidgin language derived from real German with English mixed into it, a product of hundreds of years of being the minority among English-speaking people.

Wunder. Wundfieber. Wundstarrkrampf. Wunsch. Tim rattled off a row of words pronounced correctly, then grinned, his hand going to his mouth unthinking, a motion to hide his decaying teeth. Anna watched him, her eyes slanted downward on his thick blond-streaked hair, then pulled the quilt around her thin shoulders. That began a volley of German words and their meanings, arguments, fists banging on chair arms, resorting to the dictionary many times, accompanied by raised fists and shouts of glee.

Mam spread the afternoon snacks across the table. There were oranges and grapes, coffee and punch, Chex mix, pretzels, a cheese log, and too many cookies to count, besides all the different candy.

Tim and Reuben soon got up to load their plates, then went to the basement to start a game of Ping-Pong. Anna watched Tim go. Sadie sat beside her, putting both arms around her and squeezing, quilt and all.

"How you feeling, Sissie?" she asked lightheartedly.

Anna fixed her gaze on Sadie's face.

"S…Sadie, you know what Tim said?"

"What?"

"A girlfriend of his had to live in a mental place because she was so bad. Wouldn't eat, you know."

"What?"

Anna nodded miserably. "Is that what happens?"

"Anna, yes. Of course it is. I often tried to tell you."

"Yes, but…Tim saw it happen. You never did."

"True."

"I'm not like that though." Sadie watched her face. "Am I?"

"Are you?"

The quilt lifted slightly, then fell as Anna shrugged her shoulders. How it happened, Sadie was never sure, but the remainder of the day, Anna followed Tim and Reuben. First, she shrugged off the quilt, then slyly, quietly, she went to the basement. After that, Sadie found her playing Monopoly at the kitchen table, sipping tea. She stepped back as she watched Tim break a cookie in two, offer Anna the other half. Anna lifted her eyes to his face, held his gaze, then slowly reached out and took it. It was a peanut butter cookie with a Hershey's kiss on top, the chocolate candy staying on Anna's half. Deliberately, she reached out thin fingers, loosened it, and put the whole thing in her mouth, letting it melt, savoring its sweetness,

watching Tim's expression. His eyes spoke his encouragement. Anna blushed faintly.

Reuben looked from Tim to Anna, then blurted out,
too emotional to stay quiet, "You better eat about two
dozen more of them things!"

"Maybe I will!"

Reuben howled with laughter. Tim laughed, his hand
going to his mouth.

Chapter 16

THE STORM RAGED. THE WIND BLEW GREAT WHITE whirls of fallen snow into restless, never-ceasing drifts that obscured anything in the line of visibility. Pine trees bent and waved, shaking off any accumulation on their branches. Snow swirled off rooftops, the wind moaned and howled around the eaves, the fire burned high until the wood stove in the living room gave off a tremendous heat, logs being added every few hours. The family popped fresh popcorn, made hot spiced cider and leftover ham sandwiches.

Reuben won the first Monopoly game, then went to check on the horses. He was gasping for breath when he came back, saying this was not a snowstorm, it was a blizzard, like the one in the Laura Ingalls Wilder book called *The Long Winter*.

So they all stayed for the night, Sadie acknowledging happily that it was the smart thing to do. Mark fretted about frozen water pipes at home, but Dat assured him if they filled the stove with wood before they left, it should be all right for a few days. The horses would be hungry and thirsty, but they'd survive till Mark returned.

They sang Christmas songs, then all gathered around the table in the light of the softly hissing gas lamp and drank hot chocolate. For some reason they began talking about cream of wheat, that soft white cereal mixed with brown sugar and creamy milk poured over it until it had the right consistency. Tim's eyes shone. He said Aunt Hannah used to make it for him after his egg sandwich, and he put a slice of shoofly pie in it. Dat said he'd like to try that, so Mam produced a pot of cream of wheat and, of course, a freshly baked shoofly, which was almost a staple in the Miller family. They all tasted it.

Anna watched, swallowed. Sadie urged her to try it, then watched as she looked at Tim. He met her eyes and held them. You can do this. Go ahead. The message was there as plain as day.

She smiled slowly, then scraped the last of the cereal from the pot, added a teaspoon of brown sugar, a dash of milk. Slowly, she cut only a sliver of pie, let it fall into the cream of wheat, then took up her spoon in those pitiable white fingers. Again she looked at Tim. This time Sadie couldn't watch. It was too personal. Almost sacred. Slowly, she lifted the spoon. "Mmm," she whispered, then ducked her head, embarrassed.

During the night, Sadie began coughing, an annoying itch in the throat, and couldn't stop. Mark snored, rolled over, and grabbed all the covers, so she gave up, scooped Leah's flannel robe from its hook, and made her way downstairs to the kitchen. She needed some honey and lemon or some over-the-counter cough medicine, even a lozenge of some kind. She was surprised to find a kerosene lamp on in the living room. Someone forgot to turn it off, she thought, and she walked through the wide doorway to take care of it. No use wasting kerosene.

"Oh!" They scared her.

Tim. Anna. They were sitting on the floor by the fire, both looking up at her. They were clearly at ease, innocent, neither of them offended by her appearance, waiting to hear what she wanted.

"What are you two doing still up?" she asked.

"We're talking." Anna offered shyly. "Reuben just went to bed."

"Oh. Well, I can't stop coughing, so I need some medicine."

There was no answer, so Sadie decided to leave well enough alone, found her medicine, and returned to bed. She shook Mark awake, whispering her concerns about Tim and how good was it that he sat down in the living room with Anna? And how could they know he was sincere? Just because he came to the Christmas dinner with Mark's clothes on didn't mean he wasn't the same lost teenager he'd been when they met him, and he knew how vulnerable Anna was, and how in the world could they ever feel comfortable having those two together? Mark told her to go to sleep, they weren't getting married, and hadn't Anna eaten that shoofly pie?

After Christmas, everyone dug out of the snow and life continued. Tim cut his hair, becoming quite embarrassed when Sadie made a fuss about how neat he looked, how manly, so much older. Mark's praise brought a grin, a punch on the arm, and Sadie knew his eyes smiled the rest of the evening. They paid for his dental work.

He went to church for the first time, making sure no one else knew he was planning to go. Sadie hoped she could see Anna when he walked in and was completely surprised to see how strong Anna's reaction really was. She watched the row of boys file in, then sat up straight, shocked, visibly shaken at the sight of Tim with his hair cut. Just as suddenly, she lowered her head, embarrassed, trying hard to hide the onslaught of feelings.

Ah, Sadie thought. And then she prayed for both of them. The long prayer, after both sermons were over, was extra meaningful. The prayer for a godly life, to be more Christlike. It was all a plea for her own life, the wisdom to deal with Tim as well as Anna. Was it God's will? Would they be able to make it work, in spite of all the adversities in their lives? And what about Neil Hershberger? He always managed to reappear somehow.

Erma Keim remained sedate, walking quietly through the kitchen, beaming her happiness, a halo of angelic goodness following her. She praised Dorothy's biscuits, and Dorothy acknowledged her praise with a bowed head, then proceeded to tell her she should never have turned her back on that Dollar General, that their shortening was still the best and cheapest by far.

"Ya see, Erma, I can't drive by the Dollar General, keepin' the grudge against them shoes. They's still good shoes. I'm jus' gittin' old, is all it is. I like my Crocs, don't get me wrong, but I gotta return to the Dollar General. It's muh store, so it is. You know they got toothpaste, Colgate, for a dollar? Now I told you, they're gonna hurt Walmart, you mark my words. And sauerkraut to cook with my pork? Ninety-nine cents!"

Erma nodded her total agreement, buttered a biscuit, and proceeded to tell them both about her first date. She started out humbly enough.

"We went out to eat in his horse and buggy. We could

tie at the hitching rack behind Lowell's in town. He ordered a steak, and I had roast chicken and filling. We talked and talked. He's so easy to talk to. He intends to stay in Montana, asked if I'm happy here. I said I am. So I figure we'll get married. He sees me here at work, knows what a good worker I am. I'm old, though, so likely we won't have a big family. I plan on having fried chicken and dressing at my wedding."

Dorothy snorted. "What's dressing? You mean, like French and ranch and stuff?"

"No, it's filling. Like stuffing, only better. It has chicken and carrots and celery and potatoes."

"Sounds like slop to me."

Erma's halo slid off center a bit before she could catch herself, and she told Dorothy she shouldn't say that before she tasted it. Dorothy said she wasn't about to taste it anytime soon, and what, pray tell, is wrong with plain old stuffing anyhow? The halo disappeared completely when Erma wagged a finger under Dorothy's nose and said that's what set Amish cooking apart, the know-how passed down through the ages that English people knew nothing about. Sadie was seriously afraid Dorothy would pop a blood vessel after that. She became highly agitated, telling Erma it was all a matter of acquired taste, that alcoholics liked the taste of alcohol, too, and it was slop, same as dressing.

Luckily Steven Weaver came in with a box of turnips from the Giant in town, and Dorothy was beside herself with joy, saying she hadn't had a good dish of mashed turnips in a coon's age. Erma smiled sweetly and said she bet they were delicious, although she had never acquired a taste for them, which mixed Dorothy up a bit, unsure how to take that comment, so she let it go.

Sadie decided it was why she came to work, this constant sparring between these two interesting characters whom she loved. Richard Caldwell and his wife were good friends, too, not just employers, and every day at the ranch held some new adventure, argument, or challenge.

After Steven left, Dorothy asked Erma what made her think Steven would ask her to get married. Erma said it was just the way he looked at her when he asked if she was happy here.

"Just such an intimate look," Erma finished, clasping her hands across her stomach, looking reverently at the ceiling.

"That don't say nothing," Dorothy said, not quite loud enough for Erma to hear.

Sadie had to go clean the steam table, so if there was more drama after that, she was blissfully unaware of it.

At home that evening, Mark bent over Paris's hind foot, prodding gently as Sadie came over to look at the swollen tissue inside the hoof. Mark smelled the infected area. His eyes were clouded with concern when he released the foot and straightened to his full height. Sadie stroked Paris's flank, her eyes going to her husband's.

"Should we call the vet again?"

Mark sighed. "I don't know."

No amount of antibiotic, salve, hot water baths, or any other remedy would heal that foot. Sometime Paris had become foundered or eaten too much grain, perhaps made her way out of her stall while unattended and broken into a sack of grain. Whatever the cause, the result was swollen, red, infected tissue, causing severe pain and lameness. Sadie had felt so confident when Paris returned, so glad to be able to nurse her back to health.

But the Paris of old was not to be found ever since.

Her coat still shone after the extended grooming and the minerals on her portion of feed. But the foundering had slowly progressed to a serious case of laminitis.

Now when Sadie entered the barn, she could smell the infection. Paris no longer threw up her proud head, nickering that soft rumbling of her nostrils, her eyes bright, alive, eager to see Sadie, wanting to run down the driveway with Sadie astride her back. The thing was, she was in pain.

"How bad is it?" Sadie asked finally.

"It's pretty serious."

"Isn't there anything you can do? Can't we call another vet? Someone who specializes in horses?"

Mark answered wearily. "We did."

"Someone better?"

Sadie laid her forehead on Paris's, taking both hands to massage each side of her face.

"Good girl, Paris. You're doing great. You're a brave lady," she murmured, her throat swollen with unshed tears.

Mark walked her, but it was too cruel, so Sadie made him stop. "Mark, it's not just one foot anymore. It's both front feet, too. It's like she's walking on eggshells."

"I hoped you wouldn't notice."

He held her securely when she let the tears come, releasing the tightness in her throat. She had to accept this, she knew, but why had God allowed her to return, only to put Sadie through this pain?

"We'll try a different vet," Mark said, kissing the top of her head, stroking her back to console her.

He made the phone call that evening, Sadie by his side as they ran their fingers through the Yellow Pages, looking for the best equine veterinarian available.

Tim returned from his job, cold, his face wind-bitten, his hands blistered and bruised, his beanie lowered so far Sadie had to lift it to find his eyes. Laughing, he said it was warmer that way.

"Doesn't the wind ever stop in Montana?" he asked.

"Never," Sadie answered.

She dished up the barbequed meatballs, fried potatoes, and green beans, adding a side dish of pickled red-beet eggs. She watched as Mark and Tim loaded their plates, slathered homemade ketchup all over the potatoes, bent their heads, and ate without saying a word. They were so much alike, these brothers. Yet so different.

Since Tim had gone to the dentist and had teeth filled, capped, and cleaned, he smiled so much more often, so effortlessly, that it endeared him to her more than ever. He was definitely a work in progress. He had fewer scars from his early childhood years than Mark, but he was still a child adrift, without biological parents, anchored to Aunt Hannah in some ways, yet left to find his own way through the maze of a life divided by two cultures.

He had never stolen from anyone, but he had spent a few weeks in jail for repeated underage drinking arrests. Sometimes he talked of these things. At other times, he would retreat to that dark place, brooding silently for an entire evening for no apparent reason. The next day he would grunt to Sadie's "Good morning," wolf down his breakfast sandwich, and head out the door with his plastic cooler containing vast amounts of food. He'd return in much better spirits. Sadie just never knew. They talked about it, and Tim tried to explain it, saying he wasn't really angry, just tired of trying to be happy, in plain words.

"It's sort of like walking along a narrow road that's

slippery, and for a long time you can keep going, stay out of the ditch. Then you get tired and let go, fall in it, and stay there awhile. You know it's not good, that you can't stay there, but for a while it rests your spirit to remove yourself from everything."

Sadie shook her head. "But why?"

Mark's face was taut with suppressed emotion. "It's the remembering. It's the thinking back to times when life was a battle, when it took every ounce of energy to stay afloat, when circumstances were so overwhelming you will never, ever forget it no matter how hard you try. It's a scab you pull off repeatedly. It heals over, sort of, but sooner or later, you'll pull it off again."

Tim nodded, his eyes moist. "I probably had a much more normal childhood than anyone thinks I did. For one, I went to a one-room Amish school. Even if the children tried to make fun of me in any way, Aunt Hannah would report it, either to the teacher or the parents. So, in a way, I had that protection, which you probably never had."

Mark nodded agreement. "Still, there were good people. I remember the butcher on Second Street. He was a Jew. Had all those kosher meats. Different days they did different things. But he was good to me. He used to call me in if I stayed outside his windows, looking at the cheese and meats, my mouth watering like crazy."

Tim smiled.

Mark continued. "He used to give me a paper bag full of cheese rinds, pieces of little beef sausages, and a stack of dark brown rye crackers. His accent was so different I could barely understand what he said, but we'd communicate somehow. Sometimes he'd throw in a jar of pickled herring, and I'd eat them with mustard. He was a kind man, devoted to his stout wife and all their good-sized children."

Tim laughed. "At least they had enough to eat."

"Right."

Sadie could not begin to fathom the times of hunger, of not having the security of Mam and Dat, her sisters, the loving home. Yes, their family had problems, still had, but not without the foundation of God and good parenting. The path Mark explained was completely foreign to Sadie. That same evening they sat up late discussing the Amish church, the rules of the *ordnung*, the new birth, what was expected of Tim when the time came and he dedicated his life to God, accepted Jesus Christ as his personal Savior, took up instruction class, and was baptized into the church.

It was a long and serious conversation. Tim stumbled as he tried to explain what kept him from committing his life to God. The year of not being good enough, mostly. Mark told Tim how that had been the biggest hurdle for him as well. Grasping the fact that God loved him just as he was. That just blew him away. He explained the years of counseling, the difficulties after he met Sadie, his inadequacies.

Tim kept nodding, understanding. Then, "How's Anna?"

Sadie looked up sharply. "Why?"

Tim shrugged his shoulders. "It's been awhile since I heard anything."

"You think she's pretty bad?"

"Yes, she is. I'm not sure if my girlfriend was any skinnier when they hospitalized her."

A dagger of fear shot through Sadie. "You can't mean it."

Tim nodded. "She desperately needs counseling. Although ... I don't know. I learned a lot with my former girlfriend. If I could see her more, talk to her, I might be able to help her some."

"We can invite her over."

"She wouldn't come if she knew I was here." Tim kicked the table leg self-consciously, resorting to his usual sniffing.

"She might."

Then Tim lifted his head and asked a completely surprising question, "Do I have to change my life completely to be able to date…um…someone?"

"You mean follow the Amish way?"

Tim nodded.

"It's encouraged, but not every couple is a member of the church before they begin dating," Mark answered.

Tim kicked the table leg again, then left abruptly and went to bed.

The new veterinarian came out, prescribed a different antibiotic, and left, leaving a 200-dollar bill before driving off in his new red Hummer. Mark ground his teeth in frustration. Sadie bedded Paris with extra straw to relieve her feet from any hard surface. She felt as if her heart could break into pieces, watching Paris change positions painfully from one foot to the other, over and over, her head bent, her eyelids half closed as she patiently bore the excruciating pain. Wolf would enter the barn with Sadie, then whine and cry outside her stall, as if he wanted to help but was unable.

Mark talked to Steven Weaver, who said he remembered hearing an old remedy for foundering, but he forgot who said it or what it was. He'd write to his grandfather in Indiana. Richard Caldwell got on the Internet, his remedy for everything, but said he couldn't find any information other than what the veterinarians had told them.

Mark said he vaguely remembered the Jewish butcher on Second Street coming up with old remedies for animals, but for the life of him, he couldn't remember what it was.

Sadie brought apples and carrots, bits of cookie crumbs, even a few raisins, which Paris lipped off her extended palm halfheartedly, then turned her head away. Sadie even braided her mane and tail the way she did when she was a single girl at home. She braided a length of pink ribbon into the creamy colored hair, then stood back to admire it.

She would get better, wouldn't she? These antibiotics would work, surely. For awhile, it seemed as if they would. Paris was eating better, her eyes looking only a bit brighter, but definitely not clouded with the same pain as the week before. Sadie was ecstatic.

Anna came to check out Paris's progress, only to be completely struck when she saw this poor, sick horse sagging against the wooden slats of the stall's divider. Anna tried to contain her emotions, but the tears spilled over on to her pale cheeks. She looked over at Sadie beaming proudly through the door.

"She's getting better!" she announced confidently.

"Sadie! She's so sick! I had no idea."

"Oh, no, Anna. She's a lot better than she was."

And now Anna understood. She could not reach Sadie to tell her Paris was dying.

Was Anna the same? Sadie could not reach her to tell her she was starving.

Sadie was blind when it came to relinquishing her desperate hold on her horse.

Was Anna as blind when it came to seeing why she controlled her determination to be stick-thin? For Neil?

For that controlling person who hurt her over and over?

Anna's heart cried out for help, for herself as well as for Paris. I'm so stupid, God. Sadie is so pathetic, God. Humans are all pretty much in the same boat, aren't they?

When Tim came to the barn, he found two sisters holding onto each other as they grappled with the bitter struggles of their lives. He backed away silently, lifted the iron latch, and slowly moved through the door out into the biting cold.

Chapter 17

H E TURNED AS THE LATCH CLICKED AGAIN AND watched as Sadie stumbled through the door, then bent her head to gain momentum as she started running to the house, her only thought to be with Mark as soon as she possibly could. Tim waited, and when Anna did not appear, he turned back, hesitant at first, then decisively. He found her with Paris, a bewildered look in her eyes as she raised her head to find Tim watching her.

"She's not going to make it."

Tim nodded.

"Sadie will grieve terribly."

"Yeah."

Anna gave Paris a final pat, sighed, then turned, her eyes luminous in the flickering yellow light of the kerosene lantern. She stood, her arms loose inside the too-large sleeves of her heavy, black coat, her thick, dark hair too heavy for her thin, almost translucent face. She shifted her feet self-consciously, bit down on her lower lip, then, as if reaching an agreement, said his name too loudly.

"Tim."

"Yeah?"

"Do you think … do I … ?"

There was a long, painful silence as Anna tried to muster all her courage, her low self-esteem putting up a visible battle. She cleared her throat, jammed her thin, white hands into her coat pockets, then raised her head quite suddenly.

"Paris is going to die, right? There is no such thing as a miracle, right?"

Tim gazed at an object over her head. He would not meet those large eyes, so full of hope already lost.

"They're few and far between."

She nodded. She looked behind herself, then lowered her small frame to a bale of fragrant hay. Tim reached down and pulled another bale out, facing her as he sat down, his large hands on the knees of his jeans, as if he was unsure what he should do with them. Neither said anything. Truman scraped his halter across his wooden feedbox with a heavy rumbling sound. Duke snorted, a wet slobbering sound from the automatic water trough built between the two stalls. A black cat slunk along the stable wall, saw them, and quickened her slow creeping pace. The wind rattled a loose piece of spouting in a quick, staccato rhythm, then quieted down. Anna pulled a loose piece of hay out from beneath the baler twine, chewing it reflectively.

"You're eating," Tim observed dryly.

Anna looked startled, then caught the twinkle in his eye, her lips parted as she smiled timidly. "Guess I am."

"Feel free to eat the whole bale."

Anna laughed. The sound was new to Tim. It was the loveliest thing he had ever heard, a gentle, deep-throated, genuinely delightful sound from this frail, captivating girl. He had never heard her laugh.

She paused, tilted her head sideways, and said, unexpectedly, "Am I so thin?"

Tim searched for the right answer, took his time. "You're too thin, yes."

"How much too thin?"

"Hospital thin."

"No."

"Yes."

"You are not serious."

"Yes. I am dead serious."

"Well … "

Anna stopped, looked at her black, fur-lined boots, then lifted her head to find his gaze, kind, patient, and above all, understanding.

"I … sort of … back there with Paris, when Sadie stood there with all that false … believing … hope, whatever it was, making herself believe her horse was getting better, when in reality she's dying. I … Well, Tim, that's me."

She said his name! The most unique way he had ever heard it pronounced. Tee-yum. Oh, say it again, he thought. Please say my name again. But he said nothing.

"That's me," she repeated. "I have to stop forcing myself to throw up. I do it a lot. It's so repetitive, it's like going to the bathroom or washing my hands. Eat enough to suit Mam or Dat or Leah, whoever, feel like I weigh 300 pounds, wash dishes, slip away, and … and … well, it's easy to make your stomach obey after you get the hang of it. Am I out of control, do you think?"

"Sounds like it."

"I don't do it every time I eat something. Just mostly. I was dating Neil and he … he … He's really cute. All the girls wanted him. He likes his … girls thin, he said. I guess it was Neil's fault. I just tried to get too thin."

Tim shook his head. "Wasn't the guy's fault."

"Why not?"

"Your own, more than likely. You were trying to control him, yourself, your whole life, feeling if you were only thin enough, he'd settle down, quit his ways, marry you. Am I right?"

Anna nodded, the pain of hating herself contorting her beautiful mouth.

"He never loved you."

"He said he did!"

Her head came up, her eye's black with rebellion.

Tim shook his head.

Anna spluttered, searched for words, then dropped her head miserably.

"Sorry. Don't mean to hurt you. I had a girlfriend once who was probably about as thin as you. She was hospitalized. We almost lost her. She had to remain hospitalized, went for extensive counseling, nothing helped. She died."

Anna's eyes were very large and dark. Her thin hands came up to cover her mouth. "No!"

"Yes. She died so completely mixed up in her own world of suffering."

"Was she a Christian?"

Tim shrugged. "She was very young."

"Do you still love her?"

Tim said nothing.

"I miss her, I guess," he said finally.

"I won't die. I'll eat."

"You have to stop making yourself throw up first. Go for counseling."

"I'll ask God."

"You feel as if he'll hear you?"

Anna shrugged.

"Did you ever become a Christian, Anna?"

"Amish people are Christians always. From the time that we can sit on our Dat's knee and listen to Bible stories, we're Christians. We know who Jesus is and God and the devil, and the end of the world and hell and heaven. We're just sort of raised with all of it."

"Yeah, Aunt Hannah, the church, the neighbors, all of that, I know what you mean. But sometime, we have to go through that time of taking responsibility. We're lost, need a Savior. I'm about to start…thinking I need something…or somebody."

"You mean, get married?" Anna asked, innocently.

"No, I mean, I'm seriously thinking of giving my life to God. Repenting of my past life, accepting Jesus, that whole bit."

He could feel his face becoming warm. He felt ashamed, lowered his head, his hands hanging loosely between his upturned knees.

"Was your past life very sinful?"

"Yeah. It was bad."

"Then you need to go talk to Jesse Detweiler. He's one of the best ministers for the youth to talk to."

"Will you join the church if I do?" he asked boldly.

"I'm young."

Tim nodded.

"Why are you going Amish?" she asked.

He found her gaze, held it. She lowered her eyes first, a slow blush creeping up her cheeks.

"Anna, I was raised in the Amish church by my Aunt Hannah, a single, maiden lady. As small and round as a barrel, and rolling around her house, gaining momentum as the day wore on. She was a spitfire! Energy to spare. The house was immaculate, her garden a picture of tilled soil producing tons of vegetables. She'd yell at me for tracking mud into the house, for spilling juice, for everything. But she loved me fiercely. She'd fight with parents of kids who made fun of me, protected me. I had no Mam and Dat.

"It's Hannah who makes me want to come back. Everything about her life I want for my own. The peace she had. She'd rock on her front porch, listening for the whip-poor-wills behind the house in the mountain. She loved her birds, as she called them. Could tell the name of every bird she heard.

"She chewed people out when she thought they deserved it, but she'd go to their house with a huckleberry pie the next day. She loved God, said she couldn't die until I became a born-again Christian."

"How are you going to do that?" Anna asked.

"I don't know. I guess just tell God that I want to be a new person, accept Jesus, then go talk to Jesse Detweiler like you said."

"Some people have a very big experience, as if God is talking to them. Did you?"

Tim could tell that Anna was a very innocent, young Christian, not sure exactly how much she understood.

"No. I just have a sincere feeling about ... I don't know, I guess taking care of my soul."

"Good way to say it," Anna said, nodding.

Then, "Well, if you're going to become serious, then I guess I need to pray for help if I'm going to lean on God to help me overcome my ... What did you call it?"

"Bulimia."

"No, the other word."

"Anorexia."

"Yeah, that. You said I can't blame Neil. Why not?'

"Because he was not the one rebelling. You were."

"He was, too."

"You were."

She became very quiet then. So quiet, in fact, that he watched her face, afraid he had upset her.

Then, "I want to be like Sadie." It was only a whisper, but he caught it.

She stood up to get away before he saw the tears. He heard the sob that rose in her throat and stood up awkwardly, his arms hanging loosely by his side, watching intently as a tear balanced on her dark lashes, then slid quickly down her pearl-hued cheek, leaving a small wet trail, the most exquisite sight he had ever encountered.

He wasn't going to put his arms around her. He wasn't even going to touch her sleeve. Not even put a finger on the black wool coat. He just wanted to let her know it was all right to want to be like Sadie. It was okay.

What he did say thickly was, "Anna, I ... "

When she looked up, another tear shivered on her lower lashes, made another irresistible trail down her shadowed cheek, and he only wanted to feel the beauty of it. He reached out, one large fingertip tracing the wetness on the pearl cheek. He stopped tracing it, his fingers slid to her chin, and without knowing what he would do, lifted her face. Her eyes became dark and wide, her breath quickened. His eyes told her everything. They told her he was attracted to her, she was lovely, he wanted to be with her, protect her, love her to the end of his days.

Had she ever been kissed? Neil? Ah, but the Amish were strict about purity. Some of them. His hand fell away, the spell was broken. The strict rules had spoken. Still, they stood. Suddenly afraid she would go, he could not bear to part with her now or ever. He moved, pulled her close, held her shoulders, lowered his hands, and crushed the too-thin body to his, murmuring things he didn't know he said.

He remembered saying, "Stay with me, Anna, don't go. Please stay with me, here, now."

He wanted to say "forever." Her frail, thin fingers stayed on his coat sleeve, then, like a hovering butterfly and just as lightly, went up his sleeve to clasp his shoulders with a surprising strength.

Tim never understood the meaning of true love until he held Anna in his arms. He was shaken to the core of his being, the huge difference in what he had always thought was love and this tender caring, this passion to be a better person for her sake. He saw with new eyes the scepter of her love being held by the strength with which her arms encircled him.

Who let go first? It wasn't him. When they did, they smiled silly, crooked smiles, and both started talking at once, saying what they had wanted to say weeks ago. How good he looked with his dental work. How beautiful she was. How she couldn't help being attracted to him the first time she saw him. Even if she told him to go brush his teeth? When she became flustered, apologizing, he laughed, a sound so genuine she wasn't sure she had ever heard it before.

They talked most of the night. The kerosene steadily lowered by the small rectangular flame burning steadily inside the chimney, but still they talked. They decided people like Aunt Hannah and Sadie went on with their lives and never really knew the huge influence they had on other people. They were genuine individuals who were not perfect but had a kindness, a sort of goodness about them, like an aura of peace and calm that made you want to be like them. They cared absolutely.

They talked about Paris. They couldn't bear to think of Sadie parting with her beloved horse.

"Couldn't we drench her with some home remedy?" Anna asked, in a desperate voice.

Tim held very still, not even blinking.

Drench?

What was it about that odd word? He remembered it from somewhere? Was it Aunt Hannah? What was "drench"?

When the lantern sputtered, sending sparks up the glass chimney and creating a sort of film around the glass, they knew the kerosene had been used up. The night was over. They walked to the house in the bitter night, the sky black with another approaching storm, the earth still and sharp with the aching cold.

Suddenly shy, they thought of Mark and Sadie lying side by side in their big, cozy bed, creating an intimacy they knew was not theirs to have. They separated quietly, a whispered good-night their only parting.

In the morning the snow was already falling, thinly, but with the same drive that makes real storms start with a vengeance. Sadie was down at the barn trying to lead Paris out into the snow, thinking the soft coldness might reduce the swelling of the *laminae*, that soft tissue so painfully red and swollen, protruding down into the base of the hoof, causing severe pain. Sadie knew Paris was simply buying time. Some horses would already have stopped breathing. She was convinced it was Paris's will, that strong spirit, that kept her alive.

Whoever had stolen her, wherever they had taken her, had not been good, leaving her in poor health. Likely she had had a diet of corn, too much protein, or black walnut shavings as bedding. She may have had access to too much grain, which would have foundered her, then because of exposure and a poor diet had fallen into the dire case of laminitis.

Paris lowered her head, sniffing at the cement floor of the forebay as if to determine whether she had the strength to place her painful feet on top of it. Courageously now, she stuck a foot out, then another, the pain forcing her to place her feet quickly, lightly, as if she was literally walking on eggshells. Her back was bent, her haunches tucked in, as if to touch only the front of the hoof on the unforgiving concrete.

"Good girl," Sadie coaxed.

When they hobbled out to the snowy whiteness, Paris extended her neck, kept going bravely as Sadie led her in circles, something the last veterinarian had told her to try. But when her breathing came in short, shuddering gasps, Sadie could not bear to listen to the sounds of her intense pain.

Circling once more, she slid open the barn door. A lump built steadily in her swollen throat as she struggled to resign herself to Paris's fate. She could no longer dismiss the grim reaper on the horizon who would come to claim Paris. She looked up as the door opened and Tim emerged, poking his arms into his coat sleeves, pulling on his beanie sloppily, as if he had to be somewhere in a great hurry. She was puzzled, this being Saturday.

"Sadie! Sadie!"

It was Anna, racing after Tim. Incredibly, Mark emerged, pulling on his clothes with every bit as much haste.

"Sadie!"

"What is going on?" she asked.

"*Drench*! I remember that word! Aunt Hannah's neighbor—he drenched his horse with mineral oil! He said it purges the bad bacteria that causes laminitis. Cleans the stomach! Sometimes it works. Sometimes it doesn't. He cured Harry, his draft horse. He got laminitis from being too fat!"

Tim was shouting, the veins standing out on his neck. "What?"

"Mineral oil! Do you have any?" Tim was still shouting.

"No. Oh, my! No, I don't have any. Please, Mark, somebody! Go get some somewhere."

"Call a driver?"

"Fred Ketty's store?"

"Go to town?"

They quickly decided town was the most trustworthy. The driver was called, Anna riding to town to procure it while Sadie rubbed Paris down with clean cloths. Mark paced, unable to watch Sadie as she crooned over her beloved Paris, promising help. It seemed to take forever, but finally the four-wheel drive pickup came through the whirling whiteness, and with a glad cry, Sadie straightened and came toward them.

Together they worked, pouring the oily liquid into a long-necked drenching bottle, deciding Sadie would be the one to open Paris's jaws wide enough to allow the intrusion of the bottle to the back of her throat. Would Paris allow it? Some horses fought violently.

It was heartbreaking to watch Sadie, the intensity with which she massaged the neck, speaking to Paris as if she were human, explaining every step, telling her to be good and let this mineral oil do its work. Her white scarf circled her face, and she had never been more beautiful in the light of the gray, white storm outside. She had eyes only for Paris, unaware of those around her. Paris stood, thin, breathing hard, yet her coat shone from the constant brushing. Slowly Sadie cupped her chin, put gentle pressure on it, enough to lift the face. It would be easier to get the bottle down farther if she lifted her face.

"I need a stool. Or a bale of hay," she said tightly, the only way they could tell she was under stress.

Tim hurried to comply.

"Just hold the bottle, and when I say, 'Okay,' put it in," she said quietly.

Mark nodded, gripped the bottle till his knuckles turned white. Anna looked at Tim. He raised his eyebrows. Up came Paris's head. The horse barely resisted. It was as if she knew Sadie would make everything better. That, or she was so weak, she had no strength to fight against anything.

"Okay," Sadie said, evenly.

Mark held the bottle as Sadie's thumbs remained imbedded in the socket behind the jaw bone, enabling him to slide it into the well-opened mouth. They all watched, holding their breaths as the clear, oily liquid gurgled down the dying horse's throat. They heard the swallows, saw the neck muscles contract, then broke out in triumphant cheers of accomplishment when Mark extracted the empty bottle.

"She did it!" Anna cried, beside herself now.

"We'll try another bottleful if this one doesn't work," Sadie said. Mark looked at her, hiding the doubt he felt.

They all leaned on the stable wall watching Paris. When she groaned, then heaved, her legs folding under her, and she settled down hard, they rushed into her stall. Mark stood helpless.

Tim watched Sadie as she got on her knees beside Paris, stroking her neck, talking to her. Anna hid her eyes in her hands, peeping between her fingers. Sadie decided Paris would relax if they all left her alone for awhile, saying mares would foul best when left alone, so why wouldn't this be the same? That mineral oil could churn around in there by itself. They would go to the house and make waffles for breakfast.

When Mark put a protective arm around Sadie's shoulders on the way to the house, Tim jammed both hands into his coat pockets to keep them from going around Anna to protect her from the cold and snow and to keep her by his side as long as the world revolved on its axis.

Chapter 18

THE WAFFLES TURNED OUT LIGHT, PERFECTLY caramel-colored. They'd be slathered with soft butter and soaked in maple syrup. Anna fried small patties of sausage, swallowing her hunger, dreading the act of pulling up a chair to Sadie's table, inserting a fork into that lard-laden sausage and putting it to her mouth. Couldn't she just have a poached egg? Eliminate the yolk the way she did at home? Mam allowed it.

Mark manned the orange juice pitcher. Tim sat on the recliner, put up his feet, and said there was no use four people tried to make breakfast, three were enough. Mark set down the pitcher of orange juice, made a mad dash for the recliner, grabbed Tim's ankles, and pulled with all his strength. Tim yelled but was pulled across the glossy oak floor at an alarming speed, until they both crashed into the dining room table, dangerously rocking the orange juice pitcher, which brought a resounding "Hey!" from Sadie.

After "patties down," Anna took a small sip of juice, then shifted her fingers between the knife and fork, nervously trying to portray some semblance of normalcy. Sadie helped herself to a large waffle, topped it with an outrageous amount of butter, and called across the table for Tim to please pass the maple syrup.

Anna slanted her eyes in the direction of Sadie, who was swallowing as she lifted a huge forkful of waffle to her mouth, leaning over her plate to avoid the dripping syrup. Anna took a deep breath. Sadie stopped eating, reached over, and calmly picked up Anna's plate. She placed half a waffle on it, then dabbed on a small amount of butter and a drizzle of syrup. She cut a sausage patty in half, added a small amount of scrambled eggs, and plopped the plate back in front of Anna.

"Eat."

Anna looked to Tim for help.

"Go ahead, Anna. I would love to see you put on 20 or 30 pounds."

"Seriously?"

"Of course."

Slowly she inserted the fork and pulled away with a sizable chunk of waffle attached. Anna's hand trembled as she lifted it to her mouth, but she put it in, chewed, swallowed, and closed her eyes as she savored the taste. Tim smiled at her, the corners of his brown eyes crinkling exactly the way Mark's did. She never thought she would be able to do it, but she ate everything on her plate and wanted more. She sipped juice, then pushed back to go to the bathroom and get rid of all the lard-and-calorie-laden waffle. Then she remembered.

Paris was in her stable, struggling to stay alive, the mineral oil slowly churning in her intestines. Without its help, she would die. Without calories, so would she. She needed to talk to someone.

They all acted as if they weren't aware of her eating, talking and laughing as if she wasn't present.

Clearing her throat, she said, "I ate everything, Sadie."

Sadie looked, then put a hand on her shoulder. "Good, Anna. You know you can do this."

Nothing effusive, no big fuss, just sincere encouragement. And when Anna leaned over the commode and purged all of it, she was pleased that some of it stayed in her stomach, but also pleased that she had shown all of them who was the boss. That's what they got for acting as if they didn't care, the way they talked and laughed, ignoring her totally. Tim didn't care nearly as much as he let on. He never loved her. They had only just met.

That evening Sadie walked to the barn, her shoulders drooping wearily. The thing was, the mineral oil wasn't working. She had lost her temper at Mark when he said to wait to administer the other bottle till morning, telling him Paris would be dead by then. What was he thinking?

Tim was upset about something, and Anna had suddenly grabbed her duffel bag and gone home, as if she couldn't get out of there fast enough. So now Mark was pouting, averting his eyes, not going to the barn, and as usual, her whole world had gone black the minute she knew Mark's dark mood had descended.

Why, oh, why could she not learn to keep her mouth shut?

Paris was standing. That was unusual. Just when her hope soared, Paris grunted, heaved, her legs folded, and she rolled into a heap, then stretched out on her side, her breathing coming in hard gasps. Was it fair to allow an animal to suffer this way? In addition to her three infected hooves, her stomach was churning and roiling with the slimy mineral oil. She should be walked, which would help her digestion, but on those feet, it just was not feasible.

Opening the gate, Sadie lowered herself, then slipped Paris's head in her lap. This time she would be strong enough to say good-bye. She would call the vet in the morning, and she'd stay with her as he plunged that needle into her neck. The last thing Paris would feel would be Sadie's touch. She'd have to let go.

Paris heaved, her breathing labored, then relaxed, breathing more shallowly. Sadie stroked her neck, braided her mane. She put pink ribbons in it, then said good-bye.

"I have to go to bed, Paris. Mark is mad at me, which I'll just have the rest of my life, I guess. It's his way. Just so you know, you'll never be replaced. I'm never getting another horse as long as I live. It's only you, Paris. This is good-bye. I won't leave you in this pain after tomorrow. I love you, Paris. Good night."

One final kiss on the sunken eyelid, with tears raining down her face, she struggled to her feet, closed the gate blindly, stumbled out of the barn, slipped and fell into a snowdrift, then just sat there crying. Her whole world had never looked darker. If she hadn't married Mark and all his stupid complexities, she would have been a lot better off. Smarter for sure. She wished the horse thieves would have kept Paris. Why let her come home to put her through all this? She cried on.

Tim was in a foul mood the following morning, which was still pleasant compared to Mark. He drank black coffee and grunted instead of saying good morning, his nose stuck in *Outdoor Life*. Sadie decided she had nothing to lose and told him he'd be better off applying himself to his Bible to find out how to get over something.

She felt completely unpeaceful, her eyes swollen from last night's crying, her mind made up to call the vet, Sunday or not. They would pay the bill when it came in the mail. Crows were wheeling about the pine trees by the barn, which was a bad omen. Crows always gave her the shivers. Big, black with greedy eyes, stealing eggs from pretty birds' nests, they reminded her of harbingers of evil.

"Go away! Shoo! Get on out of here!" she shouted.

They merely settled on the top branches, opened their long, black mouths, and cawed fiercely.

Resigned to her fate, accepting the crow's bad prophesy, she opened the barn door. A repulsive odor, so strong it made her hand go to her mouth and nose, slammed into her senses. Paris would not have decomposed so suddenly in winter. Gasping, she slid back the bolt, her eyes adjusting to the dim light in the stall. An unbelievable amount of excrement lay steaming in the far corner of her stall. The stench was worse than anything Sadie had ever smelled. She looked at Paris. She caught her breath. Paris was up, still in pain, there was no doubt about it. But there was a difference. She was lipping her feed box, making that snuffling noise Sadie loved so much.

"Paris!" she cried.

As if in answer, Paris lifted her tail, hunched her back, and expelled a stream of foul liquid, sending Sadie gasping for air, the latch sticking stubbornly as she struggled to get out of the barn. How could one beautiful horse smell so disgusting?

Racing to the house, she flung open the door and stopped, breathless.

"Mark! Tim! You have to come see! Quick! It's Paris! She's making an awful mess. The mineral oil is working."

For a moment, she thought Mark was going to ignore her, but he dutifully laid down his magazine, shrugged on his coat, and walked to the barn. Tim followed on their heels.

"Sure enough!" Mark said.

"Pee-yoo!" Tim backed out the door, refusing to come back in.

Mark shoveled the odorous mess out the door, spread clean straw, lifted Paris's hooves, shook his head.

"Should we … give her more?" Sadie asked, lifting pleading eyes to Mark's face.

"I don't think so. Let's see how she's doing tomorrow."

Paris was chomping hay on Monday morning. Her ears were pricked forward, and she let out that soft, rumbling nicker when Sadie opened the barn door. Her hooves were still hurting, but not as badly. Mark lifted her feet and said he would put on four new special shoes to aid in the healing process. Sadie threw herself into his arms and kissed him so soundly he had to pick up his straw hat afterward.

"Thank you, Mark. You're too good to me," she called as she went out the door, hearing Jim Sevarr's pickup truck turning into the driveway. Her whole world had turned from a despairing blackness to this vibrant, sunshiny, color-infused day.

"Jim, she's better!" was her way of greeting.

"Aw, no! Ya mean it?"

Jim was so pleased he actually took the toothpick out of his mouth, rolled down his window, and threw it out before thinking what he'd done.

The ride to work was a joy. She prattled on and on, describing the whole emotional roller coaster to Jim, who promptly put on his dark glasses, saying that sun on snow was about more than he could handle, his eyes were getting old. But Sadie knew better. They all loved Paris.

Richard Caldwell said he'd heard about mineral oil.

He just figured it wouldn't work as long as she'd been sick. He warned her that Paris might never be the same; her hooves would always be a little iffy. Sadie said that was all right, she wasn't the young girl who raced around the field of wildflowers anymore either. At least she had Paris.

Dorothy rejoiced with Sadie the way a true friend will do. Erma Keim said her dad had a "Belgiam" draft horse that they had to put down. Foundered, he was.

Dorothy winked at Sadie, said the word was "Belgian," not "Belgiam," and they got in such a fierce argument, Sadie crept into Richard Caldwell's office and looked in his enormous horse book, then had to lug it all the way to the kitchen to show it to them both.

Of course, instead of being a gracious winner, Dorothy's eyes gleamed, and she let out a resounding, "Aha! Told you!"

Erma Keim ducked her head and acknowledged her mistake, leaving Sadie open-mouthed with admiration. My, what a change Steven Weaver had brought about!

Before the day was over, Dorothy told Erma it was a fair mistake, a lot of people said "Belgiam."

Erma smiled such a smarmy grin that Dorothy stayed suspicious all week. Until she found out Steven had proposed. Steven Weaver actually asked Erma Keim to be his wife. The wedding was only six weeks away, so they could move and have everything completed and tucked into their home before spring planting.

If Erma had seemed quiet and reserved before, tiptoeing about in all her righteous goodness, she was elevated to an almost angelic height now. She sang, hummed, and whistled. Her feet slid quietly along the floor, a sort of studied gait that made her appear to float a few inches above the linoleum. She took on every menial task that no one else wanted to do. She scrubbed, cleaned, peeled, chopped, all without complaint, until Dorothy took to calling her Cinderella, which sent her into hysterical giggles, finally saying yes, her prince had arrived. After much eye-rolling and sighing Dorothy told her to go peel some onions, marriage wasn't exactly living happily ever after, so get down off yer high horse. The whole kitchen was a delight.

Sadie helped Erma scrub the dining room floor. Together, on their hands and knees, Erma became very serious. "Sadie, do you think I'm too excited to be married to Steven?"

"No, Erma. I'm so happy for you. Of course not."

"But you're thinking things you're not saying, right?"

Sadie paused, then sat on the floor, throwing her rag into the bucket of warm, soapy water. "Erma, marriage is a good thing. I love Mark with all my heart and soul. But it can be tougher than anything you've ever encountered. Personally, I don't think it's fair to us young girls to read books that portray an unrealistic version of living happily ever after. It just isn't true.

"But then I live with a man who had a very unusual childhood, and he's flawed, although only sometimes. We have many good times, but it's not the way I always imagined it to be. I read so many happily-ever-after books, and I think for some people, it is almost true. But for me … I know we will always have our dark days."

"But … "

Erma lifted miserable eyes to Sadie's. Oh, my. Something personal. She hoped she would have the wisdom to deal with it.

"But … do his feet smell okay when he takes his shoes

off?" Erma whispered this, a bothersome question that had clearly bugged her for some time.

Sadie kept a straight face and told her Mark did not have a foot odor problem, thankfully. Erma rolled her eyes, then launched into a colorful account of Steven's foot odor, until Sadie's eyes were squeezed shut and she was holding her sides laughing.

"The poor guy!" she gasped, finally.

"Well, if it's all right, I plan on doing something about it. He's not going to sit in my living room with his feet propped on a footrest, smelling like a skunk."

"Talk to Steven about it."

"I can't. I'm afraid he won't marry me then. And I do so want to be Steven Weaver's wife."

When Sadie arrived home from work that evening, there was a message on the voice mail, Mam's speech hurried, breathless, saying they were coming over for the evening. She'd bring ingredients to make soft pretzels.

Mam dropped the bomb only five minutes after they arrived, when Dat was still out in the barn with Mark. Kevin and Junior had *both* proposed. But they did not want a double wedding.

"It'll get the best of me!" Mam almost wailed.

"When? When are they planning on getting married? Surely not both of them in one month?"

"No, but just as bad. One in May and one in June. You know Leah had planned on being married last fall, then Kevin's grandmother died and his mother was so sick with her arthritis, so they put it off, and here Junior pops the question. *Siss net chide!*" (It's not right!)

Mam threw her hands up helplessly, then got up and began tossing ingredients into a bowl, soaking yeast in warm water to make soft pretzels, talking as fast as she could. Sadie smiled to herself, knowing Mam would get through this. The way she handled stressful times was to work hard and keep moving constantly, planning, taking notes.

"You'll do well, Mam," she said, reassuringly.

"I'll go mental again," she said, softly.

"Do you ever feel that way?"

"Oh, my, no. I'm so much better. I just have to take my medication."

She said it so humbly, so gratefully, Sadie loved her more than ever.

Dat was full of news from the community. David Troyer was building a huge 40-foot by 100-foot shed and was planning on building storage sheds. He shook his head, wondering if it was wise, but then, you never knew if something would go if you didn't try. And David was a manager. Sam and Clara Bontrager had another little girl named Dorothea, but something was wrong with her heart. She had been flown to Bozeman. Dat asked, what was a young couple to do these days, with medical costs like that? They'd be apt to spend a hundred thousand, depending on the seriousness of the situation.

The Amish community was fairly new, so the alms collected at church would not be any significant amount, although they could always depend on other communities for support. Dat told Mark it was a wondrous thing, this *arma geld* (money for the poor) a blessing, for sure. No one would begrudge this young couple the help that was rightfully theirs. Mark told Dat that was one of the things that brought him back to the Amish. The sense of safety, the love of community, the protection that this love of fellow men really was, coming from the place he had been in his teen years.

The soft pretzels were buttery and salty, everything a soft pretzel should be. Mam flushed with the heat of the oven and Mark's praise. The kitchen was bright and homey, Mam and Dat both in good spirits at the prospect of being held in high esteem, having two daughters getting married in one year. That was really something, in Dat's book, Mam said.

When they smiled at each other, a song started somewhere in Sadie's heart, and she knew 30 years from now her marriage would still survive, become stronger, sweeping them along on the tides of time. God was still on his throne, same as he had been for Mam and Dat, and Mommy and Doddy Miller, and their parents before them. They would have their times of anger, pain, despair, but they were stepping-stones to the good times, when the love and trust were remembered, appreciated.

God had a plan for a man and a woman. A union that was perfect, bringing a blessing on the children, so their lives were sanctified as well. The husband gave his life for his wife (as Christ gave his for the church), doing things to make her happy, giving up his nature to love and cherish his wife. In turn, she was called to give up her own will, submit to her husband's, as the weaker vessel, which really was not hard if the husband stayed in his place, subject to God's will.

The perfect circle of harmony could be ripped apart if the wife rebelled against the will of her husband, or if the husband rebelled against the will of God. That sweet, loving circle of kindness and love could turn into a vicious circle of anger and pain, the husband struggling to be the loving provider he should be, if his wife nagged, complained, and belittled him, or if the wife rebelled against choices her husband made.

It all sounded so doable the day you became husband and wife, but to actually live day by day with another person was something else entirely. When the minister said we will have rainy days and days of sunshine, he was definitely skimming across the top, sort of like spying the top of an iceberg from the crow's nest. In actuality, it was much greater and deeper and darker than anyone knew. The thing was, people were people. They all struggled to be saintly, living for each other, but they couldn't always.

Amish marriages were meant to stay. Divorce was out of the question, a sense of duty deeply imbedded, as it had been for Dat and Mam. Their days were not perfect. Their time together was good, their lives blessed, but not without the occasional air of tension, Mam tight-lipped, Dat pouting, perhaps a major disagreement erupting at the dinner table. They both knew it was wrong, but it happened anyway. Still, the good times far outweighed the bad. With Mark, Sadie had definitely bumped into the iceberg, knew its width and depth, and respected it.

Take Paris's health. Why had Mark become so aloof? Pouting in his chair when he could have supported her so many times. It was as if he tried to turn a knob and make his life go away when a situation arose over which he had no control. The resentment boiled like a pot being carefully watched, but boiling nevertheless. She wanted to shake him, scream at him, make him see the error of his ways. Why sit there like a bump, an obnoxious sort of anger permeating out of his very head, even his socks, when he should have been in the barn with her, supporting, encouraging?

But no, all he could think of was himself, what a poor victim of cruelty he was. Then he blamed her for this laminitis. How could she take the blame, when quite clearly, it was the neglect Paris suffered while the horse thieves had her?

Shouldn't Mark be getting over the fact that he had a rotten childhood as he approached middle age?

Sadie's thoughts spun away as she listened to Dat, watched Mam's flushed face, and kept an eye out for Tim. Where was he? Sadie still wondered what had happened to make Anna leave so suddenly, and Tim looking like a volcano just before eruption.

Chapter 19

As if Tim knew she was thinking of him, he sauntered into the kitchen, sleepy-eyed, his dark, blond-streaked hair tousled, his T-shirt hanging over his Amish broad-fall denims. He was barefoot, something he would not have been when he first arrived.

He had been terribly self-conscious. His feet were always hidden, he had a shirt on, and he had that constant sniff, averted eyes, the hand going to his mouth to guard against anyone seeing his decaying teeth. He had eaten quickly, his eyes downcast, sliding in and out of his chair, very seldom adding to the conversation.

Now he smiled widely, a relaxed greeting, an affirmation of his state of acceptance. He was comfortable among them, which was a God-given miracle.

"How's it going, Tim?" Dat asked jovially as he upended the mustard container on a warm pretzel slick with melted butter.

"Good! Hey, you sure you need all that mustard, man?"

Tim was teasing. Dat accepted it good-naturedly, patted a chair beside him, told him he didn't know what he was missing. Tim lowered himself into it, bringing Mam like a magnet with a plate of pretzels and some cheese sauce. Did he want coffee or tea? Some deer bologna?

Sadie smiled to herself. Mam would always be the same. Her whole life, she had *fer-sarked* (taken care of) others. Bustled about, softly whistling, sweeping, cooking, cleaning, serving, seeing to her family. Everyone must be fed, have clean clothes to wear, a clean bed to sleep in at night, shoes on their feet, coats in the winter-time, the list went on and on. But she was happy doing exactly what she did best. Serving those around her.

Dat was telling Tim about Reuben's mishap at work, tumbling backward 12 feet off an aluminum ladder, landing in a snowdrift so deep he was afraid he'd suffocate instead of breaking limbs from his fall.

Tim's eyes sparkled, then he laughed a deep down, genuine laugh, thinking of Reuben floundering about in the snowdrift. In the short time they had known each other, they had discovered a shared sense of humor that had grown and escalated.

"Why didn't he come along over tonight?" Tim asked.

"Oh, you know. He's his own boss now, too old to ride in Pap's surrey. I think I heard him ask Anna to accompany him over, so I don't know if they'll be here or not."

Tim nodded and stayed quiet. There was a space of silence, not awkward, one of those comfortable silences when slurped coffee, the chewing of soft pretzels, a cleared throat, were only sounds of companionship, an evening inside a snow-covered house surrounded by pine trees, the white moon rising above them, creating light on the snow almost as plain as daylight.

The light hissed softly, then slowly turned darker. When a gas lamp ran out of propane, you weren't sure at first if it was your eyes or if the light was becoming dim. Soon though, you could tell as the light became increasingly insufficient.

Mam swiped a hand over her eyes. "Either I'm passing out, or we need a new propane tank," she announced.

"I'll get it," Mark said as he rose from his chair.

The door burst open, and Reuben and Anna literally spilled into the house.

"Where's the light?"

"We thought no one was here!"

Sadie hurried to light a few candles till Mark got the extra propane tank and the wrench he always used to change it. This was nothing unusual, only an evening enjoying candlelight until the tank was changed.

The candlelight, however, did nothing to stop the flow of words spilling out of Reuben's mouth. Anna stood beside her agitated brother, her eyes large with remembered fright, twisting the tassels of her cashmere scarf in thin, cold hands. Mark stood, the wrench in one hand, the propane tank in the other, forgetting the work he had been about to do.

"I mean it, you guys have no idea what we just saw!"

Dat licked the mustard off his fingers before remembering to use a napkin and said it couldn't be that bad.

Sadie motioned Mark to go ahead with the propane tank exchange, then wished she'd kept quiet when he glowered at her.

"Seriously."

Reuben paused, pulled off his gloves, took a deep breath, then launched into a colorful account of their trip across Atkin's Ridge with Charlie and the buggy.

"What I can't figure out is how could they have done this for so long, right under our noses?"

"What? Who? Done what?" Mark asked, as he squatted to open the oak door of the lamp cabinet.

"We were just driving along, Charlie slowing to a walk up the steepest part of the ridge road, when these two vehicles passed, and I mean, not just passed, but zoomed past, slipping and sliding, zigzagging, fishtailing, whatever you call it. They were flying! We no more than rounded the curve, you know, just before you get to the place where Sadie and … well, you know, where the buggy went down over, that night."

He looked at Sadie apologetically. She gave him a smile of reassurance.

"Just before you get to that steep place, these vehicles slowed and turned sharply into a space I had no idea existed. Their cars, well, one was a pickup, bounced up and down terrible. You'd think they'd have busted a tire. I had a feeling … I don't know. I asked Anna if she wanted to watch Charlie. She didn't. So we pulled off. You know the right side of the road has a big turn-off before that bank goes straight up?"

Sadie nodded.

"We tied Charlie to a tree, put a blanket on him. I told Anna I was going to find out what was going on down there."

Sadie shook her head. Mark told him he had more nerve than common sense. Dat said he was nuts. Mam said that about Anna.

Reuben ignored them all and went on with his story.

"It was rough going. The rocks and ravines, no road to speak of, and it was all covered with snow. There is a road, sort of, though. I don't know why we never noticed it before. Anyway, it goes way down, through the rocks, trees, an open field, then takes a sharp right. You have to cross a creek. It's frozen though."

Sadie was horrified.

"Reuben, what were you thinking? What about Anna? Suppose she would have fallen in? You could have been shot!"

"Oh, you're a good one to warn me!" Reuben shot back.

"Now, now." This was from Dat.

Mam shook her head.

"Am I allowed to continue or not?" Reuben asked, slapping his paired gloves on the table top.

Anna reached out and grabbed them.

"So these vehicles had already gone out of sight. They went the long way out around, but we sort of took a shortcut. We had to climb another ridge, then walk through the snow another, oh, I don't know, quarter of a mile through the trees. We couldn't hear a thing. Then all of a sudden, below us we could see the lights of the vehicles."

"And Sadie...!" Reuben was fairly vibrating with intensity. "You're not going to believe this. I guarantee it's exactly where Paris was! There were vehicles' lights shining, a trail of light, rickety metal gates sort of wired together, a rough shed open on one side, more like a lean-to. Some bales of hay, some rope, some rusted drums, you know, those old oil barrels, drums, whatever.

"We heard horses then. They came crashing through the trees, strained against the metal gates, and pawed the air with their hooves. You can hardly tell they're horses. Their hair is so long they look like donkeys. And skinny! Sadie, you couldn't stand it. They're so skinny they look like walking fossils. Some of them pawed the air, but most of them had already lost their spirit.

"They just stood there, their skinny necks hanging out, barely supporting their heads. Some men got out, pitched in a few bales of hay, and those horses went crazy. They fought, tore at the hay, but a few of them were so far gone they just stood there and...I don't even know what kept them on their feet."

Reuben's voice ended on a note of desperation, and Sadie knew if he was 12 years old, he would have cried. He was crying inside now, but he was too old to allow any emotion to escape.

The usually quiet Anna forgot herself and burst out, "It's awful. Seriously. There are at least 30 or 40 horses, and if nothing's done, they're all going to die. It simply makes no sense."

Tim watched her face and couldn't take his eyes off her.

"Two bales of hay, that was it. The hay disappeared in less than 10 minutes. I was shaking all over. The guys got into their vehicles and left. We just stood there. We didn't know what to do."

Reuben took over. "Finally, we went down. We got to the fence. The horses stand on frozen ground, their unshod hooves are cracked, bleeding. The burrs in their manes and tails, the filth, there's so much disease. If we do decide to help them, where do we start? Who do we call?"

Dat shook his head in disbelief. "We all thought the end of the horse-thieving had come. None of the Amish have had their horses stolen for a long time. Where do they come from and why? If they wanted to make a profit, surely they'd feed them better, care for them, and not hide them away like that."

Mark spoke up. "The first thing would be to call the police. They would know of any organization to rescue the horses."

Tim nodded, his eyes dark. "We have to do something. We can't let those horses starve." His eyes met Anna's, and she lowered hers first.

All talk of wedding plans, community news, or any other subject was dropped, forgotten, as the men planned the following day's activities.

They would call the police in the morning, meet at Dat's house, and proceed from there. They would need direction, not knowing the course that would need to be taken.

After the good-byes were said and the buggy lights turned left onto the main road, Mark came back into the laundry room, kicked off his boots, hung up his coat, and found Sadie washing dishes, Tim beside her with a dish towel, drying. She was telling him about the misadventures of the previous years, more animated than he'd seen her in a long time.

When she heard Mark's approach, she turned, her eyes glad to see him. They clouded over with bewilderment when she received only a scathing look, a back turned, his whole being telling her he disapproved of something. Immediately her voice died, she became intense, her dishwashing taken to a tremendous speed.

When Tim went to bed, he could tell Mark was not in a good mood, and he vowed to treat his own wife better. That guy had his times. Big baby.

But then...

Tim was like a fledgling bird, his wings not used to supporting his weight in flight. God was not an intimate friend; his Christian life had just begun. He stood by his dresser, running his hand over and over across the chest Sadie had given him to keep his deodorant and cologne, his loose change, keys, or whatever.

She was too good for him. He wished he'd met her first.

Ahh...no, he was too young.

But...Mark...

"Okay, God, I don't know for sure if you'll hear me, but you need to watch that Mark."

With that, he climbed into bed.

Sadie swiped viciously at the table top. Now what?

Well, she had had enough. Being submissive was one thing, but Mark was simply acting terribly toward her, and enough was enough. He could be so friendly, the life of the evening when Dat and Mam were around. But the minute they left, he continued his dark mood, which had been hanging around for days now, while she scuttled around like a scared rabbit trying to make his life better. This scenario was not working out.

It was going to take courage, but this would have to be dealt with.

Instead of heading for the bathroom and a long, hot shower she hung up the dishcloth, straightened the mug rack, and almost tripped over the rug as premature fears blinded her. Quickly she swiped at them before kneeling beside Mark's chair, reaching out and taking his magazine away, firmly placing it in the oversized crock with the others.

Mark looked up, surprised.

"Okay. What's wrong?"

"Nothing."

"You know there is."

"Just go away. Leave me alone. I don't want to talk."

"No, Mark."

"What?"

"This is not what I bargained for when I married you.

There are no instructions for your husband treating you with complete disdain. I think it goes beyond what the minister called a rainy day. It's more like a monsoon with hurricane-force winds."

No answer. A log fell in the stove, the sparks pinging against the glass front.

"What did I do wrong now?"

"Nothing."

"Then why do you hate me?"

The word *hate* got his attention. It was a strong word, one he would never have chosen to describe his feelings toward his wife.

"I don't hate you."

What had happened? How had it come to this? That day when Nevaeh lay sick and dying in the snow, the jays screaming in the treetops, hadn't her knees gone weak with…what? His perfect mouth, that cat-like grace with which he jumped down from the cattle truck. Could she ever remember that feeling? Here was this same person, the perfect mouth in a pout of self-pity, slumped dejectedly in his lair, that same recliner he always slouched in when he was in a bad mood.

Was love meant to be this way? Was it truly all her fault? She knew firsthand what it felt like to be heartsick. She was shaken when Mark sat up quite suddenly, slapped down the footrest of the recliner, grabbed the armrests but stayed seated. His face changed color as he spoke. Why did she remember the color of his anger when the words pelted painfully in a hailstorm of hurt?

"It's all about you, Sadie! You and Paris. You and Tim. You and Anna. That's all you care about. I mean tomato soup one evening, Cheerios the next. You don't care how my day went, you don't even ask. Tonight, when you

talked to Tim, you were happier than you've been with
me in weeks! You don't care that I come home from work
with my back aching from shoeing horses, you're too
worried about Paris or Anna or Tim. You don't love me;
you never did."

Somehow Sadie could picture her spirit being hit by a
flying object, blown off course, righting itself, and con-
tinuing.

"Mark, that is simply not true. How am I supposed to
smile and talk animatedly at length with a person who is
always blind to anything or anyone other than himself?
You walk around the house like an angry wolf, and in
plain words, I'm scared of you. All right, I confess. I have
spent too much time with Paris, and I do worry about
Anna. But … "

Suddenly she burst out. "How in the world would you
ever cope if we had a baby? Babies take much more time
than Paris ever did."

"Maybe that's why we don't have one. You don't want
a baby as long as you have Paris."

Sadie's mouth literally fell open in disbelief.

"Mark! Are you … jealous of Paris?"

There was no answer as he wrestled visibly with his
pride. Sadie sat back, watched Mark's face. When he lowered it into his hands, she held her breath. Muffled now,
his words came from beneath his fingers.

"Sadie, I'm jealous of everything and everybody
around you."

His words tumbled over each other then, dark muddy
waters that crashed around rocks, assaulting her ears. Pain
of his past. A mother who chose to leave with a stranger
rather than care for her children. Always, he searched
for her love. If he found a tiny morsel, it evaporated the

minute she left him alone with five hungry siblings, the
responsibility a life-sucking parasite he could never get
rid of.

Now, if he loved Sadie and she did not return it, the
only thing that kept the monster of failure at bay was
his anger. Anger slashed through failure and disappointment. It made people do what you wanted them to. If he
got no respect or attention, if Sadie didn't act the way he
thought she should, anger brought her around. It made
her submit. So he lifted his dagger of anger and everyone
straightened up, including himself. He didn't have to be
afraid of responsibility. Of feeling unloved.

Through his volley of words, Sadie shook her head
repeatedly, completely incredulous. How could she
explain? She understood, then, a vital part of living
with Mark. He did not have the solid foundation of
two parents' love for a child. Instead he'd been left alone
in a cold, filthy house with his needy, hungry brothers and sisters, watching his mother leave, succumbing
to the terror of responsibility and never being enough.
Having to put cherry Jell-o in Tim's bottle instead of
good, wholesome milk that a loving mother warmed in
a saucepan.

When Sadie talked and cared for others around her, he
felt left out and wrestled with falling down a deep dark
hole of discrepancy. The Cheerios. Cherry Jell-o. How
could she be so blind to his unending sense of loss and
inadequacy?

But he had been okay with it. Said he wasn't hungry. He had even smiled. She had offered a grilled cheese
sandwich. He waved her away, and she was glad, ran to
the barn, grateful. But...inside, he was churning with
resentment. It was her turn then.

She apologized for any wrong she had done, but warned him that using anger as a means of controlling her would not work. Yes, she was afraid of his pouting, more than she could ever explain. And, yes, it made her submit to him, but more out of fear than anything else, which in the end brought loathing.

"You know, Mark, when you lie in that recliner and pout, what I really want to do is hit you over the head with a broom and seriously knock some sense into you. But I have to realize, you're not normal."

Mark snorted, asked her what she meant by that remark, and she told him. The fat was in the fire now, she said, and kept right on going. A good hard thunderstorm clears the oppressive heat in summertime, and so a good long talk does the same in a relationship. They ended up at the kitchen table, dipping cold soft pretzels in congealed cheese sauce, making sandwiches of deer bologna, mayonnaise, bread and butter pickles, and onion, drinking the rest of the sweet tea, and talking some more.

They talked longer than they ever had. The clock struck midnight, the moon began its descent down the star-studded night sky, casting rectangles of ghostly light across the rugs on the oak floor, and still they talked.

Mark told her the worst part of his life was trying to overcome it, which clicked in Sadie's understanding. Excitedly, she told him maybe that was his whole problem. He couldn't give up. But he *had* to give up and accept his childhood. Stop trying to get away from it.

It had happened, through no fault of his own. Why God chose to single out one small boy to suffer in such a harsh way they could never know. God's ways weren't their ways. He could not blame other people now. Yes, they had done wrong. But it was over, in the past, and they were in God's hands. Not in Mark's hands. The past was over, as soon as he accepted it.

Tomorrow was Saturday, and they could sleep in. Sadie had a long, hot shower sometime after one o'clock, while Mark put logs on the fire, checked on Paris, and locked the doors.

As Sadie covered herself with the heavy quilts, her whole body ached with fatigue. It had been a long day, scrubbing floors with Erma Keim, having her parents visit, but far above all of it, she had the opportunity of taking a giant leap in the journey of understanding her husband.

When he came to bed, she asked him if he thought Tim would ever fall in love with Anna. When he laughed and said Tim had already fallen so hard he'd never get over it, Mark took Sadie in his arms and told her he knew the first time he saw her he couldn't live without her. It was like God's hand came down and used an enormous eraser, obliterating every hurt that had ever been between them. The beauty of a relationship was not in the outward show, but in transforming the dark valleys to new heights of joy and love, brought about by the ability to forgive.

Chapter 20

THEY DROVE TRUMAN TO SADIE'S PARENTS' HOUSE after a late breakfast, their necks craning to find the secret enclosure containing the horses. At one point Sadie thought she saw a pair of tracks but couldn't be sure.

They unhitched the horse, and Sadie slipped and slid along the walkway to the house, scolding Dat for his lack of work shoveling the sidewalk. She could have fallen. Wasn't he ever going to improve? He laughed as Mam welcomed her warmly, reminding her what a treat this was, being with her last evening, and here she was again!

"Can I go along to see the horses?"

"Guess you can ask Dat. Or Mark."

As it was, they all piled into the buggy to drive to the location. Reuben was acting as if he was the town hero until Anna told him to get down off his high horse. He was acting like a banty rooster.

There was no doubt about it—Reuben was on to something. When they followed him down the side of the ridge, over the creek, and up the adjacent hill, Sadie's heart was pounding more from excitement than the strenuous climb.

She watched Anna's face, afraid she would not be able to make it in her weakened condition. But there was a healthy flush in her face, her eyes were bright with excitement, and her gloved hand slid guiltily out of Tim's when Sadie turned to look at her.

And then she saw them. It was a concentration camp for horses. It was a scene of deprivation, heartlessness, and just plain cruelty. The horses stood in their long shaggy coats, pitiful sentries of death, calmly awaiting its arrival. Some of them milled about, snuffling the snow, lipping it as if it were nutritious.

They made their way down slowly. A cloud of disbelief led them over the fallen logs and debris. How long had these horses been here? How many horses had come and gone since this lean-to had been erected?

No one spoke at first as they absorbed the sadness. It was the same as when Nevaeh was sick. What broke Sadie's heart entirely was the calm acceptance of these animals, the way they patiently endured the hardships men inflicted on them. They existed in this squalor and neglect, living in the only way they knew how, to be obedient, grateful for the few bales of hay thrown to them on an irregular basis.

Dat spoke then. "It's enough to make you sick."

Reuben was talking, talking, but the words faded for Sadie. She saw the rib cages, the jutting hipbones, the poor bleeding feet, and then knew she was going to fall into the snow in a completely uncharacteristic faint.

The cold of the snow was a rude awakening. Mark bent over her, calling her name. Dat assured him it was all right, she'd come to. He could believe this was too much for Sadie, the way she loved horses and all.

Tim leaned on the heavy steel gate, extended a hand,

but the horses kept their distance, the whites of their eyes showing their fear.

Anna yelped, pointed with a shaking, gloved finger. "There ... beside the fence," she said softly.

They all turned to look and saw the gory sight of a freshly ravaged carcass, the bones protruding from the mass of unchewed flesh where the carnivores had eaten their fill, leaving the remains for a later snack.

Nausea overtook Sadie, and she stepped aside to deposit her breakfast neatly into the snow. A hand patted her back, and Anna said dryly, "I stopped doing that. Don't you start now."

Sadie wiped her mouth, then smiled. "I wasn't planning on following your example."

Mark was very attentive, searching her eyes, asking her if she was sure she could walk back to the buggy. She assured him everything was fine, but for the remainder of their stay she sat on a bale of hay and refused to look at the horses.

Anna sat beside her. "I quit *cutsing* (throwing up)."

"Really?"

"Yep, I'm eating, too. I ate a whole entire slice of bacon."

"One whole slice?"

"Yep. And one slice of whole-wheat toast."

"When did you decide to change?"

"I didn't. Tim made me. He said if I don't quit doing this, he was going to go back to New York."

"You don't want him to?"

"No."

Sadie closed her eyes as another fresh wave of nausea approached her senses. She just wanted to leave. Get away from this sadness, these poor creatures. It was more than she had bargained for. She should never have come.

Later they called the police and Reuben escorted them to the location. Dat told him it was all right to do that, but he was not supposed to talk to reporters or have his picture taken. The ministers had warned strictly against it. They had hoped all this publicity would stop after the horse thieves had been arrested and sent to prison, so Dat was very stern with Reuben, who, he knew, was much too fond of the limelight to begin with.

So when Reuben's full length picture landed on the front page of the local paper, along with members of the Humane Society and the police officer, he had an awful time explaining it to his father. But, as usual, he talked his way into Dat's good graces, was forgiven, then had the audacity to tell Sadie he thought he looked pretty tall standing beside that officer, and how did she like the way he wore his beanie low like that?

Sadie began waking up at night, crying out, covered in cold sweat. She had never experienced nightmares like this, even following her accident. When her nausea persisted, Mark became extremely concerned, but she assured him it was only the flu and nothing to worry about. She'd just have to get the whole scene of those starving horses out of her head.

How had Paris ever managed to escape? Sadie was convinced she had been there, her emaciated state being a dead giveaway. She would have been close enough to her home that she would have been ferocious in her will to escape. Over and over, Sadie mulled this subject, playing out one scene after another. She imagined Paris running at breakneck speed, and, in desperation, clearing that fence at the last minute. That terrible, rusted, filthy gate.

She shuddered as she leaned on Paris's gate, watching

as she lifted a right front hoof daintily, as if to remind Sadie that she was healing nicely.

"Yes, I know. You're a royal wonder, Paris. All you need is a tiara, and you'll be the princess you think you are."

She turned, her ears tuned. What had she heard? Someone calling her? Quickly, she stepped outside, looked up and down the driveway and toward the house, but the sun shone on the snow with blinding intensity, so she ducked back into the barn, shivering from the cold. She swept the forebay and was reaching up for the small canister of saddle soap, when she heard it again. Voices.

Then a pair of boots hung over the ladder that went to the haymow, followed by denim trousers, which turned and crept down the ladder, followed by black, fur-lined boots.

Tim! Anna!

When Anna completed her descent, she was holding her right arm close to her body.

Tim said, "Hey, Sadie. What's up?"

Anna looked at Sadie completely guileless, as innocent as a child. "Look. I knew your Mama Katz had kittens somewhere."

Sadie was furious. "What were you doing in the haymow? Anna, why are you here this early in the evening, and Tim, why aren't you at work?"

They were completely taken aback, surprised at Sadie's suspicion.

"Come on, Sadie. Grouch. Look at these kittens. Can I keep them after they are weaned?" Anna begged.

"No."

Tim frowned, watching Sadie's face. He couldn't believe the mood she was displaying.

"Hey, just calm down. Anna wanted to look for these kittens last week already, and I promised her the first Tuesday I'd be off early, I'd help her, and today it worked out. Why does that make you so angry?"

"It doesn't."

And then because they just stood and looked at her, she began to cry, slammed the barn door, and went to the house. Someone had better tell that couple what was proper and what was not.

When the nausea worsened, the moodiness increased. Mam figured it all out, telling her she honestly thought they would soon be grandparents. Dat grinned behind his paper, Leah and Rebekah whooped and giggled and ran around the table, hugging each other with sheer excitement.

Reuben grumbled and told her in no uncertain terms that he had been right. What else could she expect, getting married the way she did, just out of the clear blue sky? Now he was peeved at this improper celebration.

When Sadie found Mam's predictions to be true, she was scared, excited, flustered, and caught completely off-guard.

When she told Mark, after Tim had gone upstairs, he took a long, deep breath, tears came to his deep brown eyes, and he said there was no way he could express his feelings just then. He held her in his arms with a new tenderness, almost a sort of reverence, and told her this was the happiest day of his life, besides the day she promised to become his wife.

He got his coat and went outside. He didn't return for a half hour or more, and when he did come in, his eyes were swollen, although he kept them hidden whenever he could. He soon showered and went to bed, which was puzzling to Sadie.

During the night, the bed shook with the force of his sobs till Sadie lit a kerosene lamp and forced him to look at her. She saw all the emotions in his dark eyes, a roiling mass of joy, pain, remembrance, hope, resolve, and she knew he was letting go, bit by bit, of his self-hatred.

"If God lets us have a child, he must think I'll be an okay sort of dad, don't you think?" he asked.

The humility in his voice was unbearably sad. Was this, then, how low his self-esteem really was, as he made his swashbuckling way through life much too often? She assured him this was so true, and it was wonderful of him to think along those terms.

Dorothy was not pleased, making absolutely no effort to hide this fact. She fumed and scolded, asking Sadie what she was thinking, and just who did she figure would take her place helpin' in the ranch kitchen. Huh? Just who?

Erma Keim was taken by surprise at Dorothy's reaction, so she said nothing.

Sadie went to work, slicing the cooked potatoes for home fries, then smelled the raw sausage Dorothy was shaping into patties for frying, gagged, swallowed, and made a desperate dash for the bathroom.

Dorothy brought her a cup of hot ginger tea with two teaspoons of sugar in it, saying, "Drink this. Put some peanut butter on these saltines. Eat 'em."

Sadie knew she'd come around, although grudgingly for awhile yet.

"You won't be able to be table waiter at my wedding!" Erma hissed when they were away from Dorothy.

"Yes. Yes, I will. I won't always be nauseated."

Work in the ranch kitchen became a challenge, then an unbearable drudgery, as her nausea worsened. She only had to smell the dish soap and her day was ruined. She finally told Dorothy if she fixed her one more cup of ginger tea she was going to turn it upside down on her head, and Dorothy became so insulted she didn't speak to Sadie the remainder of the day.

Then they found out about the horses. Richard Caldwell exploded into the kitchen, his face ashen, his mustache bristling with indignation. It took a long time for Sadie, white-faced and trembling, to explain in full detail Reuben's suspicion, his discovery, the resulting visit from the police, the professional individual who knew exactly which steps to take.

There was a huge article in the paper with the news, Richard Caldwell said. Why hadn't he known it was Reuben? The Amish had some strange ways. And he should have known Sadie would be in the thick of it, the way she always was.

He did not say this unkindly, but it hurt Sadie somehow. Richard Caldwell was a good man, devoted to his wife, Barbara, and their young daughter. He had always treated Sadie with respect after he learned to accept the ways of the plain people. Why this frustration now?

He told her, then, that he still worried about her safety. Clearly this ring of horse thieves was not giving up. The jail sentences had been handed down to the guilty individuals, but a remnant of them was bolder than ever. It made no sense whatsoever.

Sadie bit her lower lip and tried desperately to keep from crying. Richard Caldwell eyed her still face, then asked if there was anything at all she found unusual about the gates, the lean-to, the animals themselves.

Sadie shook her head. "But, then, I…don't want to admit it, but I passed out. Fainted. It was…too much.

I don't remember much, besides, perhaps the snow, the carcass."

Richard Caldwell nodded.

"I still think you need to bring Reuben to the ranch. I need to question him and your sister, is it Anna?"

Which was why they accompanied her to work the following week. They were to have an interview with Richard Caldwell, the three of them.

Reuben grumbled the whole way. He was perturbed, having to leave Dat with too much concrete work in the basement of a log home they were building. Anna didn't mind a day off work, and Sadie was feeling too sick to care either way.

Signs of approaching spring were in evidence, the way the snow was creeping away from the fence posts. Patches of gray shingles appeared on roofs where the snow had been blown to a thin layer. Water dripped off the spouting as the sun became a bit warmer each day.

The ranch had grown and added buildings every year. It was still beautiful. Sadie loved the handsome brick ranch house surrounded by well kept shrubs and trees, tended lovingly by Bertie Orthman, the master gardener.

Sadie knew, however, that her work days at the ranch were numbered. In the near future she would spend her days at home doing laundry, cooking, baking, keeping her home clean, making their own clothes on her treadle sewing machine, following the footsteps of Amish mothers all over North America. They did not work outside of the home, unless necessity demanded it. Like Fred Ketty, they might start a dry goods store or a greenhouse, perhaps a small bulk food store, but then when a baby was born, they spent their days at home, caring for the child, making do with the money their husbands provided.

Sadie embraced this future; she was thrilled by it. She loved the ranch, especially Jim and Dorothy, but there was a time for everything, in Dat's words. She was ready to devote her life to Mark and their children, the years coming like gentle waves lapping at the sands of time, living her life the way Mam always had.

There would be quiltings and sisters' days, shopping trips, frolics, and school meetings, all patches of the quilt, sewn securely, forming the essence of the community. The people would rejoice when they became first-time parents, bringing food, visiting, plunking baby gifts in Sadie's lap.

Dorothy would come, too, and Richard Caldwell. They would remain friends, but the ranch and its activities would slide into the distance, a memory to be examined time after time. It was the way of it.

When Richard Caldwell ushered them into his office, Sadie kept close to Anna, who looked as if she was being taken to the gallows, her face pinched with fear.

"It's okay," she whispered at one point.

Reuben, of course, who had reached the maturity of 16 years, walked resolutely into the office, his hands in his pockets, his neck craning as his head swiveled constantly, taking it all in—the massive oak beams, the taxidermy, (a mounted bighorn sheep, Sadie!) the huge flat-screen TV, all things he saw in the ads from Lowe's or Home Depot that fell out of the daily newspaper. But to see a television of those dimensions protruding from the wall like that was truly unbelievable. He'd never imagined them to be that big.

And when Richard Caldwell turned it on to show them the news reports he had recorded, Reuben was glued to his chair, his eyes never leaving the screen.

"Watch closely now. Isn't there anything that seems

unusual to you? I mean, this thing is chewing on my nerves. It can't be just about horses. Why horses? If you're going to steal them, shoot them, mistreat them ... "

His voice trailed off as he shook his head in frustration. He recovered when an image of the carcass flashed on screen, the pitiful bones swelling up from the snow.

"I mean, look at that. How can you make sense of it? Why steal horses if you're not going to make a profit?"

They had no answer. Not Reuben, either.

They watched the different scenes and news reports. Sadie shuddered, wishing it would stop. She felt a thin elbow in her side and turned to find Anna, her eyes huge in her thin face, pointing at the screen with shaking fingers.

"What?" Sadie whispered.

Richard Caldwell was quick to notice the disturbance. "Speak!" he ordered.

Anna obeyed, her voice gathering strength as she spoke. "The ... dead horse? The head, lying in the snow. I noticed the day we were there. The dead horse has no halter. And ... I thought it seemed weird that every horse, no matter how thin and sick, all wore an expensive leather halter, the leather, the straps, extraordinarily wide and thick. But who removed the dead horse's halter? And why?"

Reuben sat upright, his eyes wide with understanding. "Yeah!" he burst out. "I thought about those halters, Anna. But I figured it was people from a wealthy stable. Like the place the horses were taken from was a ranch like this and all their horses wore those halters."

Anna nodded agreement.

"But still, those halters aren't worth that much. Why not remove the halter? Why are they all wearing them?"

Richard Caldwell nodded, his eyes sharp, observing Sadie's face. "What do you think?"

He had respect for Sadie's opinion, having been involved in the episodes that had occurred from the very first.

Sadie shook her head. "Would it be worth trying to find a horse? See if you can examine the halters?"

Instantly Reuben was on his feet, his hands waving, as he told Richard Caldwell he bet anything those halters were made of some expensive substance and were worth a few thousand dollars apiece.

Sadie cringed when Richard Caldwell stroked his gray mustache, his eyes twinkling, hiding the smile that wanted to form.

Sadie knew Reuben was just being Reuben, completely carried away by his own enthusiasm, his guilelessness making him blurt out any nonsense, a man of the world like Richard Caldwell seeing straight through him.

"It would be worth a try."

Sadie exhaled with relief.

"Hey, you know those Chinese? What were they? Japanese? Those people whose horses were shot? You remember? We had a benefit auction for them? They got one!"

Reuben was shouting now, but it was no louder than Richard Caldwell's own booming voice.

Dorothy glared out the kitchen window, washing celery at the sink, wondering where that Sadie was traipsing off to now, riding around in the boss's diesel pickup that way? She told Erma Keim to come look, and Erma said it was likely none of their business. Dorothy said it was, too, her business. Sadie going off like that without her lemongrass tea and peanut butter crackers. She'd fall out of the pickup in a dead faint, and then what? Her well-kept secret would be out, the boss would know and make her quit her job. Then where would they be?

Erma Keim told her she'd be nauseated, too, if she was given a cup of lemongrass tea every morning, and didn't she know Sadie only drank that vile brew to please her? Dorothy said if she didn't know anything about tea it would be better for her to keep her mouth shut, so Erma did, for the remainder of the day, the fear of losing her flesh and blood blessing named Steven Weaver, a very real fear in her life.

Chapter 21

THE DIESEL TRUCK STOPPED AT THE BARN, THE vehicle's occupants spying the small, lithe form in the barnyard—a horse on a long rope loping in a relaxed circle around its owner.

The barn was small, old, but in good repair, the long pieces of sheet metal replaced with a newer variety, shinier, but with the appearance that someone cared about the place. The small ranch house was covered with new gray siding, the shutters black, a new oak-paneled door on the front. There were curtains in the windows, a tidy front porch containing only a snow shovel and a stack of firewood, neatly piled along the left side of the door.

An older pickup truck was parked beside a four-wheel-drive SUV that was also not a recent model, but it was clean and well kept. Two dogs came loping out of the barn, their tails wagging, their barking friendly.

The girl in the barnyard pulled the horse, a lean appaloosa, to a stop, then turned to lead him into the barn as they all stepped out of the truck. Effortlessly, she climbed over the fence, a weather-beaten one but in good repair, her hair tied back in a ponytail, hatless, her ears red with the cold. Her flat, dark eyes in the flawless face shone a welcome as she reached down to hush the dogs.

"Hello!" Richard Caldwell's voice never failed to take strangers by surprise. It was just so strong, so powerful. He put out a huge hand, swallowing the small gloved one. "Richard Caldwell from Aspendale East."

The girl nodded, recognizing him.

He turned. "Jacob Miller's kids," including them all with a wave of his arm.

They smiled their acknowledgment, voiced their greetings politely. Richard Caldwell told her their mission, and was it true that her family had been given one of the stolen horses?

"Doo!" Proudly, she held up two fingers.

"You got two?"

She nodded and motioned for them to follow her. The barn was well lit, smelling of fresh shavings and the molasses in the horse feed. Sadie never tired of that good, pungent odor. There was no one else at the barn, she informed them. Her parents had gone to work at their restaurant in town, but her brother was at home, coming to exercise the horses as soon as he finished his schoolwork.

"Home-schooled?" Sadie asked.

"No, no. Medical studies. Home for short time."

Sadie nodded. Hardworking, so industrious. An admiration for this family made her heart glad. Many immigrants, people seeking better lives generations before, were what made this country so good. An undeserved blessing, she thought.

The horse was brought out. Still undernourished, his neck so thin, the hairs long, every rib visible. He snorted, the whites of his eyes showing as he tossed his head in fear. Sadie had to hold her hands behind her back to keep from reaching out and stroking that thin neck, to try and calm this animal that remembered too much.

The halter was not there. Reuben caught Sadie's eye. She shook her head. The horse was wearing a blue nylon halter, a typical, ordinary one bought at any animal supply store.

Anna could not be patient.

"Was … Is this the halter the horse was wearing when you received him?" she blurted out much too eagerly.

Innocently, the girl shook her head. "Oh, no! Leather. Much doo 'eavy!"

She walked to a cupboard, opened it, and took down a brown leather one, which she handed over for them to examine.

Richard Caldwell lifted it up, turned it around to the light. His fingers felt along the leather, the side panels, the chin strap. He rolled the thick leather between his thumb and forefinger, his shaggy eyebrows drawn down in concentration. Suddenly, with urgency, he asked for a knife.

The girl ran to the adjoining shop, returning with a retractable utility knife, which Richard Caldwell grasped firmly. His eyes intense, he lowered the halter to the floor, grunting as he got down on his knees. Instantly, Reuben and Anna followed, as Sadie's eyes met those of the girl's.

"Your name? I forget," Sadie offered.

"Kimberly See. Kim," she said, smiling.

Richard Caldwell was slicing expertly along the seam, severing the heavy thread that held both pieces of leather together. A strangled cry emerged from his throat, followed by words Sadie had never heard him use. Reuben whistled. Anna gasped. Sadie bent to see.

A small trickle of … what was it?

"If these ain't diamonds, I'll eat my hat," he ground out, a visible tremor in his hands now.

Sadie could feel her heartbeat in her temples as she saw the trickle of whitish-blue objects hitting the concrete floor of the barn. Reuben whistled, then looked over his shoulder, as if already the thieves knew they had stumbled on their secret. Anna remained quiet, which was her way, keeping strong emotions to herself. Sadie had to know why.

They all began talking at once. Kim See was genuinely alarmed, asking them to call someone, anyone, immediately. She would not be going to prison, would she? Reuben must have felt such a genuine sympathy that he assured her no one was going to prison, everything would be all right, obviously savoring his moment of being a hero in her eyes.

Kim gave the second halter to Richard Caldwell. It contained a dark red jewel, spilling out like fractured frozen blood clumping on the hard barn floor.

"We need a bag. A pouch." Richard Caldwell said, urgently.

Kim ran off as lightly as a deer, returning with a Ziploc bag. Carefully they scooped the glistening jewels into the plastic bag and handed it to Richard Caldwell, who ran his fingers thoughtfully along the closure.

Sadie stood back, deep in thought, remembering a time in the Caldwell's bathroom when she was depositing the ragged garments into the laundry chute. Marcellus and Louis. Those dear children who had shown up at the kitchen door dressed in filthy clothes, carrying a bag from a designer shop, a bag with a small drawstring pouch of jewels. Why jewels? Was there a connection?

"It was too far out," she said aloud.

When they all turned to listen, Sadie realized she had spoken out loud, then told them about the blue drawstring bag.

Richard Caldwell nodded, then shook his head. "It does seem crazy, but... "

He seemed to connect his train of thought, then, saying they'd take these to the police station, assuring Kim that everything would be fine. Her family may be questioned, and of course, they'd have the media to deal with, but she was not to fear anything. She nodded soberly, her eyes wide, waving as they made their way to the truck.

Richard Caldwell took them all home for the day, telling them he had a feeling this was the beginning of the end. Justice took awhile, he said, but there was far more to this than horse thieving.

Lots of questions rolled through Sadie's mind. Why didn't the horse thieves take better care of the horses they had stolen? Maybe they were thrown off track when they discovered jewel-packed harnesses, Sadie reasoned. Greed makes people do crazy things, she thought, trying to imagine the mind of a horse thief.

She wondered if maybe they had a disagreement among themselves, remembering how panicked the fat man became while he was guarding her in the mansion. Maybe some thought the horses were more valuable and others got carried away by the glittering jewels. Dumb stuff happened when people grabbed things that weren't theirs.

Sadie could not face the day at home alone, so she got off with Reuben and Anna, exploding into the kitchen the way they had done as children, all three of them talking at once.

Mam had just put on her glasses, thankfully sinking

into the soft, brown recliner with *The Budget*, the Amish newspaper she hadn't had time to read all week. She had planned on a long wonderful nap, covered with the blue fleece throw Sadie had given her for Christmas. She hadn't even opened the newspaper when the diesel truck wound its way up the drive, three of the children (as she still thought of them) tumbling out and crashing her peace and tranquility. It was motherhood, she thought, as she reluctantly laid down the paper, folded the throw, and stood to face whatever had them all in a dither now.

They ate hot dogs slathered in ketchup and mustard, piled chopped onions on top, drank tall glasses of orange soda, and munched piles of potato chips. They all agreed it was the best, most unhealthy meal you could think of, especially rounded out with a huge slice of Mam's fresh chocolate cake spread with caramel icing, a small river of fresh creamy milk poured over it.

Mam said she had eaten after doing laundry, and Anna ate mostly ketchup, mustard, and onions on half a roll. But it was home, where you could say anything and everything you wanted, and you didn't need to worry about offending anyone or being responsible for black moods. Everyone laughed about the same thing, and you could punch someone if they said something wrong. They could punch you back the moment they felt like it.

They talked endlessly about the horses, the jewels, the what-ifs, the might-have-beens, adding, embellishing, but always coming back to the basic truth. It was a ring of horse thieves to begin with. It was bigger, now, as Richard Caldwell always knew it was. Reuben said he was a smart man. Anyone that owned a ranch that size was plain down brilliant. Or lucky. Maybe both.

Sadie told him Amish people wouldn't be allowed

to have a ranch that big, which Reuben corrected, saying they'd likely be allowed, they just wouldn't have the brains to do it.

"Fred Ketty would," Anna observed dryly.

"She'd be way too lazy," Reuben said, stuffing another potato chip in his mouth.

"Now," Mam warned.

Being called lazy was not allowed within Mam's earshot. Folks were relaxed about their work, which was not always a bad thing, being talented in other areas of life, and no one was to judge. Some of them who hurried and scurried their way through their work, living in immaculate homes, may be missing the roses along the way.

"But, Mam, Fred Ketty's store is a mess. She needs a *maud*," (maid) Anna said.

"Why don't you apply?" Reuben broke in, wagging a finger.

"Oh, no, I think Richard Caldwell will be asking for Anna to take my job this summer," Sadie spoke up. "She'd be perfect, working with Dorothy and Erma Keim."

Turning to Anna, she said, "You'd listen to them and never say a word."

"I won't work at that ranch. It's much too scary. Richard Caldwell reminds me of the giant I was always so afraid of in Jack and the Beanstalk. He even looks like him."

Sadie burst out laughing, then related a vivid account of the Pledge furniture polish bottle flying out of her hands when she started her job at the ranch.

Reuben said he was going to start shoeing horses with Mark, and Mam said, oh, no, he wasn't. Who would help Dat? And Reuben said that was the whole trouble with being Amish, so much emphasis on being obedient, and if you were English you were allowed all kinds of choices. Mam snorted and told him quite forcefully that English children were obedient, too, that they just naturally had more choices in their world.

Reuben went upstairs to his room. Sadie remembered the exact same feeling. At 16 you were pretty sure the whole world was full of people telling you what to do, and you were a pitiful victim of abuse, which was laughable now.

At home that evening they lingered around the table, discussing the day's events. Mark and Tim were incredulous. Tim said it was like a television show; Mark said they wouldn't know.

"It's not a part of our lives, remember?' he said sternly.

Sadie looked up from her plate of green beans and ham, surprised to see her young husband display such harsh judgment. His face was inscrutable, so she shook off the feeling of consternation, changed the subject, and let it go.

Her life with Mark was full of uncertainties. She was often left guessing what he meant, and to dig for answers was not always the best, often resulting in frustration and a sense of being left outside a barred door and being too dumb to know where the key had been left the last time.

Sometimes, trying to figure out his feelings, she discovered things about herself in the process. She did not always have to know. Just forget it, you can't understand, she'd tell herself. Until the next time.

The news swept across Montana and way beyond. The Amish community stayed out of it as much as possible, except for Reuben's picture on the front page, his beanie lowered thankfully almost to his nose, eluding Richard Caldwell even. Sadie read articles in the paper, the half-truths as well as genuine ones.

The law was busy, the way it sounded, but events of this scale took time and patience, so life went on. People lived their lives the way they do, going about their work and events, putting the horse thieves in the background until another article was printed in the paper.

Erma Keim's wedding was only two weeks away now. Sadie was eagerly looking forward to being a table waiter with Mark, her handsome, complicated husband.

She made a new dusty purple dress, the color and fabric Erma had chosen for her table waiters. She spent many hours at the sewing machine, getting the dress just right, using a wet handkerchief placed on the fabric, pressing it with the sad iron heated on the front burner of the gas stove in the kitchen.

She traveled to the town of Butte to buy Erma an expensive sheet set and bought a drip coffeepot from Fred Ketty, who informed Sadie it was the single most brilliant non-electric appliance anyone had ever come up with, saying she never had a bad cup of coffee since she owned one. Sadie laughingly told Fred Ketty she was going to miss Erma Keim terribly and planned on having coffee with her on a regular basis, before realizing she had almost given away her secret.

Her eyes narrowing shrewdly, Fred Ketty asked, "Why?"

"Oh, I…I…She'll likely be quitting at the ranch," Sadie answered, completely flustered.

"But you don't know."

The eyes behind the plain glasses bore into hers, until Sadie was every bit as uncomfortable as a guilty person at a cross-examination. She exited the store as soon as she possibly could and vowed never to go back until the news was out.

No doubt about it, that woman was one shrewd person. If you forgot Mam's words about judging someone, her store could be much better if she put more physical labor into it, which sounded better than the word "lazy."

Jim and Dorothy were invited.

Dorothy was in a stew, buying a new dress at Sears for herself and one for March, as she had taken to calling Marcellus. Dorothy was never able to pronounce the name properly, often saying Marcelona. Jim had a good Sunday suit, and Louis was fitted into one last fall for Sunday school, so he could wear that.

She was worried about the seating arrangement, saying there was no way she was going to sit on a hard wooden bench for three hours listening to a minister talking in German, unable to understand a word he said. Sadie assured her there were always folding chairs for the English people, and they wouldn't need to arrive until the service was half over. And no, she would not have to get on her knees. Sadie said she could sit while the congregation knelt for prayers, fervently hoping she would have the humility to keep her eyes downcast, instead of checking everyone out with her bright, bird-like eyes.

And then, because she knew how much she would miss Dorothy when her time at the ranch was over, her nose burned and quick tears sprang to her eyes, and she had to turn her head away so Dorothy wouldn't see.

The day of the wedding arrived, the morning frosty, the sun bursting over the mountaintop as if it shone for Steven and Erma alone. Spring was on the sun's rays, warming Mark and Sadie through the windows of the buggy, Truman trotting briskly, his coat shining from Mark's careful brushing.

The lap robe felt cozy on her lap. Mark looked so handsome in his white shirt and black suit, his beard neatly washed and trimmed, his black felt hat just right. The back seat held the wedding gifts wrapped in silver-and-white-striped paper, with white ribbon and bows, a large wedding card attached with Scotch tape.

As they approached the home of the Detweilers, the family who had kindly offered to host the wedding service, teams were arriving from both directions, the occupants dressed in their wedding best, smiling happily, everyone glad to participate in Erma's special day.

The wedding dinner was to be at the Yoder home about a half-mile away, so that was their destination, being table waiters, helping with the preparations in the morning, then sitting in the congregation to see them being joined together as man and wife by the minister.

Sam Yoder had a large shop that was painted and cleaned to perfection for the wedding. Long tables were set up along each wall, with tables in the middle of the room as well, seating as many as 150 to 200 people at a time. White tablecloths covered the tables, with white Corelle dishes at each place. It all looked so clean, white, and elegant.

When Sadie spied Steven and Erma's corner, the table where the bride and groom would be seated, she put a hand to her mouth, reducing the gasp to a mere intake of breath. Oh, my goodness, she thought. Fiesta-ware! Typical of Erma Keim. The dishes were every color of the rainbow, brilliant colors meant for a very modern, young kitchen or dining room. The plates were fire-engine red, the dessert plates an electric lime-green. The serving bowls were about the color of a cloudless summer sky, the water pitcher a Crayola yellow. The tablecloth, thankfully, was off-white, with orange napkins. But would it have made any difference if it was a lilac purple?

When she heard a girlish whisper behind her, followed by a genuine snicker, she turned on her heel and frowned at Lavina and Emma Nissley.

"Hey, it's her day, her choice. If she likes these colors, then we need to respect it."

She marched off, her thoughts tumbling over each other. There had been a time when she may have been those girls. No more. Erma Keim was as close to a saint as she could imagine anyone to be. She may be short with her temper at times, but she would do anything for anyone, uncomplaining, happy to be of assistance to the lowest of people. So what if her hair was never combed quite right or her covering was wrinkled? So she was over 30, marrying a man of questionable appearance. They would be happier than most other couples, of this she was positive.

And when she sat amid the congregation and listened to the minister pronounce them man and wife, she cried. When they stood to pray for them, Sadie added a fervent prayer of thanks for providing a husband for this deserving girl.

Surprisingly, Erma's hair looked decent on this day of her wedding, as did her covering. Steven was smiling all day, his small blue eyes radiating joy alongside his glowing bride. And when they sat down to enjoy their wedding dinner together, the glow of the brilliant dishes could not have matched better.

With Mark beside her, Sadie served dish after dish of fried chicken, mashed potatoes mounded high in serving bowls, a river of browned butter dripping down the sides, bright peas and carrots steaming in separate dishes, piles of thick, buttered noodles, stuffing, and salads arranged on oblong platters. They filled and refilled hundreds of water glasses, took away empty serving bowls, passed gravy and homemade dinner rolls.

The air was festive and joyous, the community celebrating this day of love and happiness for Steven and Erma.

When they saw the piles of wedding gifts, Erma let out such an unladylike roar of surprise. A few babies began crying. She clapped both hands to her mouth, then apologized and just stood there, rocking back and forth from heel to toe, her eyes protruding scarily, her hair completely gone awry.

Erma's day had come. She was the center of attention. Her mother and the dear relatives all knew what this day meant to her, and they had given lavishly. Sixteen-quart stainless steel kettles, more than one! Large wooden racks to dry their laundry! A laundry cart to put the clothes basket on so she wouldn't have to bend over, which Sadie knew she would never use, as bending over came easily to Erma, her tall sturdy form fluid in its movement. There were clothes hampers, a canister set, a mountain of Tupperware products, lanterns, shovels, hoes, a wheelbarrow, a gas grill.

After the initial shock, Erma seemed to remember to preserve her blessing, becoming quite sedate, a murmured word of joy in Steven's ear, a humble thank you to a special cousin, her manners completely restored, a sense of the angelic settling over her.

Sadie could only remember to thank the good Lord that Dorothy had already gone home, saying she couldn't stand one more minute in these ridiculous shoes, knowing it was more the crowd of people that drove her crazy.

When Erma opened the large gift and found the plastic flowers covering the Styrofoam cross, she spluttered and struggled, her smile becoming lopsided until she read the wedding card from the Dollar General and found Dorothy's signature. As Sadie smiled at her reassuringly, her smile returned, her day restored.

It was a few weeks after the wedding that she confided in Sadie that she thought it was someone's crude joke about their age.

"Sadie, they're graveyard flowers," she whispered.

"I have some exactly like it in the attic with the same card," Sadie whispered back.

Dorothy was so glad they liked their wedding gift, saying you just couldn't beat that Dollar General.

Chapter 22

SADIE WAS HUMMING UNDER HER BREATH AS SHE shoved the heavy scoop into the feed bin, coming up with a tad too much, giving it a vigorous shake, a small shower of grain sliding back into the bin. Paris tossed her head, stamped her front feet against the concrete, whinnied, and just made a big fuss in general.

"Paris, you're getting fat! You're only getting one block of hay."

Paris buried her nose in the sweet-smelling grain, chewing happily, her long eyelashes quivering with the rhythm of her teeth. Sadie threw one block of good hay into her rack, then opened the door, putting both arms around her neck for a long, solid hug. She laid her head against the stiff hairs of her mane and told Paris how glad she was they had beaten back the evil laminitis.

"We'll have many years together, Paris—you and I. Someday, you can give my children a ride, and they can feed you apples and carrots. You're still my favorite, most bestest horse."

She stopped to scratch Truman's face, then hurried out when she heard Jim Sevarr's pickup grinding its way up the driveway.

Spring had finally come, the warm breezes tugging at her covering strings and lapping at her skirt as Jim opened the door of the pickup. She took a deep breath, the odor of the pines reminding her of the field of wildflowers on the ridge in the spring. There was just something about wet pine needles that left a sweet, spicy odor in the air, as if the cold and snow had preserved the scent to make everyone happy when the warm breezes melted it.

Her usual "Good morning" was met with a grunt, a toothpick shifted, then no attempt at conversation. Sadie tried, failed, then gave up, enjoying the lovely air. The green spring emerged out of bare brown nothingness, as new life was pulled up and out of the ground by the sun's rays.

Sadie knew her days at the ranch were numbered, so each day was special. Her friendship with Dorothy had grown after she accepted the fact that Sadie was leaving her job in September, making them closer than ever. Sadie knew Erma (now Weaver, since the wedding) would take her place after Dorothy learned to accept her.

This morning, however, she met a glum Dorothy, her face drooping, her eyes red-rimmed, heavy-lidded, her mouth set in a straight line of disapproval, the very hairs on her head electric with displeasure. So Sadie swallowed the greeting on the tip of her tongue, hung up her light sweater, and tied on her apron. Dorothy was beating the biscuit dough with so much vehemence that Sadie looked for what there was to do rather than ask. Bacon done. Sausage gravy not started.

She still had the same song on her lips but hummed very quietly. Life was good. Truly. The nausea was past, leaving her energized, ravenously hungry, enjoying her food more than ever. She read cookbooks, tried new recipes, offered to bake pies wherever church services were held, always appreciating the fact that she was no longer sick to her stomach.

She was crumbling the sausage into the brown butter, the steam rising to her face, when Erma breezed in, her hair looking worse than ever, her covering sliding off the back of her head, her face pink with the pleasure of being alive.

"Good morning, my ladies!" she yelled, stopping to receive their returned well wishes.

Sadie lifted a finger to her lips, drew her eyebrows down, and rolled her eyes in Dorothy's direction. Erma raised her eyebrows, lifted her shoulders, then lowered them. Sadie shook her head.

"Sorry I'm late. We got up a bit later than usual. I told Steven we're starting to make it a habit."

She said it with so much happiness that Dorothy told her abruptly they didn't need to know they got up later than normal, in a voice that left no doubt to her objection.

There were no breaks, no coffee, just quiet, efficient work. Sadie cleaned bathrooms until lunchtime, a pleasure to scrub and polish, the bathroom cleaner's scent no longer making her ill.

At lunchtime she was ravenous, returning to the kitchen to fix herself some food. She remembered last night's pot roast, planning the sandwich she would build. She stopped short when she found Dorothy, her face buried in her hands, her plump shoulders shaking.

"Dorothy!"

Immediately, Sadie was on her knees beside her.

"Don't cry. Dorothy. What's wrong?"

"They're takin' my children," was all Sadie could fathom between the loud honks into her handkerchief.

"What? Who? Who's taking the children?"

"They. The people. Their mother."

Sadie got to her feet, sat down heavily, disbelief in her eyes as she met Dorothy's swollen tear-filled ones.

"But…how can they? We weren't sure they…their mother was alive."

"Oh, she's alive all right."

This was said with so much bitterness, so much dejection, it was hard for Sadie to grasp the depth of this great-hearted person's disappointment.

"Sid down!" Dorothy commanded, so Sadie sat.

With a sigh Dorothy got up, bringing a cherry pie and a gallon of whole milk. Heavily, she went to the refrigerator, rummaging, searching, finding cheese, ham, a container of onions, then slid them onto the table.

"Git yerself a plate."

Again Sadie obeyed, grabbing the whole wheat rolls sitting on the counter. As they ate, the whole miserable story unfolded. It had all started with a phone call, the foreign-sounding voice saying she was Louis's and Marcellus's birth mother—and how soon could she come for a visit?

"I knowed it would happen. I had a feelin'. Somepin' about that there bag o' jewelry. It jus' seemed to run alongside them other ones, sewn in them horses' halters. I pushed it back, thought it was ridiculous, or tried to.

"Well, she came. Yesterday. It'll be all over the news. This woman, she's a beautiful lady, looks like Louis. She was a victim. Her husband's the brains, the whole mastermind, Jim said, behind all the thievin' and goings on. Her and the children knew too much. The husband threatened them.

"Oh, Sadie, the evil! Like the devil himself. She feared for her life and those children's, so she did what she thought was best. She knows Richard and Barbara. She figured if no one knew where they came from, they'd never be found, and Richard Caldwell would never turn anyone away.

"She left the country, went to Spain or someplace Spanish. I ain't certain. It all worked out for her. They caught the … forget what Jim calls him. Anyway, the husband. They got him. They's a bunch of 'em. They brought her back to reunite with the children.

"The costly diamonds in that blue sack? They were to keep the children from harm. Some strange belief. I think she figured it would help provide for them, if you sold them anyhow. She don't seem pertickler religious to me.

"So, think about it. The whole horse-thievin' thing was right under our noses. Kin' you think about it, Sadie? My children's daddy! He was the one gittin' rich. Stolen horses, jewels, cars, anything he could get away with, dozens of people working for him. Livin' in a mansion. Like a king. Livin' off stolen goods. These poor innocent children."

Dorothy's voice drifted off as grief overwhelmed her. Sadie's mind raced. Was it the mansion where she had been held? Could it be?

"Them children, though. It was a sight."

She cut a wide slice of cherry pie, slid it carefully onto her plate. Taking the knife, she cut a sizable chunk off the point, lifting it carefully to her mouth, expertly sliding the knife away. She chewed methodically, then swallowed.

"Needs sugar," she stated dryly.

"Them children. The joy of the angels came straight down and settled over 'em. They jus' stood there against my couch. I'll never forget. The mother came through that door. She's beautiful. Did I tell you? Black hair, dark skin, her dark eyes. She was dressed nice. She couldn't talk. She couldn't move.

"Them children knew her. Right away, so they did. You could see it in their eyes. Louis didn't say anything. But that Marcelona, ya know how she is. Quick. She said as plain as day, 'My mama.'

"That's when it all broke loose. They just crashed together and hugged and kissed and carried on. It was a sight. I may as well not even been in the room. Ol' Dorothy was forgotten."

Sadie nodded, understood.

"We talked then. Understood. Said she'll owe me for the rest of her life. The little blue sack? They ain't stolen. They … "

Here Dorothy looked away. When her gaze returned, her eyes meeting Sadie's, her blue eyes were clouded with guilt.

"They're mine now," she said, her voice barely more than a whisper.

"What?"

Erma chose to make her entrance at that moment, announcing in her booming voice that she couldn't get the gardener to believe those pine needles were killing the hostas. Too much acid.

"Sid down!" Dorothy commanded.

Erma sat.

"Eat your lunch."

"Thank you, I will. I'm starved. That Bertie, he doesn't listen to anything I say. He thinks he knows everything. He needs to transplant those hostas. Otherwise, they'll die."

"You said that before. Get on with your lunch. We have matters to discuss much more important than Bertie's hostas."

Sadie nodded soberly. Erma picked up a slice of Swiss cheese, turned the mustard bottle upside down and squeezed, pushing the whole slice into her mouth, chewing a few times before she swallowed.

"Like a frog eatin' a minny," Dorothy told Sadie later.

Sadie told Erma Dorothy's story as briefly as she could, then Dorothy resumed quietly.

"It's hard. It's jes' terrible hard. They stayed till evening to make things easier for me. She brought boxes. We packed up their things. But in the end, I had to let them go.

"They're going to live with her mother and dad, in New Mexico. She's gettin' a divorce. Well, an annulment. They're strict Catholics. He'll be in jail for a long time. Maybe always. She cried, said he was a good man till greed, pride, got in the way. She says he fell in with the wrong people. A horrible, bad influence. They preyed on his weakness. I think, in a way, she still loved him but knew she had to get away from him.

"I kissed them good-bye, told them to be good. We all cried, all of us. Even the children, bless their hearts. Now I'm left with them jewels. I feel so guilty. Jim says I shouldn't. I don't know how much they're worth. Jim says I can retire. I'd rather have my children. My angels, I always said. It'll break my heart at this age. I can't take it."

She cut herself another slice of pie, shaking her head.

"I'm gonna give the money to the church. Go right on workin' here till I die."

"Dorothy, why? I'm quitting here in September. It

might be a good time for you to retire."

"Retire? What would I do? Crochet? No, that's not fer me. Where would I get my paycheck? Money don't grow on trees, ya know."

"The jewels."

"I'm givin' 'em to the church."

"Dorothy, the Bible says to tithe a tenth. Just a tenth would be perfectly honorable."

Dorothy ate more cherry pie, drank milk, wiped her face, then said she was in no shape to make decisions. She taped pictures of Louis and Marcellus on the refrigerator and on the bathroom mirror. She put other pictures in frames and set them on countertops. She asked Richard Caldwell if he wanted one for his office.

Jim came in for a sandwich, nodding his head as Dorothy spoke of her plans for the future. Jim's voice was so kind, so rough with emotion when he told her it was her choice, that he'd be here for her no matter what she decided to do. When he laid his large, gnarled, work-worn hand on her shoulder, calling her "Ma dear," and she lifted her weeping, red-rimmed eyes to his, the beauty of it brought a tightening to Sadie's throat.

Oh, Dorothy would work on, saying she needed the paycheck. She'd feel guilty about the money, the jewels. In September, though, she wouldn't last long. She'd sputter, falter, then say her sciatica was flaring up, and the doctor gave her orders to stop working.

She'd be happy, making many trips to the Dollar General for her necessities, enjoying herself thoroughly, tooling that old car all over the Montana countryside, visiting Sadie, taking her places, finally freed from the pressures of her job, wondering why she hadn't done this a long time ago. That was just Dorothy.

It was all over the news, then. Dat read his paper and whistled, low. Reuben almost popped a blood vessel in excitement, saying he should be given a large reward for tracking those vehicles through the snow that night. Mark and Tim bent over the paper, reading out loud to each other, exclaiming, talking until their supper was completely over-baked.

"Dumb! I mean, what were these guys thinking?" Tim asked.

"I think they actually got to the place where they felt invincible," Mark answered. "Like, well, we're big horse thieves and got away with it all these years, so who would care about a few million-dollars' worth of jewelry heisted here and there. You know? Don't they say something like this is usually found out because of their brashness, the longer it goes on, the bolder they become? That's their undoing in the end."

Tim nodded.

Sadie sat at the kitchen table, her head in her hands, feeling tired and drained after the day's emotional toll.

Dorothy developed a headache after lunch, but Sadie knew it was more a heartache, mourning the loss of her "angels." Yet the way she had described the children's mother, how could you not be happy for them? To be returned to their rightful place, with the mother they had never forgotten, was, after all, a tremendous gift of God. It would take awhile before Dorothy could accept this, but Sadie knew she would.

Dorothy had gone home early leaving Erma and Sadie scrambling to prepare the huge evening meal. Erma made meat loaf with green peppers and bacon, a lavish sauce spread thickly on top, served with fried potatoes, coleslaw, green beans, and onions cooked in a cheese sauce.

Sadie told her the grease and calories were stacked to the ceiling. Erma hooted and chortled, saying nothing would be left, that all men loved meat loaf and just wait till the compliments came rolling in.

Sure enough, one by one, friendly, grizzled, weather-beaten faces appeared at the kitchen door with grins of appreciation. "Great meal!" "Thanks!" all of which Erma answered without the slightest trace of humility. She was the perfect replacement for Dorothy. No one could handle it better. She had self-confidence to spare, was a fast worker, and clean-up time was cut in half when she was there to help.

Sadie's head sank lower into her cupped hands, her eyes became heavy lidded as Tim and Mark exchanged remarks about the article. It was the talk of the community for quite some time. The elderly among them shook their heads in the wise way older people do, saying surely the world was encroaching into their way of life. They had to be more careful.

Well, that Jacob Miller's Sadie was married, at least, and the way it looked, she wouldn't be going on with too many shenanigans anymore, which was a good thing. She was the one that started the whole thing, taming those wild horses, now wasn't she?

Fred Ketty told them sharply that Sadie was as innocent as the day was long, she was just a victim of circumstance. But then old Henry "Ernie" said "God chasteneth those he loveth," and with Sadie riding around like that against people's advice, he definitely took her in hand. That shut Fred Ketty up.

The minister spoke a stirring sermon that Sunday, setting right any misplaced blame. As was their way, he was thankful. Thankful for the *obrichkeit* (government).

Thankful for rulers who still enforced the law. A community of caring English people who worked together to eschew evil.

On this Sunday, the usual thanksgiving for being allowed their freedom of religion held deeper meaning. To live among the English people, preserving their way of life as much as possible, was something, wasn't it?

Change would come, but slowly. The adherence to the old ways seemed worthless to some, but they had structure, tradition, order, all the things that kept the people together, dwelling in the Montana countryside. He thanked God for the people of the community, wishing the blessing from above for them all.

It was a moving sermon, the main topic being thankfulness. Hearts were full of gratitude as they assembled at the dinner table. The old practice of having a light lunch after services was more meaningful that day.

The steaming coffee poured from silver coffeepots, the pungent aroma of small green pickles, spicy red beets, platters of meat and cheese—it was all home. It was a place on earth where you belonged, and it belonged to you in return. A safe place to grow, to mature, to learn, to stay.

Being Amish, you knew there were boundaries. If you overstepped these boundaries, you got in trouble. Was not that the way of the English, as well? Of course it is for every person. Here on earth, because human nature is our burden, we all need boundaries. It was when the fear of those boundaries is replaced with audacity, boldness, lack of respect for authority, that's when people get themselves into trouble, just like the horse thieves, Sadie thought. So our boundaries are a bit stricter, tighter, but if it's a way of life, it becomes a culture, she knew.

She loved her people, from Dat and Mam to Fred Ketty. She loved Dorothy and Richard Caldwell the same. It was the way God intended, to be friendly, share God's love, and dwell among the English in peace.

Mark was in a pensive mood driving Truman home from church, the reins loose in his hands, the warm breeze stirring the short, black hair surrounding his tanned face.

"What would you like to do this afternoon?" he asked Sadie.

"Could we pack a picnic lunch and go riding?" she asked.

"I don't know. Is it okay for you?"

"Certainly. As long as we take it slow. But let's stay off the road. No use getting anyone all riled up."

Mark laughed. "You already did rile up a lot of people with your riding."

"No more," Sadie said, soberly.

And so they did go riding. It was the most memorable ride in Sadie's life. The sheer beauty of the country, the gratitude in her heart for Paris's health, for her husband, her church, the minister's message, the sun's warmth, the waving of the wildflowers, was almost more than Sadie could bear.

And when Mark rode Truman close to Paris, reached out and held Sadie's hand in his strong one, she burst into tears of joy she could not contain. When Mark's eyes teared up as well, and he told her he loved her today more than ever, that he was thankful for having her as his wife, she sniffled and had to wipe her eyes with her sleeve. She cried and laughed at the same time and said she guessed she was a little crazy, being in the family way, but he was not to worry when she got like this.

They stopped their horses on a high rise, the valley spreading before them in colors of green, blue, brown, and purple, the hills undulating, the colors interwoven, a tapestry no one could duplicate. The wind sighed in the pines, that sweet, mournful sound that was so achingly beautiful. It stirred Paris's mane, and Sadie reached down to grab a handful, which she held in her hand, loving the feel of the long, coarse hair.

Mark grinned at her. "You'll always love horses, Sadie."

"Just Paris. I usually have only one. Like husbands."

Mark's eyes darkened with the love he felt, and then he came close and kissed her, sending her heart into a lovely little flutter filled with rainbows of promise.

Chapter 23

TIM WAS NERVOUS. HE PACED THE FLOOR, WISHING Mark and Sadie were home. At least Sadie could tell him what to do. A huge question lay heavily on his mind, and it was driving him crazy. How did one go about asking a girl for a date? The real thing? Not just hanging out with a bunch of his friends, Anna among them. He wanted to ask her for a date, the beginning of a serious relationship. He knew in his heart he loved her. He cared about her very deeply and worried about her battle with anorexia.

He had started instruction class, his heart yearning for God, wanting a personal relationship with Jesus Christ, his Savior. He felt at home now, knowing this way of life was what he wanted. So with all the peace he felt, why was his heart banging around somewhere in the region of his ribs? He was short of breath, his head hurt, the palms of his hands were perspiring, and he couldn't hold still. He was completely miserable.

He sat on the couch, punched a green pillow, then sent it flying across the room. He wished Reuben would show up, just to take his mind off this looming mountain labeled "a date with Anna."

Finally he went upstairs, leafed through the shirts in his closet.

Brown? Nah. Blue. Not that blue. And on and on. Indecision is a terrible thing, he decided.

When blessedly, Reuben did show up, driving Charlie to the hitching rack and then jumping out and yelling, Tim began laughing before he opened the window and stuck his head out.

"Come on up!"

"Right!"

In a minute, Reuben was clattering up the stairs.

"Where are Mark and Sadie?"

"Went riding. They left a note."

Reuben was hungry and couldn't believe Tim wanted nothing to eat, insisting that he had eaten, which wasn't strictly a lie. He had choked down a slice of bread and peanut butter after church.

When had this conviction started? This steady pulverizing of his insides, this nervous churning of his thoughts? When he saw Anna sitting in church? Dressed in that dark royal blue with her snow-white cape and apron, her hair as smooth and dark as the night sky? Her eyes downcast, perfect dark half-moons framed with eyelashes. Her complexion was like pearls. Her mouth so perfect. Her innocence, the way she lacked confidence, made him want to stand tall by her side the remainder of her days.

But he was only who he was. That was the scary part. He checked his appearance in the mirror. Bad skin. Flat, nondescript eyes. Hair nothing that would turn heads. He was a nobody, really. What made him think he would ever be good enough? He knew that when a youth asked a girl for a date, it was supposed to be prayed about. He was supposed to seek guidance and obtain God's leading and wisdom. But whenever he prayed about it, he got the same bunch of butterflies he had today.

He would just go ahead and ask and get it over with.

"What's eating you?" Reuben wondered, opening a bag of potato chips with his teeth.

"Nothing. Why?"

Reuben shrugged.

✿ ✪ ✿

The supper crowd was a nightmare. Neil Hershberger was there, looking better than ever, the most confident youth in attendance. Anna stood beside him to play volleyball, the whole game making Tim so miserable he left his place for someone else to take.

The hymn singing was no better. Anna sat across from Neil, her eyes alight with happiness, Tim watching the two of them from his vantage point at the end of the table. Finally when the singing came to a close, he knew he couldn't take one more week of this. He was going to jump off this cliff of uncertainty. A flat no would be better than living like this.

Outside the night was almost heavenly. Every star in the sky twinkled and shone, spreading enough light with the help of the white half-moon, to be able to discern faces. Would she be out soon? He figured his best chance was to detain her as she went to Reuben's buggy. He had brought his own team, which took some heavy explaining to Reuben. He needed the experience, his horse needed exercise, he wanted to get home earlier, they had a big roofing project to start in the morning. He could tell Reuben didn't believe any of it.

Suddenly she was there. Straight across from him.

"Hey, Tee-yum!"

He thought he would crumble away in a dead faint, his heart's rhythm being so severely taxed the way it was. Steady, now. In his mind, he felt like the captain of a ship, using every keen sense to guide it safely through uncharted waters.

"How are you, Anna?"

"I'm good."

"Really?"

"Yes. Getting better."

"Good."

He kicked at the grass at his feet, already wet with the night's dew.

"Can we ... would you ... "

He stopped. This was all wrong. His ship had hit a sandbar.

"Anna, I'm too nervous to make any sense, okay? Would you allow me to take you home tonight?"

When her head went a bit sideways and she caught her breath, her hands going to her mouth, then a slow shaking of her head back and forth, his ship settled into the sandbar, broke apart, and sank to the bottom. His hope was gone. Maybe he hadn't worded that right.

"Anna ... "

She was whispering something. He stepped forward, lowered his head.

"I said ... I thought you would never ask."

The ship became buoyant; all the pieces miraculously slammed together. It burst out of the water and went full steam ahead with every light on and all the music playing as the stars danced and sang a chorus of their own.

He wanted to grab her and crush her in his arms. What he did, his voice shaking now, was say, "Thank you, Anna. I'll get my horse."

In the barn his knees shook so badly he could barely walk. His hands trembled so severely he couldn't get the bit in Reno's mouth. Neil Hershberger swaggered over and offered assistance, but Tim told him he could get it, he had a new horse, not used to the bit.

"That's your excuse," Neil snickered.

"Yeah, well, looks like I have it under control," Tim answered, as the bit slipped between Reno's teeth.

Looks like I do, he thought happily to himself, his teeth chattering.

Anna helped him hitch up, lifting the shafts so he could back his horse between them. They fastened the harness to the buggy, the britchment to the snaps attached to the shafts, the long, heavy straps fastened to the collar, which they slipped on to the short metal bars at the end of the shafts. Anna hopped lightly into the buggy, when Reuben called.

"Hey, what's up, Anna?"

She put her head out of the side of the buggy, saying Tim was taking her home.

Reuben came running up to Tim, slapped him hard across the back, crowing, "So that's what was wrong with you today!"

Tim climbed into the buggy and Reno was off with a flying leap, leaving Reuben grinning in the dark.

The trip to Anna's house was a dream, the kind where you never want to wake up, but just stay in that pleasant state forever. He couldn't remember what she said or what he said. He came down to earth after they were settled on the porch swing, slowly rocking, the chain creaking in time to the constant movement. His knees had stopped shaking, his teeth no longer chattered. This was, after all, his Anna. The girl he had spent hours with. How could be have gotten so crazy?

It was the leap from an ordinary, everyday friendship to a serious relationship, in which you had to let the girl know your intentions were completely purposeful, pursuing her in the way that suggested you may want to have her for your wife someday. That was a big hurdle.

But she was so light. So fragile. He really needed to know how she felt about her bulimia.

"Are you doing better, the way you said?" he asked.

She nodded.

"I am." She said it firmly.

"You're still thin. How much do you weigh?"

"I won't say."

"Come on, Anna."

"No."

"I'll carry you in and set you on the scales."

"You don't know where they are."

"The bathroom?"

She hesitated.

He jumped up, turned, found her hands, tugged.

"Okay. But, Tim, this is huge. I haven't weighed myself since you got mad. At least a few months ago."

He still held her hands. He loved holding those thin, delicate hands.

"Quiet," Anna warned.

They tiptoed across the kitchen. He noticed the orange glow of a kerosene lamp.

Good.

They both entered the bathroom. She picked up the scales, the large black letters behind the domed plastic lid, the elongated metal covered with black treads.

"Tee-yum?"

"What?"

They were whispering now, aware of the sleeping parents in the adjacent room.

"This takes a lot of courage for me."

"It's okay."

"You won't tell anyone?"

"Only if it's below 100 pounds. Then I will."

She stepped up, then put a hand on his arm, lifting her eyes to his.

"I can't."

She had never been more beautiful. The light of the kerosene lamp obliterated any shadows, casting her perfect face in a soft yellow light, her eyes luminous, pleading with him to help her.

How could he let her know his feelings for her? His emotions crashing and banging, the cymbals of love clashed their high sounds in his heart. He only wanted to convey his love. Slowly he lifted her hand and brought it to his lips. He kissed the tips of her fingers, then released her hand.

Her eyes were so large. What was the light in them? Did she actually feel the way he did?

Slowly his arms went to hers, his fingers encasing her elbows. Slowly he moved his hands to her shoulders, brought her small form against his chest, then searched her eyes.

"Anna?"

It was a question. A permission? In answer, her arms came up, stopped. He bent his head, his lips found hers, lightly. A feather touch.

"Tee-yum?"

He was strangling with feelings and couldn't answer.

"Let's not. I have to talk to you about ... "

"It's alright, Anna. Sure."

She sighed and looked down at the scales.

"Up you go," Tim whispered.

She stepped up, brought her hands to her face, covered her eyes. Tim bent, stared at the number.

"One-oh-eight!" he hissed.

A sharp intake of breath, followed by Anna bending over to see for herself.

"I...gained a lot of weight," she said, incredulous now. "My lowest was 93 pounds."

"It makes me happy, Anna, and relieved. You're doing an awesome job."

"Am I?"

Firmly, he led her back to the porch swing and told her many things. She told him many things.

Reuben came home and sat on the porch rocker, his grin wide, his eyes glistening in the starlight. He told Anna he knew Tim was going to take her home, as strange as he had been acting. When he finally went to bed, they were both relieved, resuming their conversation.

She told him about Neil. He told her of his "lost" years. She told him about going out with Neil, the times she had let him kiss her, the convictions she had now.

"Tim, I need something better. I don't want to be hurt again. At first, being touched, being close to Neil made me feel loved, wanted, and for a girl like me, I depend so much on that physical touch. But I do want something better, I just have to have enough courage to think some-one...you...you like me."

Tim grinned. "Well, Anna, it looks like I'm the lucki-est guy in the world. The rest of my life, I want to let you know how much I love you."

Anna gasped. "Tee-yum! Those are strong words!"

"And we're not even dating, are we?" he said, laughing. "I plan on starting next weekend, if this girl will say yes."

Anna laughed with him, then very soft and low said, "Yes."

So they spent the evening on the same wooden porch swing where Mark and Sadie had sat. The same stars and moon hung low in the night sky over the same low buildings nestled on the side of the hill overlooking the Aspendale Valley.

Dat and Mam lay in the same bed, feigning sleep, wondering who was spending the evening with Anna, but in traditional Amish fashion, would not venture out to ask. This was all in secret. Parents were people to be ashamed of, respected, and definitely kept in the background until a couple had been dating for awhile, at least.

Leah's and Rebekah's weddings were scheduled in a few weeks, and now Anna was dating. Mam sighed. Dat thought girls left the house really fast after they finally got started.

Across Atkin's Ridge, in the house snuggled under the pines, Sadie woke with a start, opened one eye to look at the face of her alarm clock—1:23.

Where was Tim? Leaping out of bed, she hurried across the kitchen, her bare feet sliding across the sleek hardwood floor. The barn was dark. No buggy. Her breath came in dry gasps now. Where was Tim? She woke Mark, grasping his shoulder, shaking him hard.

"Mark! Mark!"

He groaned, turned on his back.

"It's 1:25. Where is Tim?"

"I dunno."

Clearly concerned, he threw back the covers, stuck his legs into his denim trousers, buttoning them as he moved across the floor.

"Where could he be?"

"He may have had trouble with his horse. That Reno. He's a spirited one."

Sadie put an arm around Mark's waist, needing comfort. His arm came around hers, his love and concern warm in his touch.

Headlights? They held their breath as the bluish LED lights turned in the drive. They both exhaled, then decided to stay up, see what had happened. The washhouse door opened, shoes were kicked off, and Tim charged through the door.

"Hey!" Mark said, from the darkened living room.

"Whoa! You scared me!" Tim said.

"Why don't you light the propane lamp?"

Mark and Sadie blinked in the bluish light. Mark pointed to the clock and Tim grinned sheepishly.

"We thought you may have had an accident," Mark said sternly.

"Nothing like that."

Tim grinned again, self-consciously this time. Then, as if there were no words to tell them how happy he was, he moved across the floor, gathering them both into a bear hug, one on each arm.

"I have a date with Anna."

His words were so full of happiness, they were like music. Mark clapped Tim's shoulder, congratulating him warmly. Sadie hugged him back and said she was glad.

They made hot chocolate, Tim got the shoo-fly pie, soaking it with the warm sweet liquid, and Sadie asked if Anna hadn't offered him a snack. He said she hadn't, and they all laughed when Mark said that was what Sadie used to do, too. No snack.

And then, because there was so much happiness that the house could barely contain it all, they sat in companionable silence as little swirls of contentment permeated the air.

Sadie knew their future held trials, dark valleys, days of despair, but that was God's way. He supplied the strength and courage to face each dawning day.

In the barn, Paris whooshed her nose in the feedbox, then crumpled to the clean straw, resting, content, the happiness from the house including her.

The End

The Glossary

Arma geld—A Pennsylvania Dutch dialect phrase meaning "money for the poor."

Bupp-lich—A Pennsylvania Dutch dialect word meaning "childish."

Chide—A Pennsylvania Dutch dialect word meaning "nice or normal."

Covering—A fine mesh headpiece worn by Amish females in an effort to follow the Amish interpretation of a New Testament teaching in 1 Corinthians 11.

Cutsing—A Pennsylvania Dutch dialect word meaning "throwing up."

Dichly—A Pennsylvania Dutch dialect word meaning "head scarf" or "bandanna." A *dichly* is a triangle of cotton fabric, usually a men's handkerchief cut in half and hemmed, worn by Amish women and girls when they do yard work or anything strenuous.

Dat—A Pennsylvania Dutch dialect word used to address or refer to one's father.

Driver—When the Amish need to go somewhere too distant to travel by horse and buggy, they may hire someone to drive them in a car or van.

Fer-sarked—A Pennsylvania Dutch dialect phrase meaning "taken care of."

Gaul's gnipp—A Pennsylvania Dutch dialect phrase meaning "the horse's knot."

Goot-manich—A Pennsylvania Dutch dialect phrase meaning "kind."

Grosfeelich—A Pennsylvania Dutch dialect word meaning "proud" or "conceited."

In Gottes Hent—A Pennsylvania Dutch dialect phrase meaning "in God's hands."

Kannsht doo Amish schwetsa?—A Pennsylvania Dutch dialect question meaning "Can you speak Dutch?"

Kalte sup—A cold refreshing snack served in very hot weather as an alternative to cookies. Made with fresh fruit, served in a bowl, it contains a liberal amount of sugar, a few slices of heavy homemade bread broken on top, and ice cold milk poured over everything.

Loddveig—A Pennsylvania Dutch dialect word meaning "pear butter."

Mam—A Pennsylvania Dutch dialect word used to address or refer to one's mother.

Maud—A Pennsylvania Dutch dialect word meaning "maid."

Obrichkeit—A Pennsylvania Dutch dialect word meaning "government."

Ordnung–The Amish community's agreed-upon rules for living based on their understanding of the Bible, particularly the New Testament. The *ordnung* varies from community to community, often reflecting the leaders' preferences, local traditions, and traditional practices.

Opp-Gott–A Pennsylvania Dutch dialect word meaning "almost a god," or "idol."

Patties down—Putting one's hands on one's lap before praying, as a sign of respect. Usually includes bowing one's head and closing one's eyes. The phrase is spoken to children who are learning the practice of silent prayer.

Phone shanty–Most Old Order Amish do not have telephone landlines in their homes so that incoming calls do not overtake their lives and so that they are not physically connected to the larger world. Many Amish build a small, fully enclosed structure, much like a commercial phone booth, somewhere outside the house where they can make calls and retrieve phone messages.

Rumspringa–A Pennsylvania Dutch dialect word meaning "running around." It is the time in an Amish person's life between age 16 and marriage. Includes structured social activities for groups, as well as dating. Usually takes place on the weekend.

Schadenfreude—The feeling of gladness at seeing your enemy suffer a defeat or setback.

Shtrubles–A Pennsylvania Dutch dialect word meaning "messy, fly-away hair."

Siss kenn fa-shtandt–A Pennsylvania Dutch dialect sentence meaning "That's unbelievable!" or "That's not right!"

Siss net chide—A Pennsylvania Dutch dialect sentence meaning "It's not right."

Toste brode, millich und oya—A Pennsylvania Dutch dialect phrase meaning "toast, hot milk, and a soft-boiled egg."

Verboten—A Pennsylvania Dutch dialect word meaning "forbidden."

Voss iss letts mitt ess?–A Pennsylvania Dutch dialect question meaning "what is wrong with her?"

Ya—A Pennsylvania Dutch dialect word meaning "yes."

The Author

Linda Byler was raised in an Amish family and is an active member of the Amish church today. Growing up, Linda loved to read and write. In fact, she still does. She is the author of *Wild Horses* and *Keeping Secrets*, Books One and Two in the *Sadie's Montana* series. She has also written the *Lizzie Searches for Love* series, which includes these three novels: *Running Around (and Such)*, *When Strawberries Bloom*, and *Big Decisions*. She is also the author of *Lizzie's Amish Cookbook: Favorite recipes from three generations of Amish cooks!*

Additionally, Linda is well-known within the Amish community as a columnist for a weekly Amish newspaper.

Also in the
SADIE'S MONTANA
series!

BOOK ONE
WILD HORSES

BOOK TWO
KEEPING SECRETS

Don't miss the **LIZZIE SEARCHES FOR LOVE** series.

BOOK ONE

BOOK TWO

BOOK THREE

COOKBOOK